Release Me

IF YOU CAN

one

"He's Taylor's father."

For a lingering moment, those words hung in the air, garnering no response.

Hot tears pooled in Renata's eyes as she swallowed the urge to let them fall. It wasn't a good time for tears. She wished Quentin would do *something*. Yell, scream, curse her out... anything had to be better than the look of cold disgust twisted into his handsome face.

He was perfectly still. *So* still, in fact, that Renata wondered for a second if he was even breathing, but then he finally exhaled, and what she read as disgust warped into a look of such profound displeasure that it took her breath away.

"You slept with Damien Wolfe?"

There was no emotion in his voice, no inflection to give even the tiniest of clues to what he was feeling — other than the disappointment. *That* was abundantly clear.

His question — and it wasn't even a question, the way he delivered it, with none of his usual good-naturedness in his eyes, and his mouth set in a harsh line after — he wasn't *really* asking. He was simply saying it out loud for the opportunity to have his suspicions confirmed.

She didn't know how to answer that question.

If he wanted to phrase it that way... yes. But it wasn't fair to characterize Taylor's conception as if it were some act of shared love, or even passion. Just the thought of it made an old — but *very* familiar — sense of shame heat her cheeks, and she dropped her gaze to her hands.

"He's her father," she repeated, offering nothing new.

"So you had a personal connection with Wolfe all this time? You've... what, been feedin' him information about us?"

Her gaze shot up, and she shook her head. "No. Never. Not... not intentionally. It's always been hypotheticals, veiled questions. I've *never* knowingly told anyone outside of this team a single thing *about* this team. First rule of fight club, right?"

Quentin's expression remained impassive, and Renata's attempt at injecting a bit of humor slid right off him, shattering on the floor, along with her resolve to not shed any tears.

"Why should I believe that?" he asked, in what was nearly a growl, despite his outwardly cool disposition. "From where *I'm* standin', it looks like you sought me out for help, knowin' the connection to Wolfe and Naomi."

Again, Renata frantically shook her head. "*No.* I had no idea of your link to Wolfe until I joined this team, *months* after he took Taylor. I sought you out because I needed someone I could I trust, and I thought... Quentin, we're friends."

"*Were* friends. Yeah, you could trust *me*, but it looks like *my* trust was misplaced. I'm supposed to believe this is a coincidence?"

She lifted her hands, attempting to touch him — the only thing she could think of to assuage his fears. He backed away, shaking his head, and Renata

6

swallowed hard. She *wanted* to not take it personally, to accept that he had a right to feel angry — even *betrayed*, but…the fact remained that the repulsion on his face made a stony sense of rejection settle in her stomach.

"It *is* a coincidence. I swear to you that I didn't know my *friend*," — maybe if she kept saying it, kept emphasizing that she wasn't a stranger, something would click for him — "CrawDaddy, and you, Quentin LaForte, were the same person. We made a promise to each other, that we would never do that — look each other up—, unless we decided together. I didn't break that, not really."

Quentin scoffed. "Not *really*?"

"Yes. When I was invited onto the team, and you and I met that day… you felt really familiar to me, like we already knew each other. And then, as I found out more about you — that you were from Louisiana, you being a hacker, that you *love* crawdads… Quentin, it wasn't exactly a stretch to figure out."

With his arms crossed, and face pulled into a stern scowl, Quentin seemed far removed from the charming, flirty man Renata had encountered on her first visit to Five Star Fitness to join his and Naomi's team. Golden brown skin and a perpetual five o'clock shadow, the chiseled face of a model, body of an athlete, and mind of a tech genius… she'd thought Quentin was a dream.

This, on the other hand, was a nightmare. She watched his expression for any hint of a crack in his armor, *any* sign that he didn't want to stick her somewhere in a dungeon to rot.

She found none.

"So if you didn't know of the link between me and Wolfe... why wouldn't you tell me *who* had Taylor. These last few months, it was "they" this, "they" that. You *knew* he was the one who had her. Why the secrecy?"

Renata sighed as she lifted her eyes to his. "Because I knew you would do more than I was asking you to. Just like... before. Remember?"

Licking his lips, Quentin ran a hand over his face before letting out a sigh of his own. When his eyes returned to hers, they weren't quite as harsh and accusing as before. Subtly, he nodded.

There.

There was the softening — however slight — she was hoping for. She closed her eyes briefly, then continued.

"I had already asked too much of you. I was just optimistic that you would be able to tell me *how* to do what they were asking, so I could get Taylor back, without involving you more than I absolutely had to."

"But I told you I would do whatever was necessary — and you *accepted* that. I started pokin' around got tagged. King Pharmaceuticals has government contracts, and they *don't play*. I had to answer to SSA Black about that."

Renata nodded. "I'm sorry for that. I really never should have asked, but... I didn't know what else to do... who else to turn to. He wants me to *hack* this huge, powerful company, and I... I just went to the one person I thought could maybe tell me a way out of it, while allowing me to remain anonymous. Quentin, if I'd told you this was about Wolfe, you would've done something crazy, like emptying his bank accounts or

8

something, and then what? Where would that leave me and Taylor?"

"I wouldn't have done anything without a plan."

"A plan that would entail talking to people. *Involving people.*"

Quentin threw his hands up. "People who are *already* involved. Me, Naomi, SSA Black, Inez... we would have *helped you.*"

"I didn't *know* that," Renata said, shaking her head.

"Yes, you did. Once you got asked onto this team, to help with the Lucas job, you *knew.* You even had your own people, Marcus and Kendall, who probably would have been more than willing. Renata... you had to know this would get found out. Your only saving grace was that me and Naomi didn't know your daughter. We *looked* at those pictures from the party, wrote her off as one of Taylor's friends, or a cousin from her mother's side or something. What if Marcus had reviewed those pictures with us? What then, huh? What the hell were you thinking?"

"I was thinking that if I kept my mouth shut I would see my daughter again. I was *thinking* that her father is the worst thing that's ever happened to me... but *she's* the best. And I don't know what I'll do if I never get to hug her again. The job with Lucas is over, and as far as I know, Wolfe has no idea I was involved, no idea that I know you *or* Naomi. I thought I would go back to what I was doing before — working for the FBI, and waiting on Damien to say he's ready to move forward with this ... *scheme* of his, so I can just be done."

Quentin gave a dry chuckle, then looked at Renata with a derisive smile. "You really that naïve?" he asked, tipping his head to the side. "To think he's gonna be done with you, once you do this for him? Let me guess — he told you so."

"As a matter of fact, he *did*," Renata confirmed as heat rushed to her cheeks. "But no… I'm *not* that naïve. I'm just… trying to be optimistic. I've run from him before. Changed my name, changed Taylor's name, and we hid. But, he found us. Every. Single. Time. And every time, he made me wonder why I'd even *tried*." She paused for a moment to compose herself as her voice grew choked and hot, fresh tears rushed to her eyes. "So… again, *no*. Not naïve. Choosing to believe that this time he'll just leave me alone."

"Yeah, well… you chose to be connected to the devil— this is what you get."

Renata swallowed the urge to vomit.

"So what's next?" she asked, tossing her shoulders back with a confidence she didn't feel as she pretended not to have heard his jab. "Where do we go from here?"

"I still have questions."

"Well ask them!" she snapped, then averted her gaze as Quentin's expression once again deepened into a scowl. It wasn't that she *meant* to be indignant, especially considering her clear disadvantage, but she was starting to grow annoyed.

Really, she'd done nothing wrong. Her daughter was being held by Damien Wolfe, and she was being denied her parental rights. Both of their lives were at risk if she didn't cooperate with whatever Damien said.

10

What kind of mother would she be if she *didn't* do everything she could to protect her?

"Did you give him *any* information about our team?"

Renata's head snapped to attention. "What? Again, Wolfe doesn't have knowledge that I share any relationship with you or Naomi. So no... not intentionally."

"Not *intentionally*. So... there may have been some *un*intentional cover blowing?"

"No, not like that." Renata blew out a breath. "Um... a few days before the kidnapping attempt on Naomi... I got a call. They do it often, presenting me with a scenario to get out of, but I never know when, or who. All I do, is solve the problem. They needed to know how to disable the security, break in with no trace, all of that. When I heard about what happened to Naomi, I looked at the floor plans they gave me, and then I looked up Naomi's building and compared. It was *her* apartment."

For a long moment, Quentin just stared, and then he let out another cough of dry laughter. Shaking his head, he turned away, then lifted his hand to his temples.

"What now?" Renata asked, taking a few steps closer.

Quentin looked up, then shifted so that he was facing her again as his expression hardened. Before he even opened his mouth to speak, the anger in his eyes told her exactly what he was about to say — and it frightened her.

"We're going on a little trip."

— & —

He wouldn't say anything.

No matter how hard Renata stared at the side of Quentin's head, willing him to acknowledge that he at least remembered she was there, he wouldn't even glance her way. He hadn't said anything since they left her apartment. He'd placed a brief, hushed phone call, then demanded that she put on shoes to accompany the plain cotton tee and sweats she'd been wearing when she opened the door.

She could understand why he'd confiscated her cell phone, but handcuffing her just seemed like overkill. Did he really think she was going to open the door and pitch herself into traffic if he didn't?

Maybe not such a bad idea, she thought, and then quickly thought better. With her luck, she would injure herself just enough to be *really* annoying, but not get her out of her current predicament. So... handcuffed she remained.

Not that she couldn't have easily gotten out of the cuffs. Quentin must not have researched too far, if he thought she was just some geek, too lazy to lift a finger if it wasn't to click a mouse or tap a key. Marcus and Kendall would have both known better. They would have known that with her proficiency in hand to hand combat, she could easily give a grown man a serious problem — even if he was armed, which Renata had no doubt Quentin *was*.

But, a physical fight didn't seem the right way to send an "I'm innocent" message, so she got into the car without much fuss, although she desperately wondered where they were going. She kept her head low, hoping not to be seen, but knowing that there was a very real chance Wolfe had people watching her. If he did, she was already screwed— they'd probably seen Quentin coming in.

Renata blew out a puff of air as she searched her mind for a better way to explain… all of this. She was telling him the truth — maybe not the *whole* truth, but still the truth — and he still didn't seem to believe her. His reluctance to look at or speak to her, the fact that he hadn't called her *cher* in his sexy Creole twang… it was unnerving. Again, it crossed Renata's mind that if he blew up, yelled, screamed… some type of emotion would be better than the *nothing* she was currently getting from him.

"Quentin, I hope you understand I nev—"

The ear-splitting sound of shattering glass interrupted Renata mid-sentence, making her throat constrict with fear. She screamed at the angry zip of a bullet as it flew past her and hit the windshield, showering them in another layer of tempered glass.

Faintly, she heard Quentin yelling for her to get down, but she couldn't move.

Somebody is trying to kill me, she thought, just before Quentin reached over, with his eyes still on the road as he punched the car into full speed, and grabbed a handful of her braids. He yanked hard, pulling her head toward her knees with a command to "stay down" as he maneuvered the car into a sharp turn. She glanced up, at her seat, and the little hole through her head rest, where she'd been not even ten seconds before, made her stomach lurch.

Squeezing her eyes shut, Renata said a quick prayer, then took a deep breath.

Think about Taylor, Ren. She needs her mother.

She quickly manipulated her hands out of the loosely applied handcuffs, then looked to Quentin, who was hunched low over the steering wheel as he tried to navigate them away from danger. His eyes were focused ahead, occasionally darting behind and beside them, and then they rested for a moment on Renata.

"Are you okay?" he asked, slowing the car for just a moment as they pulled out of the side street and back onto the highway.

Renata braced herself against the dashboard as he shot up to a higher speed. "Yeah."

He eyed her again. "Good."

She caught the cell phone he tossed her a second later, then followed his directions to get Inez on the line, and put it on speaker.

"¿Qué coño quieres? Es tarde!" Inez's usually melodic voice sounded muffled, as if her head was stuffed into her pillow. Between that, and her harsh *"it's late, what the fuck do you want"* greeting, Renata quickly surmised that they'd woken her up.

"Inez, it's Agent Parker," Renata called out as Quentin's eyes narrowed at something in the rearview mirror.

"Ren!? Calling me from Q's phone this late? Que le coger?"

Heat rushed to Renata's cheeks as she glanced at Quentin. "What?! *No*, Inez, we kinda have a situa—"

Once again, the crack of gunfire took away her ability to speak, and the phone toppled to the floor as Quentin pressed the gas harder. She heard the sharp click of a button being depressed, and the glove

14

compartment opened in front of her, revealing a mini arsenal of weapons.

"Take your pick," Quentin said, his voice not edged with nearly as much anxiety as Renata felt. "Since you've gotten yourself out of the cuffs, we need the cover. *Now.*"

With shaking hands, Renata reached for the gun that looked most familiar — the same Glock 23 she was issued upon graduation from the FBI academy. A quick check told her it was already loaded, so she switched the safety off and with a deep breath, unbuckled her seatbelt.

From the floor of the car, Inez's voice rang out through the phone's speaker. "Hello?! What is happening?!"

"We've got a situation, Nez. We're on the highway headed to your house, being pursued by a black Escalade. Doesn't appear to be armored, but in just a second, Renata is gonna find out."

At the sound of her name, Renata's eyes went wide, and she looked at Quentin. He gritted his teeth as he bore down on the gas, whipping them from side to side so they wouldn't be such easy targets. For a moment, he caught her eye and nodded. Knowing what that meant, Renata pushed out a breath as alarm seized her chest, squeezing tight.

"Stay alive for ten minutes," Inez exclaimed, sounding excited. "Dios mío, I have not been in a gun battle in *forever*. I'm on my way!"

Renata carefully turned around in her seat as Quentin gave Inez a few more indicators of where they were, bracing her back against the dashboard. The back windshield was shattered, so it was easy to see the larger SUV as it bore down on them.

With Taylor in mind, Renata calmed herself, blocking out everything except one goal: kill the driver. She lifted the gun and pointed it at the pursuing vehicle, aiming precisely before she pulled the trigger.

She watched in shocked disappointment as the windshield of the other vehicle shattered, but did not break.

Shit.

Renata ducked low as another round of bullets hit their car. It was very late, and traffic was low, but there were still innocent people out. They needed to end this situation before any bystanders got hurt.

She aimed again, holding steady even as the car swayed, waiting until she saw the gunman ease his hand outside the vehicle, weapon pointed. She drew the trigger again, and smirked in satisfaction as a spray of red burst into the air, and their attacker's gun dropped to the asphalt.

She relaxed — but only a little — giving Quentin an affirmative nod when he asked if she'd gotten him. The other vehicle was still approaching — *fast* — so there was no room to lose focus. Especially when there was another gunman sticking his head out of the car. Before she could think about it too hard, she'd already aimed and shot again, putting a bullet through his forehead before he could point the menacing automatic weapon in his hands.

"Good aim," Quentin said, gifting her a brief, but grateful smile as he swerved to avoid a slow-moving Mercedes. Renata started to smile back, comforted by his slight softening toward her, but that

16

relief quickly shifted to fear. She lifted the Glock again, aiming it in Quentin's direction.

Quentin's face dropped into a glower as he looked down the barrel of the gun. "What the fuck, Renata, why are you—"

"Don't move," Renata commanded, cutting him off as she pulled the trigger.

Around her, the air exploded with the deafening crack of a gunshot. The bullet shattered his window and kept moving, striking the gun-wielding driver of the Mercedes in the neck, which sent the car swerving as it suddenly decelerated.

"Hell yes!" she exclaimed, as the Mercedes swung into the front of the Escalade, incapacitating both vehicles. She turned her gaze back to Quentin with a huge smile.

Oh my God.

Horror gripped her heart like a vice when she saw the blood splattered across Quentin's face. She dropped the gun to reach for him, to see where he was shot, but… she couldn't feel her fingers… couldn't make herself move. Dizziness swept over her, and she briefly closed her eyes. When she opened them again, she realized he was talking to her, saying something, but… her eyes were just *so* heavy. So, *so* heavy. So she closed them again.

She could hear sirens. They were in the distance, but she could hear them, and she knew that wasn't good. She had to warn — had to tell Quentin, sirens wasn't good. Sirens meant police, and police meant questions, and questions meant answers, and answers meant… she couldn't remember where she was going with that. She was going somewhere with that, if only she could remember. But sirens weren't good. They were bad.

When Renata wrenched her eyes open again, she was being pulled from the car, and the voices around her were frantic. Faintly, she registered that she was in Quentin's arms. He was talking to someone, and even though *his* tone was measured and calm, it still held a slight edge of anxiety as he carefully lowered her onto something… maybe a bed.

She groaned as he pulled away, and an unfamiliar face came into view. The woman was pretty, but she had a needle in one hand.

Get away from me.

Her thoughts drifted to Taylor, wondering if she were safe, and if she knew an attempt had been made on her mother's life. If she knew her *father* had made an attempt on her mother's life.

It was the only thing that made sense. Other than Wolfe, Renata didn't have the kind of enemies that sent armored vehicles to kill you in the middle of the night.

Only Wolfe.

Her eyes shot open again, bulging wide as pain burst suddenly through her shoulder and head. A vicious wave of nausea swept over her, and somebody, she wasn't sure who, held up a bucket as she pitched her head over the bed to relieve herself of her stomach contents.

"*Ren*, lay back, please."

She wanted to follow that instruction, but her body wouldn't cooperate. Another round of sickness struck her stomach as she began to shake uncontrollably. A few moments later, as the voices

18

around her grew frantic again, her consciousness slipped away, and she descended into obscurity.

two.

painted_pixel: g2g. Friend's annoying big sister is making us go 2 some party with her.

CrawDaddy: u can at least TRY 2 have fun, u know that right? Don't be a lame all your life p.

Painted_pixel: blah. Rowdy parties are totally not my scene.

CrawDaddy: is ANYTHING?

Painted_pixel: not really, lol. I'd much rather stay here and talk 2 u.

CrawDaddy: Same here.

Renata sucked in a deep breath as heat rushed to her cheeks. Most sixteen-year-old girls would probably be embarrassed that someone whose face they'd never seen, let alone met in person, could make them blush.

Not her.

She much preferred the safety of her just slightly flirtatious friendship with CD to the unavoidably awkward interaction with boys her age in real life.

Of course it crossed her mind that he could be some creepy old man, hanging around in chat rooms for teenage hackers to pick his next victim. But she pushed the possibility — probability — away. He'd passed every little "test" she'd thrown his way. Casual mentions of pop culture, questions of birthday, maturity level when she mentioned boobs — if he wasn't *really* seventeen, he was damn sure good at pretending. If he was... *well, Renata had no plans on meeting him in person anyway.*

Ever.

"Prettiness" was something Renata had never lacked, and her teenage body had developed to grown woman proportions early — and fast. *Nothing she could really do about it, since... you know,* biology, *and all of that, but her mother certainly acted as if Renata had stood in the mirror and telepathically given herself the womanly curves she hid under baggy hoodies and sweats. "Fast ass" this, and "think you're grown that"... one would think that Renata spent her time hanging at the mall in short-shorts with her adolescent peers, drinking at the lake, getting caught under the bleachers...* anything *that would warrant such accusations, instead of locked in her room with a book or her computer. But that made more sense than her mother actually had.*

So, Renata kept to herself. The less interaction with people her age, especially boys, the less chance there was for a rumor to start about her, and the less chance there was for something to get back to her mother. Which meant less chance of hell at home. The only exception was Stacy, her equally awkward, but much more outgoing friend — the only person in the "real world" that Renata considered such. And, the only person who didn't fall outside of her mother's arbitrary standards of a "bad influence".

As such, it was Stacy's house that Renata went to whenever her mother was out of town, since she didn't trust Renata to be home alone. Thing was, this time Stacy's parents had to leave at the last minute, and were leaving the two younger teenagers with Stacy's older sister Samantha, who was home for the weekend from college.

Samantha wasn't very fond of the idea of "babysitting" two teenagers who were more than capable of watching themselves, so she made an executive decision for the group. She was going to a party in nearby Houston, and since she'd been told not to leave them alone... they were going with her. A smoke filled, liquor filled, — probably drug filled — celebrity party was the last place Renata wanted to go, and she doubted she was old enough to get in anyway. But that wasn't her problem, it was Samantha's.

In any case, all Renata wanted to do was stay at the house, with her face glued to the computer screen so she could talk to CD. With him, none of the awkwardness, none of the presumptions about her sex habits based on her body, none of the overpowering boredom of other boys her age existed. He was funny, smart, knew his way around malicious code, and didn't treat her as inferior simply because she was a girl, as some of the other hackers did. So maybe... she crushed on him, just a little. His physical appearance was a mystery, but the way he affected her intellectually was the kind of thing her teenage fantasies were made of, and he certainly didn't help matters by claiming he would rather spend his Friday night talking to her.

Painted_pixel: srsly? U don't have a party or a girlfriend or something 2 keep u busy on a Friday?

CrawDaddy: nope. Girl who is a friend tried 2 get me 2 go spying w/her, but I'm on caregiver duty for my mom.

Damn.

Renata knew his mother was sick, but she wasn't sure with what. He'd mentioned good days and bad ones before. Today must have been bad.

Painted_pixel: go spying?

CrawDaddy: yeah, she's always n2 something. Was hoping u would be keeping me company.

Whew.

Painted_pixel: sowwy. Loud music and underage drinking await.]

Renata closed the chat after that, because she'd read in some trashy teenage magazine that she should always end conversations first, to "keep a man guessing." Why exactly she wanted to keep a boy who lived God knows where "guessing"... she had no idea.

"Hey nerd."

Renata rolled her eyes at the way Samantha chose to address her and turned her back to the computer screen to look up. At twenty years old, Sam was already a bombshell of a young girl, with honey-toned skin and hazel eyes. A "red bone" as they called them, and she had no qualms about flaunting her light skin and "good" hair around as more valuable than Renata's copper hue and kinkier textured coils.

Renata had no idea why Sam seemed to pick with her. She was four years her junior, and could only dream of the tall, slim body Samantha had poured into a tiny hot pink dress better suited for dancing on a stage than dancing in a crowd.

"Put this on," the older girl snapped, tossing a bundle of shimmery blue fabric into Renata's face. "I

24

borrowed it from my chubby roommate before I left the dorm."

Biting her tongue, Renata shot a scathing look at Stacy, who gave her a sheepish smile as she pulled a silver dress onto her slender body.

Lucky them, Renata thought bitterly as she stood, pulling her hoodie over her head. Stacy and Samantha were the slim beauties — they would get all the attention. Renata was used to fading into the crowd with her baggy clothes and somber facial expressions.

She'd showered before she left home, so all she had to do was strip down to her bra and panties. Her stomach was flat, but she had breasts, hips, and butt spilling from everywhere, it seemed. Self-conscious, she hurriedly yanked the dress on, smoothing it over her hips before she looked at herself in the mirror.

"Holy crap," Stacy whispered, staring at her friend. "You look super-hot, Ren!"

Samantha sucked her teeth. "She looks like a teenager in grown-up clothes."

"I am a teenager in grown up clothes." Indignation swept over Renata as Samantha circled her, scrutinizing her as if she were judging livestock.

"How is your body all... bootylicious," she continued, as if she hadn't heard Renata speak, "when you have the face of a twelve year old?"

"I can't help what my face looks like."

Samantha's mouth spread into a sly grin. "Oh... but I can."

— & —

25

Renata took a deep breath as she exited the backseat of the car, after giving herself one last nervous glance in the mirror. Her heart raced as she fell into step behind Samantha and Stacy. Stacy had gone to enough parties with Samantha that she knew how to walk in the scary-high heels she'd been presented. Renata had to concentrate, so she didn't look like a freshly-born foal, wobbly kneed and awkward as they headed for the front of the club.

Their small group got first, second, and third looks as they walked past the line, and right up to the door. Samantha approached the bouncer first, slinking into him with a sexy smirk as she whispered something in his ear.

He didn't appear to be moved.

The bouncer was a big man, the kind of big that tended to get nicknamed "Tiny", with heavy fists that looked capable of easily smashing a skull. If that didn't work, the visible gun at his waist would. He looked at Sam, and for a moment it seemed as if he might use one of those meaty hands to shove her out of the way, but then he looked over her shoulder at Stacy and Renata.

Renata shifted uncomfortably on her aching feet as his eyes swept up her body, lingering at her hips and chest before finally settling on her face. She still felt like her awkward sixteen-year-old self, but knew she didn't look it, after the way Samantha had applied makeup to her face. The blush created cheekbones, eliminating the plushness, and the dark, heavy eyeliner and shadow took away the wide-eyed innocence from her face. A thick layer of deep red lipstick turned her already full lips into a sexy pout that she'd barely *recognized when Samantha was done with her "makeover".*

She'd endured her share of unwelcome attention from men and boys before, but this was a whole other level of blatant lust. Renata much preferred "hey, hey, sexy, where you goin' wit all dat ass?" to the searing, almost palpable touch of the bodyguard's stare. She looked away, enduring it in silence before letting out a breath of relief when he finally turned his attention to Stacy instead.

Without a word, he nodded at Samantha, then unhooked the rope to let them in. Samantha grinned, running a hand over his beefy chest as she passed, leading Stacy and Renata behind her.

Inside, Renata's face pulled into a scowl. The air was thick with smoke, from cigarettes and something a little less legal, and the crowd was heavy. It was hot, and loud, and... Renata really wished she could go home.

All she'd wanted to do tonight was talk to CD.

They weren't on the main floor of the club very long before Samantha talked their way into VIP, and onto the lap of one of Houston's well-known underground rappers. A cheer went around the section as one of his "chopped and screwed" style songs came blasting through the speakers, and Renata took advantage of the distraction, using the time to find a semi-quiet spot with a seat.

She sat down, rubbing her temples as she looked over the balcony at the crowd. The VIP area was basically a sky box, where they could see out, but no one could see in. Renata wasn't concerned about that. She was just glad for a separation — however slight —

from the noise, and grateful that they were no longer among the sweaty, rowdy throngs of people on the main floor.

Behind her, a low masculine voice spoke in a semi-hushed tone. She didn't mean to intrude on a private conversation, so she tuned it out, turning to glance at Samantha and Stacy, who both seemed to be enjoying the attention of the up-and-comings surrounding the stars of the night, a rap duo who'd just been featured on a big *rappers song and video, which played on a big screen. Renata shook her head at the image on the screen, a party full of skimpy women frolicking on a yacht, while the men rapped about pimping.*

Totally not my scene, *she thought with a sigh. But she was here now, and the only thing to do was tough it out until they were ready to go — and hope Samantha didn't plan to bag herself a rapper.*

"Excuse me..."

Renata nearly jumped out of her skin at the deep, rich sound of a masculine voice right next to her ear. She turned, and her gaze was immediately snared by deep, cinnamon-toned skin and golden-brown eyes. His gaze raked over her much like the bodyguard, but instead of disgust, his slow perusal elicited heat in her cheeks and between her thighs, which she squeezed closed.

The man was stupid-fine, but very obviously much older than she was. His soulful eyes held wisdom, intelligence, and... something else... danger, *which made a slight chill run down her spine. But she remained rooted to her seat anyway, staring.*

His lush, full lips spread into a smile,
showcasing two perfect rows of white teeth. "Are you
alright?" he asked, placing a hand on her bare thigh.

In her mind, the heat of his touch nearly seared
her skin, and she swallowed hard. "Yes." Her eyes
flicked down to where his hand was still on her leg, and
his gaze followed, but he made no effort to move it.

"What's your name, beautiful?"

"Renata."

Why are you telling a stranger your name,
crazy!

"You have a last name?"

"Parker."

He smiled then, a smile that made her skin
crawl, but somehow made her want to move closer as
well. She glanced up, feeling another set of eyes on her,
and found Samantha looking in her direction. Sam
smirked, and then her gaze slipped away, and she
nodded.

What is that about?

Renata shook her head. Sam hated her, for
whatever reason. It didn't make sense to try to figure it
out now.

When she looked back at the man, he ran his
tongue ran over his lips. "Renata," he repeated,
dragging the syllables in a sensual tone. "Nice name.
Do you know who I am?"

She shook her head, feeling stupid. She got the
distinct feeling that she should know him, that he was
important around here. Instead of the baggy jeans,
fresh tennis shoes, and oversized tee shirts that most of
the other men wore, he was dressed in charcoal - grey
suit pants, a deep teal oxford, and a patterned tie that

29

*matched his other attire. Everything looked... new.
Even his low haircut had impossibly sharp lines,
defining his wavy hair from his blemish-free skin.*

His hand inched a little higher on her leg.

"Would you like a drink?"

*When Renata shook her head, delivering an
emphatic "no", he chuckled.*

*"What... you one of those "good Christian
girls" that come to the club, and don't drink?"*

*Swallowing hard, she shook her head again.
"No... it's just... I... I'm only 19," she lied, trying her
best to keep a straight face. He frowned a little, and
Renata wondered if she should have maybe gone
younger. Eighteen was old enough to be in the club,
and maybe she didn't look as old as she thought. If he
called security, Samantha would kill her, and probably
get her in trouble with her mom. Ah, damn.*

*"Don't worry about it, baby girl. Nobody is
gonna ask you for ID."*

"How do you know?"

*He smiled, and that dangerous glint crossed his
eyes again. "Because the owner of this club works for
me... so I own this club. And because I said so."*

*So maybe that explained why he looked so...
shiny, and out of place, compared to everyone else.
"Seriously?" she asked, feeling a hot, unfamiliar
sensation rake over her as he swept her with his eyes
again. "What are you doing here, at this... hood club?"*

*Chuckling, he shrugged a little. "I needed to
meet with a certain... element tonight, to conduct some
business. I don't want them on my usual turf, so... I
come to theirs. And I come prepared."*

30

For the first time, Renata noticed the similarly — but not nearly as well — suited men a few feet away, all pretending not to pay attention.

Security.

His *security*.

He motioned for a bartender and ordered something Renata had never heard of. A few moments later, she had a large, purple frozen drink in her hands.

"Houston specialty," he said, guiding the glass up to her lips. She took a tiny sip, immediately recognizing the flavors of sprite and cough syrup. Whatever alcohol the bartender had used was unfamiliar, but she knew without asking that she held in her hands some variation of "purple drank", popular among her partying high school peers. Renata had heard the stories, and wasn't interested.

She pulled the drink away from her mouth, but he pushed it back. She obliged another small sip, then shook her head, pressing her lips **tight**. His eyes darkened for just a moment, enough to send a prickle of fear up her spine, but then the mysterious charm was back, as he tilted his head to the side and laughed.

"Nineteen, huh? No wonder you're acting all shy."

Renata looked down at her hands as he called the bartender over again, returning the previous drink and requesting another, making sure to emphasize that it should be virgin. When she was presented with a plain cranberry juice, pineapple juice, and sprite a moment later, she took it gratefully. She closed her mouth over the straw and drained the short glass in one drag, then glanced over at her companions. Neither

Sam nor Stacy were paying her any mind, so she turned back to ... him.

"You didn't tell me your name," she said, squinting a little as another round of head-pounding music started.

"Damien Wolfe."

His hand reached the top of her thigh and inched inward. She pulled her legs away, ignoring the little voice telling her it was fine. The mention of his name... it tugged at a distant memory, but she couldn't pinpoint why. He'd mentioned that the club owner worked for him... maybe he was some type of business man?

"Excuse me for a moment," he said, as several similarly- dressed men walked up. She averted her eyes as they stepped into the corner, conducting a conversation in hushed tones. Her head shot up when Damien raised his voice, and she watched as he slammed his fist into his palm, then jabbed a finger toward the exit as he said something about "cleaning up a mess back in New Orleans". The cool façade she'd seen not even moments before had slipped a little, and he seemed angry. One of the men muttered something about "lost control", and Damien hand snatched up a handful of his shirt, dragging him forward.

Renata quickly looked away, not wanting to be caught eavesdropping and face a similar fate. Everyone else seemed to be ignoring the little scuffle, so she did too. A moment later, she felt the shift in the air around her as he sat down again, back to dapper as his hand slid over the small of her back. This time, the voice telling her it was fine spoke louder, as her eyelids dipped a little, suddenly heavy.

"So back to what we were talking about... what do you like to do for fun, Renata?"

She frowned a little, then burst into a loud giggle, leaning into his shoulder. "I don't think we were talking about that."

"We are now."

Renata laughed again. "O-kayyyy. Well... I like to use computers."

"Really now? That's... surprising?"

"Why?"

He lifted a hand, allowing it to drift up her arm, over her neck, and up to cup her face. "You don't look like the kinda girl who likes computers."

She stifled another giggle as she struggled to keep her eyelids up. "What kinda girl do I look like?"

"The kind who likes to play shy... but really... wild. Are you... wild, Renata?"

Something was wrong.

Feeling dizzy, she shook her head. She wasn't wild at all, but she was having a hard time actually saying otherwise. Her body wasn't cooperating... as if it weren't even connected to her head.

"I don't believe you," he said, with his mouth right against her ear. He was close enough now that she could smell alcohol on his breath, and a faint, shrill alarm sounded from somewhere in the back of her mind. She wanted to push away the hand he'd moved between her thighs, but her lips were heavy, her limbs sluggish, and her ears filled with a ringing sort of static.

She managed to shake her head and take a deep breath, finding a moment of mental clarity after. Barely, she found the strength to turn her head to where

Stacy and Sam were, but they were both occupied with purple drinks of their own.

She flinched as he pushed her panties out of the way, embarrassed by the involuntary way her body responded to the intimate touch. A moment later, his fingers pushed inside of her. Her brain registered pain, but her body was powerless. She squeezed her eyes tight as his liquor-soaked breath heated her neck again.

"Nice and tight," he groaned. "Perfect. Let's go."

Her vision went black as someone dragged her up from her seat. Faintly, she heard Stacy's giggly voice asking what was going one, but soon her hearing was as muffled as her vision. Shortly after, there was nothing.

The next morning, she woke up in Stacy's bed. Her head was pounding, and she was sore between her legs — a feeling she'd never before experienced, but had read enough things she shouldn't be reading to know why her thighs and intimate parts were tender. She looked around, and a moment later, saw Stacy sitting at the end of the other twin bed in the room she'd shared with Sam before she left for college.

As if she felt Renata's questioning gaze, Stacy looked up with red-rimmed eyes and shook her head. An ache that had nothing to do with a physical pain started in the pit of Renata's stomach, working its way into a thick lump in her throat that took her breath away.

She sat up, dry heaving as she wrapped her arms around herself.

34

*When she finally looked up, her throat aching
and sore from sobbing, Stacy met her eyes.*

*"I'm so sorry Ren. They took us to this big
house, and that guy you were talking to... nobody
would stand up to him, and Sam wouldn't do anything.
We were so drunk, and... I'm so sorry, Ren."*

*As a fresh wave of sobs swept over her, Renata
drew her legs up to her chest, burying her face against
her legs.*

All she'd wanted to do was talk to CD last night.

— & —

Something was... off.

It wasn't the searing pain in her shoulder or
head — Renata knew what that was from — or the fact
that the room around her was unfamiliar — she had a
good idea of where she was.

Something... *cold* was touching her.

Renata dragged her eyes open with a groan, and
as her blurry vision cleared, the first thing she saw was
Naomi. Deep mahogany skin, dark, striking eyes, and a
thick mass of kinky black hair— she was beautiful...
and deadly.

Naomi had death in her eyes.

Renata swallowed hard, frozen in place by
Naomi's lethal stare. She flicked her gaze upward, and
immediately knew what the "something" cold was.

There was a gun pressed to her forehead.

"I'm going to ask you several questions. All I
need from you is a yes, no, or the shortest possible
answer. I don't need your pitiful explanations. You can
tell the truth, or I will blow your brains all over this
room without hesitation or regret. You got me?"

"Yes," was Renata's immediate answer. She wasn't exactly scared of her, but truth be told, Naomi was terrifying. She had no doubt that Naomi *would* pull that trigger.

"Are you willingly employed by Damien Wolfe?"

"No."

"Does he have your daughter without your consent?"

"Yes."

"Have you given him any information that could be hurtful to this team?"

Renata swallowed hard. "Yes."

Nostrils flared, Naomi tightened her grip on the gun. "The information on getting past my security system?"

"Yes."

"Anything else?"

"I don't think so."

Naomi pressed the gun harder into her skin, sending a fresh wave of pain through Renata's head. "Does he know we're after him?"

"I don't know."

"*Think harder.*"

"I don't know!"

Narrowing her eyes, Naomi stared a little longer before she finally backed away a little, pulling the gun away from Renata's head, but keeping it pointed in her direction. Now that she'd moved back, Renata could see Inez — her caramel skin glowing in the dim light, blonde-tipped hair pulled into a messy bun — standing near the door of the room, her arms crossed as she watched them.

36

"Do you know if Wolfe sent those men to my apartment himself?"

Renata shook her head. "No. I never know who I'm talking to."

"Do you know who came after you last night?"

"No."

Naomi sucked her teeth. "Well you just don't know *shit*, do you?" She rolled her eyes, then swung her attention back to Renata with a scowl. "How about this — why don't you tell me how you ended up with Damien Wolfe as a baby daddy?"

"No."

The refusal was out of her mouth before she really even knew what she was saying.

Naomi's expression turned lethal again, and a second later, the gun was pressed against her head again, with Naomi's finger against the trigger. "You're in no position to be brave, Agent Parker. I already feel like I still owe you an ass whooping for telling Marcus I knew about his dad. Redeem yourself, bitch. I want some answers. *Now.*"

Tears pricked Renata's eyes as the steel bit into her skin, adding more pressure to the headache she already had.

"Naomi… *please*," she whispered. "I was sixteen years old… just a kid."

For a long moment, Naomi glared at her. Her finger danced over the trigger again as her scowl deepened.

She doesn't believe me.

But then… Naomi's expression softened, as a sudden flash of understanding crossed her face. Her eyes went wide, and she pulled the gun away, stepping back from the bed. Relief swept over Renata, and she squeezed her eyes shut, not opening them again until Naomi spoke.

"I'm sorry," she said, in a strained voice. "I recognize Damien Wolfe for exactly what he is — a monster. I'm sorry that he made you another victim."

Renata swallowed her tears as Naomi met her gaze with glossy eyes of her own before she continued.

"Taylor is... she's family. My... cousin, I guess. We'll get her back for you."

Naomi nodded, then turned and left the room, not looking back. Inez gave Renata a tight smile before she nodded as well.

"I'll get Savannah, see if she can give you something for the pain, okay?"

Renata didn't know who the hell Savannah was, but she agreed. Anything to take away the nightmares plaguing her — asleep and awake.

three.

"It's done."

To anyone observing the scene, it would appear that the man lounging on the couch, dressed in pajamas worth twice the average mortgage, hadn't heard anyone speak. He lifted his to his mouth, took a sip, then lowered the glass.

He frowned.

Too much vermouth.

He made a mental note to address his beloved about the mistake —a courtesy he was becoming exhausted with offering— then finally offered the man standing at the door — his assistant, Harrison— his attention.

"Was it messy?"

Harrison scratched his eyebrow, squinting a little before he answered. "A bit."

"Will it be on the news?"

"Already is."

The man sighed, then shook his head. He sat up straight, and beside him, his wife sucked in a tense, fearful breath.

"Will it be connected to me?"

"No."

Furrowing his brow, the man suddenly stood. His wife folded her hands in her lap, staring at her fingers.

"What makes you so sure?" he asked, his voice dangerously low as he stalked up to Harrison. "I'm supposed to believe that because what... you're always right?"

"I *am* always right."

"You're *not* always right, get the fuck outta here."

Despite his boss's harsh words and stony expression, Harrison's posture was relaxed. He smirked. "I was right about Renata."

A vein twitched at the man's temple as he scowled at Harrison — but the younger man didn't back down.

Good.

Finally, a smile cracked his face, and he clapped Harrison on the shoulder before returning to his seat. "You *were* right about Renata. But don't pat yourself on the back yet. This isn't over. She hasn't proven herself quite yet."

Harrison nodded. "Anything else you need, Mr. Wolfe?"

Damien shook his head. "For now... that's all."

When Harrison was gone, Damien turned to his wife, lifting a hand to stroke her face. He lowered the hand to her throat, and arousal swept over him at the way her breath hitched.

"You know I have to punish you, right?"

An excited gleam came to her eyes as she nodded. "Yes, please."

Good.

40

— & —

"You hit those keys any harder, you're gonna break something."

Quentin's fingers paused over the keyboard, and he let out a quiet groan in response to Naomi's interruption.

Three hours... or maybe closer to four.

Four *long* hours had passed since the first gunshot into the back of his car, and he'd still gotten nowhere with checking into the shitload of things Renata had revealed. Instead of the laser-sharp focus he usually employed when it was time to find the facts buried under lies and half-truths, his head was spinning. Maybe it was adrenaline, maybe it was anxiety— he didn't know which. What he did know was that he needed answers— *concrete facts* — to figure out if Renata was someone he could trust or not.

Before, when he'd only known her as painted_pixel, he trusted her implicitly. He may have never seen her face, never heard her voice, but... he'd known her since they were kids. She knew things he'd done, crimes he'd committed... had even played accomplice more than once over the years. But they had a code. If you get caught doing some shit you shouldn't, you've never heard of me. If you need help, ask. Don't try to find me, I won't try to find you. Don't tell any identifying details about yourself.

Quentin shook his head.

They'd trampled all over *that* one.

She knew he lived in New Orleans as a kid, he knew she lived in the suburbs of Houston. She knew he worked with a bad-ass professional criminal. He knew she'd erased cyber-crime related arrests from the system in order to be accepted into a government agency — he hadn't known then which one. She knew he'd suffered the worst pain of his life when his mother succumbed to cancer a few short months after his father died. And he knew that when her mother found out that newly-seventeen, never been in trouble, skipped a year of high school, always on the honor roll painted_pixel was pregnant... she'd kicked her out of the house.

He'd known something was wrong when she contacted him from a *public* computer, in a *public* library, terrified, alone, and in a panic. His first question was why she hadn't just gone to the friends' house she was always talking about, but she freaked out about that.

He was still going through his own shit, still processing the fact that both of his parents were gone, but he pushed that to the side. That first night, she stayed in the shelter, but early the next morning, he sent her to the bank to open an account with the few hundred dollars in birthday cash and allowance she had. A couple of hours later, once she gave him the account number, he'd put in enough to get her through the next few days.

Enough for a few weeks rent at a motel until she could find something better, enough for a new computer, which she had to sneak into her room in a laundry basket, so no one saw. Enough for clothes to hide her growing belly, so she could finish her senior year in peace. He could feel her strain, even through the screen, but he encouraged her, helped however he could, all while meticulously avoiding the knowledge of her real name.

If she wanted him to know, she would tell him.

They'd made exceptions to that no personal details rule before, but it was still part of their code. If she *wanted* him to know, he would know.

But... she hadn't wanted him to know.

After *everything* he'd done for her over the years, risks he'd taken that could have ruined his life... she'd stood right in his face as Special Agent Renata Parker, knowing who he was, and not said a word.

That was *fucked up.*

Quentin groaned again as Naomi pulled up a chair up beside him at the table in Inez's "war room". It was one of many rooms in what was essentially a — rather luxurious — secure bunker, in the basement of her house. A couple of doors down, Renata was asleep in the medical area.

That was part of why he couldn't focus.

Despite a confusing combination of anger, betrayal, and hurt, he was concerned about her. Sure, her loyalty was in question, but that didn't make watching a crimson stain blossom from the gunshot wound in her shoulder any easier. It didn't change the fact that the gunshot wound along the left side of her head would have probably taken her life if the trajectory had taken it just an inch further right.

It's just a graze, " Javi, Inez's "retired military doctor" neighbor had assured.

That didn't make him feel any better.

The thought of losing painted_pixel made a weird, dull sort of ache bloom in the pit of his stomach,

43

radiating up to his chest. Similar to the way he felt whenever something happened to Naomi, but... *different.*

Worse.

He wasn't quite sure yet how he felt about the possibility of losing "Agent Parker".

"So are you just not gonna say anything?" Naomi asked.

He could feel her eyes on him, and when he looked up, sure enough, she was staring expectantly, waiting for him to speak.

"Whatcha' want me to say, Mimi?" he asked after a heavy sigh, swiveling his chair to face her. "I told ya' everything I knew when we got here."

"I want you to tell me how you're feeling... you know, like friends do."

Quentin shook his head. "I don't got time for this shit."

He started to turn his chair back around, but Naomi caught it by the arms, stopping his rotation.

"Uh-uh," she said, twisting him right back to his position facing her. "Don't shut me out right now. Tell me what you're thinking."

Quentin lifted an eyebrow at her, and when he did nothing else in terms of a response, she dropped her head into her hands. After a short groan, she sat up, tossing her hair back from her face.

"Okay... I'll start it off: *I believe her.*"

Sucking his teeth, Quentin leaned back in his chair. "Of *course* you do. All anybody's gotta do is sell you a sob story about Wolfe, and you're ready to play superhero. Hey, cut that shit out!" he exclaimed, dodging the half-hearted kick Naomi aimed at his calf.

44

"*You* cut the shit out. Don't act like I'm out here being a vigilante. My focus has always been singular — *still is.*" She paused to scowl for a long moment before she rolled her eyes and continued. "*Anyway*, I believe her because she's telling the truth, not because I'm being conned."

"How ya' know it's the truth?"

Naomi smiled. "Because I looked her in the eyes while I had a gun pressed to her forehead. People tend to tell you the truth when you do that."

"What? She's supposed to be resting, they had to do surgery to close her shoulder up."

"So I woke her up."

"She *took a bullet.*"

Naomi shrugged. "It went straight through. She'll be fine in a few months."

"Not the point, Mimi."

"Yeah, I know." Naomi leaned forward in her chair, tipping her head to the side. "The *point* is that I believe her. And I want to help her."

"With what?"

"Umm... getting her daughter back?"

With a huff, Quentin propped his hands behind his head against the back of the chair, then turned his gaze back to Naomi. "Man... who says her daughter was even *really* kidnapped? Could be bullshitting us, usin' sympathy as leverage."

"She *could*, yes. But I don't think she is, Q. I think she's another one of Wolfe's *victims*, and he's proving himself to be just as disgusting as we all thought, by using his own child to manipulate Renata into committing a crime. Come on, Quentin... if this was reversed, would *you* have said anything, if it meant your child was in danger?"

"She'd already reached out!" Quentin sat up again, and scrubbed a hand over his face. "As painted_pixel, she'd already involved me. Hadn't given me the details, but she'd told me her kid was taken from her. *That's* what had my head fucked up on the Paris job, and a few before that! Tryna' to figure out how to help my friend. You can't convince me she thought she was alone in this. We were on the same damn side. She had *me*."

Naomi shook her head, then took Quentin's hands in hers. "She *thought* she had you. For two seconds, can you look at this from her eyes? She reaches out to her hacker friend, who she's known for years for help with her daughter. Okay, that's established. But then, as part of her job, she actually *runs into* the man on the other side of the screen. Works with him. Finds out that he works for the federal government, that he's on a Special Ops team *specifically* geared against the man who has her child... Is this a setup, or some sort of test? And even if it's not... is he being watched? Is Wolfe going to assume the whole plan is coming out? Is he gonna send someone to "clean it up"? *I don't blame her* for keeping her mouth shut. I would have too."

Quentin propped his elbows on his knees, then dropped his head into his hands. He guessed she had a point, but still... it just didn't sit well with him. Renata knowing who he was and not saying anything, the fact that she'd — under duress or not — given out information that compromised their team, and what

46

maybe bothered him most… how the hell had she ended up in a relationship with *Damien Wolfe*?

He knew women considered Wolfe appealing, if rich, handsome, and scum of the earth was your type. There wasn't a single doubt in Quentin's mind that Wolfe was willing, capable of, and probably well experienced in talking the fairer sex out of their panties, grown women and younger ones alike. But Renata seemed so much… *smarter* than that, than falling for the charm of a snake. That… he just couldn't wrap his head around.

"Just… can you just trust *me* on this, Q?"

When Quentin looked up, Naomi had her arms folded across her chest, the bright white of her bandaged wrists reminding him *she'd* been through an ordeal too, not even two days ago.

Because of Renata.

"Why, Naomi? Why should I trust her just because you do, when she's the reason you almost got kidnapped, killed, whatever they were planning to do? When *my* ass almost got killed a few hours ago because of some lunatic after her. Huh?"

Naomi held up a finger. "First of all, what happened to me isn't her fault. If it hadn't been her, it would have been someone else. They wanted to get to me, so they made it happen, end of story. *We* should have been better prepared. Second… how do you know they weren't after *you*? Could have followed you to her place, followed you two out… who knows?"

Quentin scoffed. "*Bracque.*"

"Hey! Don't you slip into patois on me. It's *not* crazy. I can think of plenty of people who would want you dead. The Russians, for when you kept replacing their *Russian* vodka with French. The Japanese, for that time you turned off the internet for the entire city of Tokyo. The —"

"I get it," he said, groaning as he sat back once more in his chair. "So… trust *you*, even if I don't trust *her*, right?"

Naomi nodded. "*Right*. Just like I trusted you, and didn't kill your ass over that Paris job. You expected my trust then — without even asking, or informing me — because you believed in her. I think you can do the same for me now."

With a heavy sigh, Quentin ran his tongue over his teeth, then reluctantly nodded. "So… okay. We've still got stuff to figure out though. Who came after you, who came after Renata," — Naomi lifted an eyebrow— "Or *me*," he corrected. "And we have to figure out what to do about Royale, because we know her ass is crazy, how to still manage taking down Wolfe…"

"And how to get my little cousin back. Taylor is family. Non-psycho killer crime boss family. I *need* her."

Quentin bit his tongue instead of letting out his snarky response, opting instead for another question. "Okay… what if we trust her… let her in…. and find out she's been lying… find out she's really *not* on the same side?"

Naomi smiled, then stood from her chair. "Then, *cher*… you get to be the one to pull the trigger."

— & —

Quentin snatched off his headphones and tossed them onto the tabletop beside his keyboard. Raising his hands to his face, he pinched the bridge of his nose, pressing hard to offset the mounting pressure of a headache. He sat back in his chair, closing his eyes to shut out the unnatural glow of the computer screen in the dark.

An hour had gone by since Naomi returned to bed, and the basement was quiet. Everyone was back upstairs, except for him, and presumably, Renata. Digging into her background hadn't proven itself the most effective means of getting answers about her. He *had* discovered that someone — presumably Damien Wolfe — had been depositing hefty checks into Renata's bank account for *years*. But… looking at her, you'd never know she had an account with a balance in the *high* hundreds of thousands.

As far as he could tell, for the last fourteen years, she'd lived modestly. Lived in middle class neighborhoods, drove a regular car, and paid regularly into her retirement accounts. There was nothing to suggest she was taking advantage of any perks from being the mother of Damien Wolfe's child. In fact… it didn't look like she touched the money at all, other than moving it into an account named simply "Taylor".

That realization, while it did increase the likelihood that she was telling the truth, did nothing to soothe the sense of anger and betrayal he felt. She was being honest? Fine. The fact remained that after *everything* he'd done for her over the years, she hadn't trusted him with this. She only divulged it because she *had* to.

A noise from the hall pulled him from his thoughts, and he straightened up in his chair, listening again before getting up to investigate. The sound led him to Renata's room, and he hesitated at the door, taking a deep breath before he pushed it open.

"The hell?!"

Renata was on the floor, sitting back on her knees, eyes closed as tears streamed down her face. At the sound of Quentin's voice, she opened them, and the distant, dazed look in her eyes told him whatever painkillers Savi had her on were still in effect.

"Why are you out of your bed?" he asked, still standing in the open door.

She blinked hard a few times, then looked up, squinting to focus her eyes. "I was thirsty... I dropped the cup, and it rolled under the bed. I can't reach it."

Her slurred words made Quentin cringe, and he stepped fully into the room. "That's what the call button is for, so somebody can help you... but I see you're allergic to that."

Renata's eyes widened a little, as if his words had a sobering effect. She looked away, and feeling guilty, Quentin crossed the distance between them. Careful to avoid her injured arm — which was bleeding through the dressing, probably due to her over-activity — he helped her up, and back into the bed.

Retrieving the cup she was after from under the bed, he took it to the sink and washed it well, then returned it to the table at her bedside.

"Call Savannah down here to look at your shoulder. You oughta be thanking your lucky stars for those painkillers, or you probably woulda' blacked out from pain down there on the floor."

He turned away from the bed and headed for the door without saying anything else. When he looked back, just before he opened it, he saw Renata struggling

50

to pour herself a glass with her left hand, while not straining her injured right shoulder. As he watched, she accidentally bumped the glass, sending it toppling to the floor.

Why won't she just ask for some damned help?

Quentin's first inclination was to continue on his way. If she *really* wanted his assistance, she would have asked, but… *shit.*

With a heavy sigh, he stalked back toward the bed, retrieving the cup again. He washed it, cleaned up the water, and poured a new cup for her without a word. When he pushed the glass in her direction, with force dangerously close to a *shove*, their eyes met for a moment. Hers were filled with a pain that Quentin guessed had nothing to do with the gunshot wound in her shoulder.

"I'm sorry," she spoke quietly, with a slight quiver in her voice. "I'm just… trying not to be a bother to anybody."

She accepted the glass, then looked away, and Quentin turned away as well. He wasn't *trying* to be an asshole, not at all, but he was having a hard time pushing past… whatever the confusion in his head was. Logically, he understood that she'd done what she had to do for her daughter. Naomi had referred to her as a victim, and… *rationally*, Quentin knew that was an accurate characterization.

But… he wasn't feeling rational. He was feeling *pissed,* because the deep, long-standing friendship he'd had with painted_pixel was slipping away fast, thanks to Renata.

Still without a word, he left the room. On the other side of the door, he called Savi himself to come and re-dress Renata's shoulder. If she wouldn't even ask for help with a glass of water now, he seriously doubted she was going to request the help she needed with that.

four.

Just knock, man.

Quentin paused, with his fist lifted to tap the door. The last few hours had been spent attempting to sleep, but the only success he'd found was in tossing and turning, then finally passing out when he was just too exhausted to do anything else.

He'd spent the night in one of Inez's guest rooms. Until a culprit for last night's attack was determined, returning to his apartment was unwise. Good thing he'd brought his laptop with him — it was the only thing he kept in the apartment that *really* mattered. Call it paranoia, or simply his nature as a hacker, but he felt neither want nor need to fill his living space with "stuff". He needed to be able to drop everything and run, with nothing except the computer, his bag, and the contents inside.

A conversation he'd had more than once with painted_pi—Renata.

Her name is Renata.

The sooner he got that through his head, the sooner he reconciled that painted_pixel and Renata were the same person... the sooner something as simple as knocking on her door to check on her wouldn't feel so... strange.

He shook his head.

This wasn't him. This *nervous* bullshit was foreign. He was the level-headed one, the one that operated on logic, and cooled *other* people down when situations became tense. Mostly, Quentin dealt in rationality, not emotion... except when it came to women.

Boy, I swear, every bonne a rienne dat come ya way, you gotta go chasin'. One a dem fast-tailed girls put a gree gree on you, don't come runnin' to me wit da oo ye yi. You hear?

Quentin chuckled a little as his grandmother's words, warning him that she would provide no comfort for a broken heart, played in his head as clearly as if she were beside him. She'd leveled that warning with good reason, when he was fourteen. He'd developed the *faintest* bit of facial hair, and was feeling himself something *tough*. Thing was, the girls were too, to the point that his mother and grandmother had taken to threatening the random girls that called the house or showed up at the door.

He enjoyed — *loved* — women, but wouldn't say he had a weakness. Very, *very* few touched him on a level that moved him to action, compelled him to comfort, or garnered more than a passing concern for their well-being. Momma and Mémère, both gone now. Naomi, who he'd known since they were *little* kids. Inez, who he considered something like a sister. And... painted_pixel.

Renata.

Finally, Quentin took a deep breath and pushed the door open, realizing a moment later that he'd forgotten to knock. The first thing he noticed was warm, rich, cinnamon-brown skin.

54

A *lot* of it.

Or not, he thought, forcing his mind out of the gutter as he stepped in. At first glance, her bare shoulders had given the impression of nudity, but further inspection revealed that she was simply wearing a strapless top.

Her eyes were closed, fist clenched, brow furrowed in pain as Savi cleaned and changed the bandages on her shoulder.

Savi looked up, smiling at Quentin as he approached the bed. "Mornin' Q," she said in her usual cheerful voice.

Even with her face contorted from discomforted, Renata was pretty as hell, but when she looked up at the sound of his name, her big brown eyes open wide, lush lips parted, she took Quentin's breath away. Her long braids were all pushed to one side, and slung over her shoulder in a way that lent an unintentional sultriness to her look.

Beautiful.

She was looking at him like she expected him to say something, but Quentin's mouth had gone dry. He swallowed, in an attempt at relief, but before he could speak, the door opened behind him.

Shit.

He tore his eyes away from Renata long enough to glance up at Kendall and Marcus as they came in, both wearing somber expressions. Almost immediately, a sense of dread washed over him as they tipped their heads in greeting, then headed to Renata's side.

"What is it?" she asked, in a strained voice. "Is it… Taylor? Did something hap—"

Marcus lifted his hands in a calming gesture. "No. *No*. We haven't heard anything about Taylor, but... you know when we left this morning, we were gonna grab some things for you from your apartment. But... there was a fire, Ren. All of the alarms were disabled, so one of your neighbors called it in when they smelled smoke, but... everything is gone."

For a long moment, Renata didn't respond. She remained... *stuck*, her brow furrowed in apparent confusion as Savannah finished dressing her shoulder, then carefully put her arm into a sling. It wasn't until Kendall stepped into Savi's place, putting a hand on her knee for comfort that Renata finally exhaled, with a ragged breath that seemed painful.

She shook her head, looking back and forth between Kendall and Marcus. *"Everything?"*

Quentin simply watched, somewhat baffled at Renata's reaction to the fire at her apartment. The stuff at her place was just that — *stuff*. Why the hell did it matter? She should know better than this... know better than to become attached to material crap. They had the same code... or used to.

"My... my baby's room... her clothes, her pictures... her baby book, all of our memories... I... my *paintings.*"

Quentin dropped his gaze. *Of course* she didn't live completely by that "drop everything and go" mentality anymore. She *couldn't*. Not with a daughter in school, becoming a teenager, making friends. Not working for the FBI, growing close to her colleagues... working towards a semblance of a normal life. She was *happy*, before Wolfe rocked her world — again — by taking Taylor from her. He knew because she'd told him — as painted_pixel — but still. He knew she was settled into a legit government job that she loved. Knew she'd been *thrilled* to find that apartment, for such a good price, so near the water. Knew that after years of moving around — for reasons he'd never understood before, but felt like he did now — she was... *settled.* She was happy.

And Wolfe took that from her when he took her daughter.

Not quite sure what to do with himself, Quentin scrubbed a hand over his face. He felt... out of place, watching Marcus and Kendall attempt to comfort Renata as she cried, rambling off things that were lost to her now. She used her left hand to brush her braids away from her face, then abruptly shook her head again.

"I... I need a minute. Can... everybody just *go,* please. I... just need a second."

"Ren..." Marcus tried to grab her hand, but she snatched away, shooting him a look that was half tortured, half anger.

"*Go,*" she repeated, glancing between him and Kendall. "Everybody. *Go.*"

Savannah wasted no time getting out of there, and Marcus and Kendall reluctantly followed. The door closed behind them, and Quentin was left there, torn between making his own attempt at comforting her, and answering the quiet voice that still nagged at him to leave her alone.

She cleared tears from her face with a harsh swipe, then her gaze lifted to where Quentin stood. Their eyes met, and for a while, neither moved. Just as Quentin was finally about to open his mouth to speak, the warmth dropped from Renata's eyes, replaced by a coldness that made him feel... dejected.

"*Everybody,*" she said, nostrils flared. "*Go away.*"

Well damn.

It would have been grossly disingenuous to pretend that her words didn't sting... but he couldn't blame her. After treating her like shit, did he *really* expect to be allowed to play comforter? He gave her a quick nod, then obliged her wishes and left, pulling the door closed behind him.

On the other side, he paused to take a deep breath, then headed back to his computer. Even if he couldn't make her feel better... he could — no, *would* — find out who was behind this shit.

— & —

Wolfe had called.

Some time after she'd been able to catch her breath from the devastating news of the fire at her apartment, Renata reached for her phone, on the table beside her bed. It had been there for a while, turned off and missing the protective case she usually kept it in. Both things told her that someone, probably Quentin, maybe Kendall, had already stripped it, checked for tracking or recording devices, mined it for any information it held, and *then* decided she could have it back.

But... getting the phone back meant that whoever held the most authority — probably Naomi — thought she could be trusted.

58

At least one person does, she thought, as she powered on the phone. While she waited for the phone, she'd leaned back into her pillows, wondering how soon the next dose of painkillers was. The bullet to her shoulder had fractured several bones before exiting her body, and the hot heaviness of the wound didn't seem keen on letting her forget. Renata breathed a heavy sigh. It was just her luck that the bullet had gone through her right shoulder, instead of the left. How was she supposed to work, live, *paint,* or do what she needed to get Taylor back with her dominant side out of commission?

Well maybe Wolfe should have thought of that before he tried to have me killed.

Because… it really wasn't very fair, if he expected her to still pull off the job against King Pharmaceuticals.

Internally, she scoffed.

If.

That was ridiculous.

Of course he still wanted her to pull off hacking and sabotaging one of the biggest pharmaceutical companies in the country, one that had millions — if not *billions* — of dollars worth of contracts with the federal government. *Of course.* He wouldn't care that she was injured — would probably call it her fault for "running" or whatever he thought she'd done that warranted a shootout. Damien Wolfe would still expect her to get it done, and he wouldn't reunite her with her daughter until she had.

That, she was sure of.

Once her phone was fully powered on, she unlocked the screen and was immediately met by several notifications. Some from various apps, a few reminders of upcoming work events and deadlines, and... two missed calls from Wolfe.

Renata's breath caught in her throat.

What did he want?

They weren't calls from the same mysteriously scrambled numbers that popped up on her screen when she was presented with another problem to solve. These were calls from his *personal* number, the one he unequivocally expected her to answer when it rang.

And she hadn't.

Twice.

With a deep breath, she pressed the button on the side of the bed that would notify the others that she needed something. While she waited for someone to come, she began turning over the possibilities in her mind.

What did he want?

Was he calling as a way to see if she were still alive? To make sure she'd heard about the fire? To inform that her services were no longer needed, and she wouldn't ever see Taylor again? Or... maybe to change her mission? If he knew for sure that she was working with Naomi and Quentin now... would she be forced to play mole, or maybe even saboteur? Her brain was still running with possibilities when the door opened and Naomi and Inez stepped in.

"What's going on?" Naomi asked, wariness in her eyes as she approached the bed.

Renata took a deep breath, then blurted it out. "Wolfe called... and I need to call him back. I don't know what he'll do if I don't call back."

60

Inez nodded, looking back and forth between Renata and Naomi. "Agreed. Especially with so much going on. The last thing we need is an assumption of anything. We know how Wolfe operates... he comes on strong, no mercy. We *need* to know what he knows."

"Okay... so what's the plan?" Naomi turned her attention to Renata. "Does he do this often, calling you?"

"Not... *often*," Renata said, allowing the phone to drop into her lap so she could rub her the bridge of her nose. "Before he took Taylor, once every six months or so, no matter how many times I changed my number. Since he's had her, he calls once a week to let me talk to her, and she texts me from her own phone sometimes."

"And today's call?"

With a heavy sigh, Renata shook her head. "Is off schedule. I talked to them five days ago, so... I think we can safely assume it's about the shooting, and/or the fire."

The fire.

Even more than the shooting, she was trying to block that from her mind. Before she'd left for her "summer vacation" with her father — as Wolfe had phrased it — Taylor had been adamant about making sure that her room, overwhelmingly girly, decorated in soft shades of peach and white, remained intact while she was gone. No surprise makeovers — as Renata had done before — no snooping, no closet purging. She wanted her room to stay exactly as she left it, and Renata had promised her that.

Now, that promise was broken.

Her yearbooks, class pictures, report cards, all of the things she'd collected as her little girl grew up were gone. The knick-knacks they'd picked up while moving from place to place when Taylor was younger, back when Renata still thought maybe she could *hide* from Wolfe— gone. And her own personal escape, the paintings that were either too private or too precious to sell or giveaway, the ones she pulled out when she needed something emotionally... *gone.*

"So, here's what I think we should do."

Renata blinked hard as Inez's voice snapped her out of her musings.

"You should call back, and just remain neutral. Naomi and I will stay in the room. Let *him* ask the questions. Don't tell him where you are, if he asks, just say you're in a safe place. We'll see where we can get from there, okay?"

"Okay," Renata agreed. "But... it's usually... he insists on video calling."

Naomi's eyes narrowed. "So... he forces you to *look* at him when he's talking?" She rolled her eyes, then lifted her hand to massage the back of her neck, mumbling a *this muthafucka*-style rant under her breath. "Okay," she said, when she lifted her head again. "We'll prop the phone against something, so he only sees you, and you don't have to hold it. It's not a big deal for him to see your arm in a sling. If he asks, just give him a direct answer."

Renata nodded, then sat up a little more in the bed as Inez positioned the phone. When she and Naomi were out of view of the camera, she gave Renata a "thumbs up" gesture, and Renata reached forward, pressing the few buttons she needed to make the call.

62

Her call was answered almost immediately, and she was unsurprised to see Wolfe's assistant, Harrison, on the screen. In another lifetime, under different circumstances, she may have considered him handsome, — skin the color of cooked caramel, brown eyes, chiseled features, and a tall, athletic frame — but as it was, he worked for Wolfe. Never had she gotten an "evil" vibe from him like the one she got from Wolfe, but... that almost made it worse, if he was just terrible for hire.

"Ms. Parker. What can Wolfe Tobacco Industries do you for you today?" he asked casually. Renata swallowed hard, trying to keep her voice steady as she answered.

"My cell was turned off, and I missed a few calls. I'm returning them. Is Taylor okay?"

The question was out of her mouth before she remembered that *she* wasn't supposed to be doing the "asking". She shot at a subtle glance at Naomi and Inez, who were both wearing grim expressions.

"Taylor is perfectly fine. She and Kennedy are getting along very well — as siblings should."

Renata resisted the urge to roll her eyes at that statement, opting instead to press her lips together until the compulsion to be snarky went away. "Do you know why he called, Harrison?"

"Ask him yourself," was Harrison's curt response. "He's done on the other line now."

Behind him on the screen, Renata could see the office scenery change as he moved, presumably to where Wolfe was. Before handing off the phone, he spoke again.

"Hey Parker," he said, giving her his usual smirk.

"What?"

He winked. "Glad to see you alive."

Renata's eyes went wide, and she opened her mouth to respond, but the face on the screen had already shifted to Wolfe.

Even through the phone, his gaze was calculating as it swept over what he could see of her. Despite her desire to appear confident, her voice wavered as she spoke.

"Did you need something?"

He grinned, then shook his head as he chuckled. "What, you can't speak? Hello, Ms. Parker. Good morning, good to see you. See... that wasn't very hard, was it?"

With a clenched jaw, Renata responded with, "Hello, Wolfe."

Again, he shook his head. "I guess that'll work... for now."

After that, he said nothing, just sat there with the same scrutinizing look as before.

"Did you need something from me?" Renata asked again, growing impatient. He'd called twice, and she knew it wasn't just for the sake of calling. Wolfe did *nothing* just for the sake of doing it.

"I want to know how far you are with King Pharmaceuticals."

At that moment, the door opened again and Quentin and Marcus walked in, carefully closing the door behind them. Already feeling a heavy sense of dread, Renata didn't look away, keeping her eyes on the screen.

64

"I'm not… *anywhere*, with KP. I'm… trying to figure my way through their firewall to gain access, but it's not a simple process. I… I need *time*. And help that I don't have. I've told you this isn't a one person job."

Wolfe smiled, a gesture that was simultaneously terrifying and pleasing to the eyes. "Help that you *don't* have? Why… Ms. Parker, I beg to differ. You see… I heard an *interesting* story recently, involving a certain family member of mine. It would seem that she has involved herself with a very… what's the term I'm looking for, Harrison?"

"That motherfucker thinks he's Mike Lowery!" Harrison's voice came from the background.

Chuckling, Wolfe nodded. "Yes indeed. Loyal, but impulsive, smart, but destructive, arrogant, but with a heart of gold. Special Agent Marcus Calloway thinks he's Mike Lowery. You know who that is, right, Will Smith, Martin Lawrence, Bad Bo—"

"I know who he is, thank you," Renata snapped. "What does that have to do with anything?"

He lifted an eyebrow. "Well… you see, Marcus Calloway is one of the agents on your team, and I know for a fact that he's romantically involved with a certain young lady I know very well. That young lady is *family*. *Blood* family. She knows someone who can help you."

"And what exactly should I say, when I ask for this assistance?"

"I don't care *what* you say Ms. Parker, I just want the job done. Tell them whatever you need to."

"And if they refuse?"

Wolfe's expression turned cold, and Renata stiffened under his steely gaze.

Off-camera, Harrison spoke up again. "She thinks we're stupid, boss."

Wolfe nodded. "Yes, she does. She thinks I don't see how *convenient* it was for Calloway and my *beautiful* Naomi to be in Barbados the same night an attempt was made on Rochas' life. Ms. Parker thinks I don't know Calloway was pretending to be a dirty FBI agent to take down Victor Lucas. She thinks I didn't notice her change in pattern, that she started spending a little too much time at that gym Naomi and Quentin own. She is *insulting my intelligence* to think I can't put two and two together."

"A gym membership is insulting to you?" she asked, fighting to keep the strain from showing in her face or voice.

Wolfe lifted a hand, pointing at the phone in a "do you believe this?" kind of gesture as he looked at something — presumably Harrison — off screen. He chuckled. "Let me make this plain for you, *Renata.* I want King Pharmaceuticals to go *down*, and I want *you* to do it."

"Then why did you try to kill me and the only person I know who can help?"

Eyebrow raised, Wolfe turned his attention back to the screen. "I wasn't behind that — you can believe or not believe that, it's your choice. But you and LaForte are worth far more to me alive, so hear me on this — it's being taken care of. I don't play about business, and I don't play about my family. Anybody who fucks with either *will* be dealt with. Ask Victor Lucas."

Immediately, her eyes went to Naomi, at the realization that Wolfe had essentially admitted to being

66

behind the death of Victor Lucas. A moment later, Renata's gaze went back to the screen and stayed locked there, as Taylor's face appeared beside Wolfe.

The similarity in appearance between her innocent, beautiful daughter and her predatory father had always bothered Renata. Still, the sight of that sweet face, which she hadn't seen in what felt like forever, made tears spring to her eyes. She cupped a hand over her mouth to choke back a sob as Taylor smiled at the screen.

"Hi Momma!" she said, with a cheerful wave.

Swallowing her emotion, Renata replied. "Hi baby. How are you? Are you okay?"

Taylor gave back a playful roll of her eyes. "Of course, Mom, I'm fine! I'm having so much fun here! Kennedy introduced me to all of her friends, since I'll be going to school with her when the semester starts."

Renata's eyes shot to Wolfe. "*What?*" she asked in disbelief.

"Well, I explained to Taylor that you have a *terribly* important project you're working on, so you wouldn't be able to give her the attention she needs, and she may be a distraction for you. When I told her that it may be best that she not return home until you've completed your project, we agreed that she would stay here for the upcoming school year." He finished with a smile that some might read as encouraging, but all Renata saw was him taunting her.

"Yeah Mom," Taylor chimed in, her face beaming "They set up a room for me and everything! I'm gonna miss you like crazy, but I'm having a blast! Thank you Daddy!"

Renata had to look away from the screen as Taylor placed a big kiss against Wolfe's cheek. *That*, the thought that Taylor thought this man was worthy of her positive opinion, made her stomach turn.

"Mom, what happened to your arm?!"

Renata turned back to her phone to see that Taylor's jovial expression had shifted to one of concern, at the realization that her mother's arm was in a sling.

"It's nothing," Renata responded, but Wolfe shook his head.

"She's not a baby. Tell her what happened."

Nostrils flared, she considered if it would be worth it to tell Taylor she'd been shot because of her father. Probably true, even if in a roundabout way, but definitely not worth the chance of Wolfe's retaliation. Not while her child was in his care.

"Mom... what is it?"

With a deep breath, Renata shot a glare at Wolfe, then focused on her daughter. "There was a fire, baby. Everything in the apartment is gone. I'm so sorry."

Taylor's mouth dropped open in shock, eyes wide, but before she could say anything, Wolfe chimed in. "But, don't you worry your pretty little head about it, baby girl. I'm going to make sure your mother has everything she needs, starting with a new apartment, and we'll replace all of your stuff. How does that sound? Would you like that?"

Taylor nodded, then gave him a big hug before turning back to the screen. "Mom, I'm so glad you decided to let Dad be in my life! See how awesome he is?!"

68

Ugh.

With a quick wave, and her sorrow about the fire already forgotten, Taylor bounced out of the camera frame, and a few moments later, Renata heard the distant closing of a door.

"What a beautiful child," Wolfe said, smiling as he turned back to the screen. "You wanna see her again… you get your new friends on board, and take King down. Figure it out."

And with that, he ended the call.

As soon as she registered that he'd hung up, Renata grabbed the phone and torpedoed it across the room with a scream, feeling no remorse as it shattered into pieces against the concrete wall. For a moment after that, she just felt… frozen, but then somewhere in her, the dam broke, and she dropped her face into her hand as she sobbed.

She didn't feel any pain, not from her shoulder or head. The pain she felt was a deep, cavernous ache of emptiness and loss. She had… *nothing.* It seemed like no matter what, she just…. couldn't escape the poison that Wolfe spread.

Somebody placed a hand on her shoulder, and without looking up, she knew it was Naomi. Tearfully, Renata turned to her, futilely attempting to dry her face with her hands.

"So," Naomi said, addressing the room, instead of just Renata. "I know we still have some things to figure out, but… it looks like we've got our next plan."

"What's that?" Quentin stepped forward, his expression a mixture of rage and determination.

Naomi turned back to Renata, lowering her hand to cup her face.

69

"We take down King Pharmaceuticals. We get Taylor back… and we kill Wolfe. I'm sick of him… this motherfucker… blood or not…. He needs to die."

Renata looked up at her with a grateful smile.

A dead Wolfe sounded excellent.

five.

If it weren't for Taylor... Renata wasn't entirely sure she would still be alive. After what happened at that party, that night, she'd been in a desolate place — mentally, emotionally, spiritually... everything just seemed... *black.*

Her mother seemed more verbally abusive than usual, she couldn't stomach the sight of Stacy, and CrawDaddy was in a gloomy place of his own, coping with the death of his father, and the worseningillness of his mother. Renata was miserably, piteously, alone.

Many, *many* times she considered ending it.

The night after the party.

The day after her period never came.

The day she told her mother she was pregnant, and got smacked in the face and called every type of whore under the sun.

But then... CD came through for her. Took care of her, sight unseen... that was *just* how much he cared, and that gave her a tiny bit of hope. For a short while, things were good. Well... better than they had been. She graduated high school, and moved to the city where she planned to go to college with a fake ID that said she was 18, her computer, and a single suitcase.

Shortly before the baby came, she hired a midwife and doula, partially because she didn't want questions at a hospital, mostly because she didn't want to be alone. She and the baby were both healthy, so there wasn't any reason for concern. When she finally had her, and the midwife placed a screaming Taylor on her chest for the first cuddle, Renata was in awe. She didn't understand how a tiny, wrinkled, *loud* little person, borne of violation, could be so... *beautiful* to her. She placed her pinky in one of the baby's flailing fists, and when the baby latched on, squeezing her finger in her miniature hand... Renata couldn't fathom how she'd ever considered ending her life.

This was life.

Taylor was life.

Which was why she needed to *do* something.

If only she *could* do something.

Lying in a hospital bed, nursing her hurt feelings wasn't doing anything toward taking down King Pharmaceuticals, which is what it would take to get her daughter back. Problem was... the injury to her shoulder wasn't just a flesh wound. Even now, she was enduring a level of pain she wouldn't have thought possible, and she wasn't even doing anything except... sitting there. With all of the nerves and tendons and whatever else had been destroyed by that bullet, using that side to type or hold a mouse was pretty much out of the question within the next few weeks... or months... or... possibly *ever*.

That brought a fresh round of tears to her eyes.

Sure, the most likely outcome was that eventually, she would be able to use her arm again, for something other than filling out her sling, but the possibility of it taking months, or years... she didn't have that kind of time. She wished that it was like in books or movies, where she could take a bullet to the

72

shoulder and scale a building a few hours later, but... this was real life.

In real life, the fact was that if she wanted to see and touch Taylor any time soon, she really had no choice other than to accept help.

She swallowed hard, and closed her eyes. There was no telling what the others must think of her by now. After that phone call, she'd slipped into what she could only describe as a mental state of desolation. Overwhelming helplessness, loss, anger, and hurt had descended on her mind, and to cope, she just *slept.* For several days, she welcomed timed dosages of painkillers, immersing herself in the artificially induced sleep. When she was conscious, she spent that time in relative silence, working on clearing her mind of worries, fears, thoughts... *anything.*

For that time, Renata wallowed in the false peace of nothingness, mostly ignoring the steady stream of people who stopped by the room. Marcus, Kendall, Inez, Naomi... even agents Barnes and Black came to see her. And then... there was Quentin, who was hardest to ignore.

She wasn't sure why, because he never said anything. She would hear someone opening the door and close her eyes, pretending to be asleep, and then the air in the room would change as he walked in. He stayed perched near the door, just looking at her, and *God...* she wanted to talk to him so badly. Yeah, she considered Marcus and Kendall friends. They cared about her, and she cared about them. Inez and Naomi were cool too. But Quentin was just *different.* He knew things about her that no one else knew, related to her in a way that no one else did, he was her *best* friend, and... they just didn't have that anymore.

And it hurt like hell.

But... that wasn't what she was supposed to be thinking about. She wasn't supposed to be pining away after a man... a "friend", while her daughter was being brainwashed into believing Damien Wolfe was actually a good man.

Closing her eyes, Renata fought back tears as she remembered the first time she realized Wolfe intended to have a presence — in some capacity — in Taylor's life.

— & —

"What are you doing in my apartment?"

The handful of diapers slipped from Renata's grip as she cautiously eyed Damien Wolfe. She'd just gone to the back for a moment, leaving two-month-old Taylor safely in her bassinet in the living room while she grabbed supplies to restock her changing area. When she left the room, the only person there was Taylor. Now, Damien Wolfe sat on her couch, cradling the baby in his arms, while his... bodyguard, maybe... stood near the door, arms crossed, giving Renata a look that dared her to do anything.

She wasn't gonna do anything.

Not while the devil had her baby in his hands.

"I came to look at my daughter," he said, not even glancing up. He stared down at Taylor's chubby little face, tickling a fat cheek. "She's nice and healthy. Are you breastfeeding her?"

Renata swallowed hard, trying to overcome the dirtiness she felt. She considered calling the police, but… what would she say? Hi, I'm a minor, who committed fraud to get into this apartment, hacked my way into a fake ID, and a whole host of other crimes to cover it all up. I need to report that the father of my child… came to see her.

"Yes." She forced the word out through clenched teeth, planting her feet to stay balanced as she trembled with a mixture of anger and fear. "She gets some formula as well though."

Damien nodded. "All breastmilk is preferable, but any is good too." Finally, he looked up, turning his piercing eyes on Renata. "Looks like you're doing well for yourself."

"I'm doing well for Taylor. Why are you here? How did you find me? What do you want?"

He smiled, sending a fresh wave of nausea over her. "I told you… I'm here to see my daughter. I found you because I always find what I'm looking for. As for what I want… insurance."

Renata raised an eyebrow. "Insurance? What does that mean?"

Chuckling, he stood, then walked over to her and placed the baby in her arms.

"You'll see."

— & —

And was this what he'd meant? There was no way he was shrewd enough to "know" back then that she would grow into the talented hacker she was, *possibly* capable of taking down a business rival. And even if he'd guessed… it was kind of extreme to keep your illegitimate child's mother on a string, waiting on the day you could *maybe* use her for her abilities. Why not just hire — or blackmail, or threaten, or whatever other intimidation tactics he kept in his arsenal — someone who had the ability then?

She had no idea *why her*, other than his cryptic response of "insurance". And he certainly hadn't lied about his ability to find her anywhere she went. He always, *always* did, with successively worse punishments. She'd been cursed at, threatened, and hit. But the time that made her stop trying to outrun him was almost ten years ago, when he'd found her, had her tied up, taken Taylor, and simply... left. For two days, she remained tied so tightly that she couldn't move, sobbing against the gag in her mouth. No food, no water, no bathroom, no *nothing*, and then... someone finally came, and Wolfe brought her back. He promised Renata next time would be far worse, and she believed it... so she fell in line.

Curiously, he didn't even bother her. He sent money that she didn't touch, occasionally contacted her about seeing Taylor, but for the most part, he just... left her alone.

Until now.

He'd taken her again, and was waiting until Renata completed this task to give her back. So... she couldn't wallow in depression. She needed to do something, *anything* towards getting into King Pharmaceuticals. But... being able to do that would take time.

And space.

And... *energy*.

Renata knew that part of her present drowsy state was the presence of painkillers lingering in her system. The other thing draining her of energy was the forced confinement in this cold, barren room. She'd had to be sedated after the phone call with Wolfe, but those effects had worn off, and it was time for something different.

She had to get out of there.

… in just a minute.

Right now, she needed another moment. Another *few* moments, to bottle her emotions, to…

Crap.

The sound of the door opening pulled a quiet sigh from her throat as she closed her eyes, turning away. A few seconds later, she felt the now familiar change in energy of Quentin stepping into the room. She willed herself to remain still, willed her heartbeat to steady, but it only seemed to surge faster as this time, instead of remaining at the door, he approached. From the sound, she could tell he placed something on the rollaway table, but then he just… stood there.

"I know you're not sleep, Agent Parker." He placed a hand on the bed, not close enough to touch her, but close enough that she could feel the pressure as he leaned forward. "You sleep witcha' mouth open a little, I've seen it. Stop pretending."

Renata blew out a frustrated breath, but didn't open her eyes. "What do you want?"

"I want you to look at me."

With her lips pressed together, Renata opened her eyes, then turned to look at him.

Geez.

Never would she have imagined that the man on the other end of the screen would be so... *sexy*. She'd always been attracted to him intellectually, drawn to the way he coded, and delighted by his sense of humor. But she'd long pictured a stereotypical "geek", *not* the man she found. He was incredibly handsome, with chiseled features better suited to high-end print ads than being hidden in the shadows of the internet. And his tall, golden-brown, muscled body was definitely not the flabby body of someone who spent most of the day on their ass, pecking keys.

Right now, he looked and smelled fresh from the shower, and as usual, she was having a hard time keeping her tongue in her mouth. And as usual — lately, at least — his expression lacked any humor.

"What?" she asked, her voice bordering on a whisper as she looked away.

"We've got work to do."

Renata scoffed, shaking her head. "*We*? What exactly do you think I can do, with... *this*?" She pointed at her injured arm. "I can't do anything."

"You can do exactly what you were doing before — without that arm." He shrugged after he said that, then looked at her plainly, as if he'd given the most obvious solution in the world.

"Are you... kidding? How am I supposed to type, run commands? I can barely even feed myself with my left hand."

Quentin shook his head, then gave a dry chuckle. "So... voice recognition software is suddenly out of the question? You can't type with your left hand now? You can't drink a damned smoothie? *Come on.* You've been down here feeling sorry for yourself for

78

three days, and we've let that ride, cause your world has been turned upside down. We *get* that. But... we can't do all of this to get Taylor back *for* you. Naomi has been in Terry King's *house*, planting cameras, bugging devices. We've got Inez on the payroll as an employee at King Pharma's headquarters. Kendall has been doing security for us, and gotten himself into an MMA league with King's son. Marcus has been working the fire investigation, watching security feeds, tracking license plates. Hell, even Barnes and Black are doing what they can from their positions. *Everybody* is on this, except you. It's time for this helpless bullshit to end. *You* have work to do."

Tears pricked Renata's eyes as Quentin finished speaking. She had no idea that they'd been so busy, because she hadn't been willing to talk about it, hadn't been willing to *think* about it. He was right, but... he was also being an asshole.

"I don't even have a computer," she mumbled, not meeting his eyes.

He slid the rollover table to the bed, then lightly rapped his knuckles on the intricately painted surface of the closed laptop that hadn't been there before he came in the room.

For a long moment, she simply stared at it, then let out a shuddering breath as she touched it herself. "How did you... did you take my bag that night?"

Nodding, he rocked back on his heels as he shoved his hands in the pockets of his sweatpants. "I took it when I thought you were a traitor, so I could strip it, and mine your files, clone you, and then put a virus that would wipe you out, along with anything attached to your tag."

Renata's eyes shot up to his face, wide with fear, growing glossier with every blink.

"But I didn't do that," he continued, and Renata's shoulders sagged with relief. "I didn't have a chance before we got involved in a shootout, and then... I just wasn't sure if it was right. And with everything that's happened *now*, I... yeah. I didn't touch it. I hope you don't make me regret that."

She looked away. Just like that, he popped the little bubble of hope she had that maybe he was coming around. He may not think she was a mole, planted into their team for the purpose of backstabbing, but... he certainly didn't seem interested in anything like friends.

"Um... do I have to stay down here?"

"No... you're not in prison, Agent Parker."

And there was *that* too. "Agent Parker". He wouldn't call her *Renata*, let alone *Ren*, or what she *really* wanted to hear — *cher* — in his sexy French Creole twang. He was willing to help her, willing to *tolerate* her, but it was quite apparent that their friendship no longer existed. It didn't even seem to phase him. He turned and walked out with his head held high, completely unbothered, and left Renata in the room alone.

Taking a deep breath, she braced herself with her left arm and sat up, then carefully swung her legs over the bed. She took another heavy lungful of air to stand up. Cringing at the pain in her shoulder, she padded carefully across the floor in her socked feet.

In the bathroom, she brushed her teeth and scrubbed her face, then carefully mimicked what Savi had shown her to cover and tape her bandaged arm in plastic for a shower. It went much longer without any help, but she was grateful to eventually get under the hot spray at all.

It took her exponentially longer to dress than usual. Panties, leggings, socks, a bandeau bra, and a tank top that she could only wear on one shoulder took up almost thirty minutes, but she felt an honest sense of satisfaction that she was able to do it herself.

She spent another ten minutes maneuvering her laptop back into her bag, which Quentin had left behind for her. Carefully, she swung the shoulder strap over her uninjured arm, then made her way across the room. At the door, she paused for a moment with her hand on the knob. Her head was pounding, shoulder aching, and she realized suddenly that she was *starving*. She could remember food being brought to her, could remember struggling to eat... but couldn't remember actually consuming anything.

Pushing the door open, she made it out of the room, into the empty hall, then slowly up the stairs. At the top, she glanced around to see if she spotted anyone coming, then continued on, peeking into open doorways until she found the kitchen.

Renata had been raised to *not* go snooping through people's bathrooms or kitchens, but this was a different kind of situation, and she doubted Inez would mind. She opened the refrigerator, and took a cup of yogurt. Once she had something on her stomach, maybe then she'd be able to formulate some type of strategy or plan to complete the job against King Pharmaceuticals.

She opened drawers until she found one that contained the spoons. With spoon and yogurt in hand, she sat down at the kitchen table, put down her bag, and... stared at the yogurt.

How the hell do I get the top off this thing with one hand?

Awkwardly, she tried to hold it place against the table while simultaneously bending her non-dominant hand to grab the foil lid.

"What *exactly* is your issue with asking for help?"

Renata's head popped up to see Quentin standing at the other side of the table, laptop in hand. He placed the computer down, then extended a hand, presumably for her to give him the yogurt.

She glanced down at his hand, and then — even though a little voice in her head was *screaming* for her to just give him the damn yogurt, and let him open it for her — she lifted it to her mouth, grabbed the foil with her teeth, and pulled it open. It took her a moment to process what she'd done, but when she finally did look up, he still had his eyes on her. She saw a flash of something... maybe...resignation, before he sighed, shook his head, and sat down.

Minutes later, he was consumed with whatever he was looking at on his screen, as Renata ate her yogurt in silence. Her own screen was covered with various open windows and documents, all related to King Pharmaceuticals, none of which she was really focused on.

Why couldn't you just let him help?

That question kept playing in her mind, and still, she had no answer, other than the fact that he'd already given *so* much. For *so* long, he'd served as a vessel for her frustrations, never judging her, never complaining about the vague details. To be fair, she'd played the same role for him, but then again... she didn't believe it

82

was *really* the same. She seriously doubted that she'd ever been the kind of emotional support that he'd been for her. He knew nothing of the abuse, gloom, and sorrow he'd enabled her to get through. Him and Taylor... and she had neither of them now.

She tucked her head low, essentially hiding behind the screen of her laptop so he wouldn't see the tears that sprang forward. Frantically, Renata wiped her face, not wanting him or anyone else to see. She'd already burdened him with *so* much... it didn't seem fair to ask for anything else... not even opening a damned yogurt.

But... she *needed* him. With the ache of loneliness and loss weighing heavy on her chest, she could barely read the words on her screen, let alone comprehend them, or formulate any sort of plan. A thought, holding hands with a little trickle of hope, popped up in the back of her mind. Before she could overthink it, she placed her left hand on the keyboard, and began pecking away.

```
[command: open private chat]
painted_pixel: hi.
...............
.........
...
CrawDaddy: .........hi. is there a
reason you're opening a chat to
talk to me, when i'm sitting
across the table?

painted_pixel: this feels
easier.
.......................
```

```
...................
............
```
CrawDaddy: okay... what's up?
```
............
......
...
```
painted_pixel: i'm sorry for not telling you who i was.
```
.............................
```
CrawDaddy: okay.
```
...............
.........
...
```
painted_pixel: okay?... does that mean you accept my apology?
CrawDaddy: if that's what it takes for you to let me get back to work.

Renata looked up, but Quentin had his eyes focused on his screen. She took a deep breath, then began tapping out a response.

painted_pixel: Q... I wish you could understand that I didn't feel like I had a choice. I WANTED to tell you, but making sure I got Taylor back had to come first. I couldn't take that chance.
CrawDaddy: I do understand.
```
...............
.........
......
```

84

painted_pixel: then... what is it?
what do I have to do to make
things right between us? I've
loved you since we were fifteen
years old... tell me what I have
to do for you to call me your
friend again.
....
....
...

CrawDaddy: You don't know ME.
You know my hacker tag. Not the
same thing.

Shaking her head, Renata looked up again,
trying to catch Quentin's eye, but still, he kept his gaze
on his computer. Running her tongue over her lips, she
swallowed hard, willing her heart to stop racing.

painted_pixel: it IS the same
thing. you're the same person,
just... with a face, and a real
name. it's still you... I'm still
me. painted_pixel=Renata. Not
"agent parker". I'm the same
girl, Q.
....
...

....
....
....

[user "CrawDaddy" no longer
exists. aborting chat.]

Renata raised her hand to her mouth, muffling
the choked sob that tried to free itself from her throat.

She dropped her head, her shoulders trembling as a dull ache worked through her chest.

That's it, she thought. After all those years, he doesn't even wan—

"Renata."

Startled, Renata looked up to Quentin kneeling beside her.

"I...," he stopped, pushing out a sigh, and scrubbing a hand over his face before he continued, "I don't know what to say to you, Renata. I don't know how to react to you, how to act around you, because I... I feel I don't *know* you. Painted Pixel? I *know* her. I *care about* her."

"I'm *her*."

Quentin nodded. "I know. Rationally, I *know* that. But... I feel like... even though there were obviously things that went unsaid, details left unfilled... we didn't have secrets from each other. If I needed you for something, you did it. If you needed me for something, I did it." He pointed up at the screen. "We *relied* on each other. Painted Pixel and CrawDaddy *trusted* each other. But *you,*" — he put his finger to her chest — " Don't trust *me*." — he pointed to himself. "And... I gotta be honest... that feels *really* fucked up."

Fresh tears sprang to Renata's eyes. "I *know*. And I'm so sorry. It wasn't that I didn't trust you, I just couldn't—"

"Take that risk. I *get* that. I really, really do. But it don't make it feel any better, *cher*."

Briefly, Renata closed her eyes as a lump formed in her throat. Before she could respond, he continued.

86

"With that said… you're right. It *has* been fifteen years. No sense in washin' it down the drain over a misunderstanding. And… I kinda miss talking to ya'."

For the first time in what seemed like forever, a little smile turned up the corners of Renata's mouth, even as tears spilled over her cheeks. "Kinda?"

Quentin chuckled as he reached up, using his thumbs to wipe the tears from her face. "Okay. I missed the hell outta you."

Whoa.

Those words made warmth bloom in her chest. "But."

Crap.

That "but" doused the warmth in cold water.

Renata squared her shoulders, bracing herself for what was coming next.

"I have to ask," he said, running his tongue over his lips. "Wolfe… as Taylor's father… *why?*"

She tipped her head back. She certainly wasn't expecting *that* question, but… she supposed she should have. She emptied her lungs with a heavy exhale, then inhaled deeply before finally meeting his eyes.

"I… I wasn't… Quentin, it wasn't something I *wanted*. I was only sixteen, and I ended up in a situation that left me pretty helpless."

He nodded. "I know you probably didn't plan to end up pregnant, but I'm trying to understa—"

"No," she interrupted, holding up her hand. "I'm not saying that *pregnancy* wasn't something I wanted. I'm saying that he…."

She trailed off, trying to figure out how to tell Quentin what Wolfe had done to her. She'd never spoken it aloud, never verbalized the violation she'd suffered at his hands. She looked up at him, sure that the confusion in his eyes mirrored hers.

"I didn't want to do it," was what she settled with, when she couldn't figure out a different way to articulate it, without saying any of the words she so desperately hated to even *think*.

Bit by bit, the bewilderment left Quentin's face, replaced by flared nostrils, a clenched jaw, and cold, angry eyes — the same look he'd had when they'd lost contact with Naomi while she was in Victor Lucas's house.

"He... forced you?" he asked, his voice low, and carrying an edge Renata had never heard before.

When she nodded, he pushed himself to his feet, and the rage hanging off of him was so intense she could *feel* it, scorching hot.

"It was something in my drink, at that stupid party," she quickly amended, holding up her hand in an effort to calm him. "It wasn't like... beating me up or anything."

"That's better?!" He turned to face her, his eyes wide with disbelief.

"No. *No*, not at all, I'm just... can you calm down?"

He looked at her with a scowl for another moment longer before his expression softened, and he scrubbed a hand over his face before he knelt in front of her again.

"I'm... sorry," he said, reaching to cup her face in his hands. "And I'm sorry he did this to you." Briefly, his face took on a hard edge again. "He *will* pay for what he did to you. I *promise*."

88

"Q, I don't want—"

"Why didn't you tell me?"

Renata shrugged, then dropped her eyes. "You were dealing with your own stuff. Your dad's death, and then your mom... You were already doing so much."

"And I would have done *more*. I wish you'd told me."

"So you could have done... *what*? If I'd told you what Wolfe did to me, the same night as what he did to your father... what would you have done?"

"I would have killed him."

Renata shook her head. "You would have gotten *yourself* killed. We were *kids*. And me, not knowing your name, I would have never known what happened to you, just that I told you what happened, then never heard from you again. And if I *did* decide to look for you, and found out you were dead... I didn't know back then that Wolfe had killed your father, so I would have thought it was just about avenging *me*. So... I'm glad I never told you back then. I wouldn't have been able to handle that."

A moment passed, and then with a deep sigh, Quentin nodded. "Okay. I *get* that. But you never told me about... any of it."

"Right," she said, with a tight smile. "I... I guess there was some shame there too. I wasn't supposed to be at a party like that, I should have paid better attention to what I was drinking, I should have fought harder... I had all these *wrong* reasons in my head that it was somehow my fault. I know *now* that it wasn't, but... back then... I didn't want you to think less of me." She paused briefly as her voice strained. "I… didn't want you to be disgusted by me."

Quentin's brow dipped into a scowl.

"*Disgusted?*" he repeated. "*Cher…* listen to me… there isn't — and *never has been* —- anything disgustin' about you."

Renata sniffled, then reached for a paper towel from the table to wipe her nose. "Not even this?"

He reached up, running a hand lightly over her bandaged head before he brought it back down to her face. "Not even."

Her breath caught in her throat as he drew her closer, and a moment later, his warm, soft lips were on hers. Heat blossomed in her chest, then everywhere else as he amplified the pressure of his mouth on hers, drawing a soft whimper from her throat. His hands drifted down to her waist, pulling her closer to the end of the chair, closer to him, as he pressed his tongue against the seam of her lips.

The heaviness of their conversation was quickly forgotten as he dipped his tongue in her mouth, stroking hers with unhurried skill. Renata draped the one arm that she could over his shoulder, gripping a handful of his shirt as he drew her against his body, mindful of her injured shoulder. Much sooner than she would have liked, the sound of heavy footsteps in the hall drew them apart, and they looked up just as Marcus appeared in the doorway to the kitchen.

His eyes went wide as he quickly glanced from Renata, her face still wet with tears, to Quentin kneeling in front of her. A second later, understanding lighted his eyes, and he turned on his heels and headed back down the hall.

Quentin chuckled, then turned back to Renata, catching her mid giggle. The look he gave her then was one that she couldn't quite decipher, but made a pleasant sort of heat wash over her.

He lifted his hand to her face again, stroking her cheek with his thumb.

"So... are we good?" he asked, keeping his gaze focused on hers.

She nodded, then smiled, nuzzling her face into his hand.

"Yeah... we are."

six.

"Okay everybody… let's get down to business."

An hour had passed since Quentin kissed her, and Renata still couldn't focus. They, along with the rest of the team, were seated around the table in Inez's war room, looking up at a huge screen. She wasn't sure if this debriefing was for her benefit or not, but in any case, she needed to pay attention. But how the hell was she supposed to do that?

Quentin had *kissed* her.

And *damn* it was good.

Guilt poked at her chest for even thinking the kinds of thoughts she had about him, for *feeling* the warm, buzzing sensations she still felt. A man she considered her own personal satan had her child, filling her head with God knows what, and she was… *horny*.

What kind of mother was *she*?

Renata shook her head and looked up at Agent Barnes, trying not to feel the magnetic warmth of Quentin's body heat radiating from beside her.

Focus, Ren.

"You a'ight, cher?"

Ohhhh, damn.

Quentin's voice sent a jolt of excitement right to her chest as he leaned over to quietly ask that question in her ear. Her gaze shifted to meet his, which were filled with concern. She gave him a quick nod, followed by a little smile of reassurance. Under the table, he put his hand on her knee and squeezed, then returned his own attention back to Agent Barnes, and Renata had to bite her lip hard to suppress the *big* smile that wanted to take over her face.

"So," Barnes said, looking at her from his standing position beside the screen, "Now that we have Agent Parker back with us, in whatever capacity she can work, we're going to run over this again from the top, and fill in some gaps that we've found answers to now, okay?"

Renata nodded at him, and once the rest of the table was in agreement, he moved forward, using a remote in his hand to change the images on the screen.

"This man is Terrence "Terry" King, owner of King Pharma. 56 years old, married, with three teenaged children. Purchased the company twelve years ago, back when it was "American Health Innovations". Saved it from bankruptcy after a huge scandal, lawsuits, and so forth. Pulled major PR moves to make sure everybody forgot that AHI's drugs were killing people, rebranded it, and turned it into the drug giant we all know today."

The picture on the screen was of a handsome man, with smooth, dark skin. Slightly questionable ethics aside, Renata thought he looked nice. She knew from TV interviews, news headlines, and her own research that he was hugely philanthropic. He was also one of the only people with the power to actually *do* anything who was calling for more affordable prescription drugs, and even had a program through his company that "sponsored" the prescription costs for terminally ill children. Everything she'd seen, in the short time she'd been able to research before everything went to crap, pointed to a standup guy.

Of course *Wolfe* would want him taken down.

"Now," Barnes continued, "We all know what the news media has shown us about Terry King. But what Mr. LaForte has discovered is… Terry King wasn't always his name. Good ole' Terrence used to be Sean Williams — partner in crime and *very* good friend of Damien Wolfe."

Renata's eyes went wide, then refocused on the screen.

Wow.

"Sean Williams is just as bad as Damien Wolfe, far as I can tell," Quentin said, taking over for a moment. "Grew up together, ran together, all of that. Mid-eighties, things shifted. Wolfe started to make a name for himself as a young guy in the drug trade. He wasn't into slinging dope on the corner, he was college educated, wanted to sling it in the boardroom. *That's* how he set himself apart. King — *Williams* — was a smart kid too. Pharmacology student, into chemistry. Neither of them *had* to do illegal things to make it, but… that's what they chose. Mid-nineties, King was working as a scientist for AHI. But… he wasn't *just* making drugs for AHI. He was also developing street shit, highly-addictive add-ins for weed, coke, whatever you can imagine."

Shaking her head, Renata turned to Quentin. "How do you know all of this?"

Quentin smiled. "Well, thanks to Mimi getting into the house, we have access to King's personal network. Homeboy likes to *journal*, and he keeps immaculate records of everything. It's all encrypted, so I haven't been able to get to it all yet, but we will. Those records are how we know that King abandoned a pregnant wife in the mid-eighties. It's how we know

95

that he had developed something, a hybrid drug that we know today as Triple-H, a mix between ecstasy and marijuana that leaves you hungry, horny, and high. He and Wolfe were supposed to make a *lot* of money off of that deal, but… King ended up cutting him out of it. He got in touch with our dads, gave them information on Wolfe, part of what they took to the FBI. Seems like he wanted to take Wolfe down *completely*, all at once, but Wolfe found out about it… and we know what happened from there."

Yeah. They *all* knew what happened from there. Wolfe had killed the three men he could get to — Marcus, Naomi, and Quentin's fathers. Williams was apparently in the wind, and had changed his name to Terry King. Maybe that's why he felt the need to go drugging young girls that same night. To work out his anger, to… *shit.* Renata didn't feel like trying to figure out why Wolfe did the things he did, wasn't really interested in rationalizing. That would imply that he was *human*, which… Renata really didn't believe to be true. As far as she was concerned, he was just a monster in a human shell.

"So," Barnes picked up, "A name change from Sean Williams to Terry King, and a bit of sabotage to drive down the value of AHI. He used the money he made — *many* millions — on that development and initial sale of Triple-H, and purchased the company. Did some building… and here we are."

Naomi cleared her throat. "So now we know *why* King Pharmaceuticals."

Barnes nodded. "Now we know."

"Good. Now I don't feel bad at all for helping take his ass down." Inez leaned forward over the table.

"I guess he feels like his philanthropy and everything today makes up for the sins of the past."

"I disagree," Naomi said, her voiced tinged with constrained fury. "He doesn't get to come up with his own atonement. Do we have a plan now?"

"We do." Barnes pulled up the next image, which was a composite sheet with pictures of, and facts about a new drug. "We're going to do the same thing to King Pharma that he did to American Health Innovations."

Renata frowned. "Wait a minute though… people *died* because of what he did to AHI. We can't do something like that."

"You're right," Barnes agreed. "We aren't. We're going to sabotage it before it ever hits the public market, and make sure the public knows about it. There will be email leaks, FDA payoffs, all kinds of things that will tank their value and their reputation with the public. Then, the lawsuits will come, once we prove that *he* caused those AHI deaths in the nineties, and possibly jail time. We went from trying to figure out how to take down a good guy with minimal damage, to taking down a criminal. It's a lot easier to get money for *that*."

Whew.

Renata felt a little bit of relief at *that*. It had been part of her concern when she was supposed to be working on this alone, that other people would get hurt, physically or otherwise because of *her*. Now, she was glad to hear that no one would be getting bad drugs, or anything like that, but still… there were lost jobs to think about, and those kids who relied on the King foundation to pay for their medicine... either way it went, the victory would be hollow.

Long after the meeting wrapped up, she sat upstairs in her "new" room, one of many guest rooms in Inez's house. Savi had cleared her to be off of the monitors, so there was no reason she *had* to stay downstairs in the med room. Being up here made her feel less isolated, more like she was part of them, instead of just a stranger.

She picked up two painkillers from her bedside table, then changed her mind and only took one. She was still dealing with a lot of pain, but the last thing she needed was a clouded mind, or a potential addiction, especially after what she'd found out about King Pharma. Laying back into a propped position against her pillows, she wondered what Taylor was doing. Someone, probably Kendall, had replaced the phone she destroyed, but neither Taylor — nor Wolfe — had called or texted.

But that's not abnormal, she reminded herself, taking a deep breath to stop from descending into a panic. Taylor was a teenager, living with her half-sister for the summer, and it was a Friday. Movies, skating, the mall... there were plenty of things Taylor probably wanted to do besides texting back and forth with her mom. Taylor was fine. And despite the *horrible* things she thought of Wolfe, she didn't really believe he would hurt their daughter, or allow her to be hurt by anyone.

He'd put a bullet through my *head in a heartbeat though.*

With that sobering thought, her mind shifted to the man on the other side of the wall. Inez had given her a suggestive wink when she led her to that room, whispering that Quentin was "just a few feet away if you need him at night" before she slinked off.

Renata had *no* intentions of "needing" Quentin, especially not at night, in a house full of people. There were more important things at hand than soothing raging hormones.

If only her *hormones* knew that.

Instead, they were indeed *raging*, especially with the knowledge that he was right next door. He'd *kissed* her, waking up feelings and thoughts that were probably best left sleeping. Especially now. Maybe under different circumstances, if she still had her daughter safe at home, she would have gone about this in a completely different way. If she'd been asked onto their team, discovered who he was… maybe a sexy little cat and mouse game until he discovered the truth? A hacker-style seduction, or something?

She rolled her eyes, and nearly laughed at the thought of *her* seducing anybody. Renata knew she was "cute", but sexy… *barely*. Not at all like Naomi or Inez, who *oozed* sex, without even trying. Inez was beautiful, badass, and fun. Naomi was beautiful, badass, and deadly. Renata was… *cute*. And smart! And… no wonder there had been a "thing" between Quentin and Naomi.

He hadn't talked about her often — for reasons that were apparent now — but Renata knew enough. Knew that they grew up together. Knew they lost their parents together. Knew they'd worked together all this time. When he revealed that he occasionally slept with his mysterious "partner", she remembered thinking that it was a bad idea. The whole "sleeping with friends" thing pretty much never worked out, but apparently, between Quentin and Naomi, it just... did.

Once Renata actually *saw* Naomi, with that gorgeous deep brown skin, and those eyes, and that *body*... she totally understood. Hell, if she were Quentin, she would have slept with her too, and thanked her afterwards for the privilege. In her view, Naomi was the kind of woman that men salivated over, obsessed over, pretended to hate so they wouldn't have to admit just how mesmerized they were — kinda like Marcus.

But, Renata had seen the way Naomi and Quentin interacted. It was an easy, *friendly* interaction, exactly the kind you would expect from people who'd known each other for so long. There were no long, pining stares, no hint of jealousy from Quentin when Naomi was with Marcus. So... it seemed like what he'd told her, that he and his "partner" may sleep together, but were really just friends, was true. And that was relieving.

Why was that relieving?

When it came down to it, the only title she held with Quentin was "friend" too. And she *barely* had that. Yeah, he'd kissed her, but... he'd slept with Naomi. Probably a *lot*, before Marcus entered the picture. So... maybe that was just the kind of thing he did with his friends?

With a heavy sigh, Renata closed her eyes and leaned further back into her pillows. It was ridiculous to even be wondering these things about Quentin, with everything else going on. Her painkiller was starting to take effect, so when a knock sounded at the door, she found it *hard* to open her eyes.

"Come in," she mumbled as loud as she could, hoping it was loud enough to be heard.

A moment later, the door swung open, and Quentin sauntered in. "Hey… just wanted to check on ya'… see if you needed anything."

Renata suppressed the filthy thought that first crossed her mind. He looked like he'd just left the weight room or something, because his arms were glistening with moisture, and his breathing wasn't quite relaxed. Her own breath caught in her chest as he walked up to the bed.

"N-no," she stammered. "I'm… I'm good. Thank you."

A little smile turned up the corners of his mouth. "You sure? You sound a little… smothered."

Renata took a deep breath, willing her eyes to stay open. "Painkillers," she managed, just before she gave in and closed her eyes. A second later, she was able to force them back open, and Quentin was already pulling the covers over her with a grin.

"G'night, cher."

A deep feeling of calm filled Renata as Quentin leaned over her, just enough to press his lips to her forehead. She was too out of it to verbally respond, but she smiled before she closed her eyes again, then heard the click of the lamp as he turned out the light.

seven.

Diligence. Focus. Agility.

Alone in her car, Naomi repeated her mantra as she glanced in the rearview mirror. She barely drove the vehicle — barely drove at all — so it was unlikely that she would be recognized or followed, but still… couldn't be too careful, with people breaking into apartments, and holding shootouts on the highway these days.

She wasn't *really* supposed to be out alone after the attempt on her life, and she knew Marcus was probably going to flip when he found out. But… she just needed some time. *Alone* time. With most of their lives in danger, and no real ideas on who the current deadliest enemy was, the entire team was spending most of their time at Inez's house. Her house was secure, in a private, gated neighborhood peppered with government agents, current and past, some covert, some not. One would have to be *stupid* to start anything there.

Out here in the wild, it was a different story. Still, whatever risk it posed was well worth it to get out of the house. It was spacious enough, plenty of room for everybody, but *still*. Unless Naomi stayed confined to her room, and kicked Marcus out, there just seemed to be people *everywhere.* As much as she enjoyed their company, she really just needed some time away from them.

Away from Renata.

Naomi believed in her gut that Renata was on their side. She seemed to be really sweet, Quentin liked her, and in spite of the threat Naomi had made, she really *didn't* harbor any negative feelings toward Renata for telling Marcus about his father. She would have done the exact same thing, probably not as quietly. Renata was intelligent, highly valuable to the team, and obviously the woman was good at keeping secrets. So… it wasn't that she didn't *like* her… it was just that being around Renata made Naomi feel sick.

"How's that pretty little girl of yours? Looks just like Noelle, doesn't she? She's what... sixteen now? Tight little body... pussy is probably still brand new... yeah... perfect time to pay her a little visit. Maybe she'll behave better than her momma."

Wolfe's parting words to her father played over in her head as she thought about what he'd done to Renata. A week had passed since everything came to light. Naomi had been able to coax a little more detail out of her — just a little — and Quentin had filled in what he could without violating Renata's privacy, because that was absolutely *not* the goal. She'd been violated enough. But the information she had was enough to make Naomi wonder… had Renata been her replacement?

She hadn't even gone home the night of the shooting, she'd gone straight to Quentin's, blood-soaked and hysterical by the time she made it to his door. What if Wolfe had gone to the apartment, looking for her? And once he didn't find *her*… any pretty sixteen year old would do? For what had to be the hundredth time in the last week, guilt swept over Naomi

104

at the thought of Renata's violation being the only reason he had never come for *her*.

Vividly, she remembered his angry declaration, *Gonna have to change my motherfucking jacket before we hit this party.* So... going to that party that night wasn't a fluke. And Wolfe had *never* struck her as the type of man who enjoyed loud music and big crowds. She knew for a fact that he was a shrewd, calculating man. So if going to the party wasn't by chance... maybe Renata being there wasn't an accident either.

Naomi shook her head. Here she was again, trying to make sense of the things Damien Wolfe did. She'd discovered long ago that only *he* understood the methods behind his madness — and she had no doubts that there *were* methods. Even in the brutal murder of his own brother, Nelson, and the violation desecration of her mother, Noelle, Naomi could — albeit vaguely — see that perhaps Damien felt betrayed. He'd seen Noelle first, had pursued her first, maybe even... *loved* her first.

But she chose Nelson.

Naomi knew firsthand that love could make you do irrational things... but she somehow saw Damien as incapable of being ruled by emotion. Or maybe... emotion was the only thing that could make someone do such brutal things?

Again, Naomi tried to shift her thoughts to something else. If she wanted to talk about logic, there *was* none in trying to rationalize Damien Wolfe. You didn't try to *humanize* a person like that. You simply... took them down. And Naomi knew exactly how to do that.

Diligence. Foc— who the fuck am I kidding?

She'd dropped the ball on *every* part of her mantra, and the paper lying innocently folded in the passenger seat was proof of that. Just glancing at it made her heart drum out a staccato beat, so she focused on the road again.

All she'd wanted to do was go to the doctor by herself. There was nothing *wrong*, just a routine visit she'd been putting off for months because of everything else. In her profession, her physical health was paramount, and with the beatings she'd put it through over the last few months, she knew it was time for a little checkup.

She had the option of using a doctor provided by the FBI, but they were in her business enough as it was. Her doctor was *very* discreet. She didn't know about Naomi's skills or profession — hell, she didn't even know her real name — but after assurance that Naomi wasn't being abused by someone, she did her job and sent her on her way, sometimes with a prescription for this ache, or that pain, none of which Naomi ever actually took.

Usually.

This time, the old superstition of nothing being wrong *until* you got to the doctor had proven itself to be true, and Naomi... didn't know how to process the news she'd received.

When she pulled into the underground parking garage a few minutes later, she hadn't come any closer to finding clarity, to grounding herself in reality. In the house, she skirted the areas where she heard voices, hoping to make it to her room unnoticed, but just as her hand touched the knob, she felt the familiar shift in energy that told her Marcus was close by.

106

She closed her eyes as he approached her from behind, wrapping his arms around her waist as he lowered his mouth to her ear.

"I was worried about you," he muttered, drawing her close against him.

Despite her silent, frantic pleas for her emotions to tuck themselves back in, tears welled in Naomi's eyes. Behind her, Marcus must have noticed something was off, because he opened the door and pushed her in, closing it behind him.

"What's going on, Beautiful?"

He tried to reach for her hand, but Naomi pulled away, shaking her head. She turned to the window, afraid of what would happen if she met those dark grey eyes. She'd already seen that they were filled with concern, and he hadn't even heard her news yet. Emotionally, she and Marcus were already in strange, foreign territory — she didn't really want to think about what *this* would do.

But… it wasn't like she could just ignore it, not when her health, and ability to perform her responsibilities for the team were compromised. Besides that, Naomi was also hesitant to keep any more important information from Marcus — not after what happened last time.

Reluctantly, she turned to face him, giving him a weak smile in hopes of softening the hard expression he wore.

"Naomi…"

She expelled the air from her lungs in a huff, then pulled the folded paper from the back pocket of her jeans and handed it to him. He accepted the paper, eyeing her with suspicion as he opened it up. Naomi chewed nervously at her bottom lip as she waited for him to react.

"Keeping yourself healthy until your next appointment... Naomi... what is this?" he asked, not waiting for an answer before he turned his eyes back to the paper and kept reading. "Take naps... put your feet up... pass some household responsibilities to your partner. Eat small meals throughout the day... bland foods when you feel nauseous... be sure to take your pre—... be sure to take your prenatal vitamins," — his eyes flicked up to Naomi's face, then back to the paper again — "Your baby is due in approximately... 34 weeks"

Slowly, he lowered the paper to his side, then met Naomi's gaze. "Our... *baby*?" For a long moment, Marcus's expression was completely blank, but then... a spark of excitement came into his eyes, and his mouth spread into a smile. "We're having a baby?"

"*No*," Naomi said, sharply emphasizing the word. Was he *crazy*?! "Marcus, I... I can't have a *baby*!" Shaking her head, she pushed her hair away from her face as she began pacing the room.

"What do you mean you *can't* have a baby?" Marcus gently grabbed her arm, stopping her stride as he held up the paper in front of her. "According to *this*, you're pregnant, so apparently you *can*. So... are you saying you... *won't*?"

Pulling away, Naomi propped her hands on her hips. "I guess so. I just... I needed time to process this before I talked to the doctor about termination options."

"*Termination* options? Are you... are you fucking *kidding* right now, Naomi? You needed time to *process* before you discussed options? Not that you needed to talk to *me* about this shit, you needed time to *process*. Oh, okay."

"It's *my* decision, Marcus! So yeah, *I* needed time to process."

Marcus narrowed his eyes. "So... the fact that it's *my* baby too doesn't matter?"

"Oh, *please*," Naomi scoffed. "Your ass wasn't thinking about a *baby* with me, Marcus. We were too horny to use a condom, your pull-out game is *wack*, and we got caught up — that's it. Besides... based on *my* calculations, this happened right before you told me you wished you'd left me sitting outside your apartment that night — *remember*?"

"I thought we were past that, and don't act like I didn't have a reason to say that shit to you."

Naomi crossed her arms. "We *are* past it, and yes, you had a reason. My point is that it's *not* like we're some settled, established couple who've been talking about, and wanting a baby. This isn't... *right*, Marcus. We can't bring a child into this... *bullshit* that's happening around us right now. I *won't*."

"So... that's just *it*?" Marcus asked, his shoulders sagging as he pushed his hands into his pockets. "We can't even talk about this? I mean... I get that the situation isn't ideal, but *come on*... it doesn't mean we can't try to make it work."

"But... it *does*." Naomi shook her head, shifting from her indignantly crossed arms to holding herself. "I *want* a family... *more than anything*. You know that. But... as long as Wolfe is alive and breathing... I can't take that risk. Look what he's done to Renata. Can you imagine if he found out I was pregnant? I have *no* idea what he would do, and I… I don't wanna think about it, don't even want to imagine."

She shied away as Marcus quickly crossed the room, pulling her into his arms, but he grabbed her anyway, drawing her close. Reluctantly, she relaxed into his embrace as he placed a lingering kiss on her forehead. "What happens if you do this… And a week from now somebody puts a bullet through Wolfe's head? What then?"

Naomi squeezed her eyes shut as she buried her face in his shirt. She hadn't even considered that yet, but then again… there was a lot she hadn't considered. She was *barely* six weeks pregnant, and hadn't even missed a period, which according to her doctor wasn't abnormal. All she knew so far was that the thought of bringing a child into a world where *that* man still had blood pumping through his cold heart terrified her.

Why he hadn't bothered her over the years was a question for which Naomi had no answers. She *did*, however, know that the man was ruthless. And unpredictable. The actions against her mother, her father, his business rivals and associates, and now Renata, were all proof of that. In that video call, he'd mentioned letting nothing stand in the way of business or family — so what if she *had* this baby, and Wolfe felt somehow entitled to be in its life?

That haunted look in Renata's eyes ran *deep*. Naomi could only imagine the emotional terror she'd suffered at his hands, because he was able to use her child — her *heart*— as a bargaining chip. Naomi didn't want that.

He probably already thought she *owed* him something, after taking care of Victor Lucas. It didn't surprise her to find that Lucas had been behind the attempt on her life and or freedom. It *did* surprise her that Wolfe had stepped in as protector. And what had Lucas revealed to Wolfe before he met his death? Was *that* how Wolfe knew about she and Marcus? There were *so* many questions without answers, so many unknown variables that it made her head spin. How on earth could she be responsible for bringing a child into that?

But then... there was Marcus. And as much as she didn't *want* to calculate his feelings into making this decision, she couldn't help it. Whether or not she cared to admit it, she... *loved* him. How could she not consider what he wanted, when as he said... the baby was *his*?

Licking her lips to relieve their sudden dryness, she pulled away to look up at his face. A sharp pang echoed in her chest at the sight of his *just slightly* glossed eyes.

"Naomi," he said, his voice strained. "I know this is your decision... it's *your* body... your health that you'll be sacrificing. And I understand your fears, baby, I swear I do. But... *please*... can you just think about it a little longer before you decide? Just... give me a little more time, Beautiful. I know we're supposed to be doing this takedown the "right" way, but if I have to walk into Wolfe's house, put a bullet between his eyes myself, I will. I didn't know this until it became a reality, but   I really want us to have this baby. If *Wolfe* is your only fear, the only thing giving you pause about moving forward with the pregnancy... let's terminate *him*... not the baby."

With those words, Naomi's dam broke, and tears flooded her face. Sniffling, she lifted her arms to wrap around Marcus's shoulders, and he picked her up, carrying her to the window seat where he sat down, then pulled her into his lap.

She buried her face against his neck as she cried, breathing in his scent, and enjoying the warmth of his hand as he ran it up and down her spine. They stayed like that for a long moment, and then finally, she lifted her head and met his gaze.

Cupping his face in her hands, she gave him the best smile she could through her tears, then leaned to press her lips to his. When she pulled back, she ran a hand over his hair then tipped forward a little, so their foreheads were touching. Then... she nodded.

"I'll give it a little more time."

Instant relief took the tension out of Marcus's shoulders, and he exhaled, as if he'd been holding his breath the entire time, waiting for an answer. He pulled her tight against him, planting another on her head before he lowered his mouth to her ear for a quietly-spoken "thank you."

Naomi closed her eyes, allowing Marcus to keep her pulled close. *"Thinking about it"* a little more sounded good, and seemed like the right thing to say, but the truth was... she'd already made her decision.

She just hoped everything would be okay.

— & —

Pregnant.

Pregnant.

Marcus turned that word over in his mind again and again, but it still barely seemed to sink in that it was his reality. Naomi — *his* Naomi — was pregnant.

She was sleeping now, tucked under his arm in the darkness that covered the bedroom. They hadn't talked about it again since she'd told him, earlier in the evening. She'd washed her face, and they joined the rest of the team for a debriefing over dinner. Visibly, Naomi seemed engaged with the conversation, but Marcus knew what was actually happening in her mind — she was freaking out about the baby.

And really, he was too. If she was six weeks pregnant, that meant that she was pregnant when she'd gotten attacked. The doctor had told her everything looked fine, but *looking* fine and *being* fine weren't the same thing, especially when it came to babies. He knew that first hand, since his niece Sophie had been born with an abnormality of her spine that none of the ultrasounds had picked up. She was barely two days old before going into her first surgery, and although she was a healthy, happy little girl now, well enough to dance in Naomi's class, that could have easily not been the case.

What if something like that happened with them?

Marcus pushed out a heavy sigh, and Naomi stirred, shifting positions to prop her leg over his thigh. She snuggled a little closer, then drifted back into her deep sleep as Marcus pushed the negative thoughts from his mind.

Sophie was only six, but there had been many medical innovations in six years. If something was wrong, they would be able to know, and prepare beforehand.

He hoped.

Just like Naomi, he wanted a family too. Yeah, he had Megan and Sophie, both of whom he adored, but he wanted... something more. Something he'd not even seriously considered before Naomi.

He gave a quiet snort.

Of course he would start thinking about a wife and kids while involved with a daredevil career thief/ undercover FBI agent / niece of a ruthless crime lord. *Of course.*

But... he wasn't sure that mattered. What mattered was that Naomi was smart as hell, interesting, and as hard as it had been to see it at first, warm-hearted. And *beautiful*. And... more important than anything else... he *loved* her.

So, yeah, he wanted her to have his child, wanted to make her his wife.

And just like with everything else he decided he wanted, he *would* make it happen.

He just had a rabid animal to get out of the way first.

"*Marcus.*"

He looked down at Naomi, surprised to see that her eyes were open. They were still slightly swollen from sleep, but she seemed wide awake as she climbed on top of him, straddling his legs. Marcus raised his hands to cup her butt as she lowered her mouth to his.

"Are you mad at me?" she asked, when she pulled away from the kiss. She stayed pressed against his chest, her expression pensive as she waited for his reply.

114

He shook his head. "Not mad... just... apprehensive. Terrified of what may happen, no matter which decision you make."

"Will you be mad if I decide not to keep it?"

Marcus closed his eyes. *That* was a much harder question to answer. "Um... I really can't say. I'm sorry. But I want you to make the decision that feels right for you... not the one you feel will make me happy."

"But I want to make you happy. I love you."

He kissed her forehead, moving his hands up to rub her back. "I love you too... which is I want you do what makes you feel secure. I want you to be comfortable."

She nodded, then slid her hands between them, to his boxers. "Can we...?"

Marcus chuckled. From the beginning, sex had been the way they connected, and it seemed like that was still the case now. He kissed her, then nodded, and she wasted no time getting his boxers down, removing her panties, and sinking onto him.

He groaned, gripping her thighs to keep her close, to keep himself buried in her damp heat. With his hands, he explored her body in the dark while she rode him, quietly whimpering and moaning her pleasure. Would he get to see her figure change, get to experience the wonder of her hips spreading, belly growing, breasts swelling to nourish their child? He drew her down, against his chest as her movements became erratic. He was teetering on the edge himself, and wanted to feel her close.

Even after their climaxes came and went, he kept his arms around her. He didn't want her to move, just wanted to stay just like this, in this moment of pleasure and peace, where nothing else mattered.

eight.

"Why doesn't he like me?"

Quentin hung back, just out of view behind the concrete block wall that separated the indoor basketball court from the tiny area Naomi and Tomiko used to dance. From where he was, he could see both girls in the mirror, dressed in spandex leggings and sports bras. He really didn't mean to be a creep, watching them — especially Naomi, who had been his friend for years — when they didn't know he was there, but... fine ass girls, dressed in next to nothing? ...It really wouldn't hurt anything to enjoy the view, just for a minute.

In response to Tomiko's question, Naomi groaned, shaking her head before she planted her feet, then lowered her upper body into a stretch. "I don't know," she finally answered, her voice carrying a slight strain from being upside down. "You'll have to ask him."

Quietly, Quentin scoffed. Naomi was lying her ass off. She knew exactly why he wasn't interested in Tomiko, and it had everything to do with her over-eager attitude. Tall, well-built, and handsome enough — even at just eighteen years old — that women between 18-30 were pretty much an all-he-could-eat-buffet, he wasn't *interested in easy. He wanted a challenge, and Tomiko was anything but.*

He watched as she cut her eyes at Naomi, then sat down on the floor to begin stretches of her own. "Don't bullshit me, Mimi. You're his best friend, you know him better than anybody."

"I don't keep up with who he's messing with though."

"But I bet you know more than you're letting on. What type of girls does he like?"

Pulling herself into a stand, Naomi huffed, then turned to face Tomiko. "Smart ones."

"Are you saying I'm not smart?"

Naomi shrugged. "Not the kind he likes. Quentin deals with a lot of girls, but he's picky. He likes pretty Grambling girls, with double majors. Hot biochemical grad students. Hell, hot computer science professors — and we've only been out of high school a month. You're pretty, and you're smart Tomiko, but I don't think you're his type."

Tomiko stared at Naomi for a moment before she threw her head back and laughed. Quentin knew why.

Tomiko was more than pretty — she was fine as hell. Pretty caramel skin, tight slender body, almond shaped eyes, and long, thick hair that she wore straightened — she had an exotic look that was the stuff of some men's fantasies, but... a fantasy she would remain, because of that damned attitude.

"So, you're saying he's like, gay? If I'm not his type..."

"Girl, hell no," Naomi said, scrunching her face into a scowl. "You know damn well that's not the

118

case. He likes a cute, funny, laid back, sweet girl. That ain't you."

"Or you." Tomiko shot those words back with a smirk as she stood and faced Naomi.

Shaking her head, Naomi rubbed her hands on the front of her leggings as she laughed. "Damned right. I'm not sweet or laid back, and not trying to be. I do just fine with men either way. You, on the other hand, are a brat. That's why you can't keep a boyfriend. But with me and Quentin, neither of us is checking for each other like that. You're the one with the crush -- my feelings aren't hurt because he doesn't like me like that."

Tomiko crossed her arms over her chest, rolling her eyes. "Whatever. He's a nerd anyway."

"Hottest nerd you've ever seen in your life," Naomi giggled. Despite the truth in her statement that they didn't like each other "like that", Quentin grinned. "Don't stand there and act like you weren't just digging for details."

"Thought you didn't like him?" Tomiko retorted, rolling her neck.

Naomi laughed louder. "I don't, but I'm not blind. Quentin is fine. Him being my friend doesn't detract from that."

Under her breath, Tomiko grumbled. "If you say so, bitch."

"I do." Walking past her to retrieve her ipod from the table, Naomi patted Tomiko on the shoulder. "But girl, if I'm a regular bitch, you're princess bitch. Have your daddy buy you a crown."

"At least I've got one."

Quentin knew those words were a mistake before Tomiko was half through saying them, but it took her a second longer to realize it. She clapped her hand over her mouth, then just barely avoided the fist Naomi aimed in her direction.

"I'm sorry, I'm sorry!" She yelped, cowering behind her hands as Naomi advanced on her with violence in her eyes. "I didn't even mean to say that, it just came out!"

"And that's why nobody wants your ass," Naomi snapped, getting right in Tomiko's face, almost nose to nose. "You're always saying some slick, unnecessary shit. Maybe if you actually tried to be a decent person, your looks would get you further, instead of fucked and left behind, which by the way, is what Quentin does. That's the other part of his type — girls who aren't clingy or desperate. Somebody has his heart already, and it isn't me, isn't gonna be any of these girls he fools around with, and damn sure won't ever be you."*

Damn, Mimi.

Naomi wasn't lying about not being "sweet", but she usually kept her vicious streak tucked in. A moment like this where she was being outright malicious was rare — and just like now, well-deserved. Tomiko knew Naomi's parents were a sensitive issue, and it wasn't like Naomi's "have your daddy buy it" comment was off base. All Tomiko ever talked about was what she had, where she'd gone, and who'd bought it for her, in a very "I get everything I want cause daddy buys it" tone. Quentin hadn't confronted her about it yet because he just didn't care enough, but "daddy" was broke, and living way beyond his means.

120

So maybe that's *why she was sensitive about it now... the money had run out.*

But... more important — and more interesting — was Naomi's assessment that someone "had his heart already". That confused him, because... who?

"Who the hell are you talking about?" Tomiko asked, the fear in her eyes replaced by rabid curiosity.

Naomi smirked. "Hacker he's been talking to for years. *Sight unseen."*

"Some hacker *bitch, probably some pale, pasty creature with bad acne? Bullshit."*

Lifting an eyebrow, Naomi turned away from Tomiko and walked away. "Whatever you say."

— & —

It was the memory of that eavesdropped conversation, twelve or thirteen years ago, between Naomi and Tomiko that told Quentin *exactly* who'd sent the anonymous text he'd woken up to that morning.

"Heard about all those... holes in your car. Should probably leave hacker bitch alone. Hope she liked the work at her apartment. – blocked number"

Reading over the message again, he sighed. He and Naomi had both suspected, after her conspicuous silence since the job at Victor Lucas's house, that she would pop up soon. They'd also suspected that she would be angry, but not at... *him.* Especially not enough to take it out on Renata.

In the past — *after* she decided to no longer be a part of their team — Tomiko's anger had been very Naomi-centered. It might have gone over her head in their youth, but Tomiko had always considered Naomi

121

a source of envy. Naomi was the better dancer, the better thief, the one who was more desired by men, because of her air of unattainability... *mystery*. Tomiko was a woman where you saw exactly what you were getting, right up front. There was no guesswork involved with her motives. Quentin had already pegged that Tomiko would backstab them, warned Naomi about it, and was well on his way to figuring out that the FBI was her weapon of choice when Naomi was captured.

This time though... this was *different*. He couldn't understand the motivation to harm Renata over a non-mutual attraction that never advanced beyond a teenage crush — as far as he knew. If she wanted to be pissed off, he would think that her anger would be — again — aimed at Naomi, who'd kicked her ass in Lucas's house twice, once while she was tied up. Now, her income source — Lucas — was dead, thanks to the retaliation of Naomi's uncle.

It wasn't that he *wanted* Tomiko going after Naomi. He just... preferred to think about things rationally, and Tomiko turning her anger on him and Renata just... didn't make sense. She didn't even *know* Renata.

But... she knew *him*.

Quentin groaned as he thought back to Naomi's assertion of the possibility that *he* had been the target of the attack, not Renata. With Tomiko claiming responsibility, there was little doubt that those bullets had been meant for anyone but him. It stood to reason that if Lucas had found out how to get to Naomi, that information was easily available to Tomiko. They were hiding in plain sight, pretending to be legit. It would

122

have taken nothing to follow him from the gym —
thank goodness they had employees, who could run the
place in their absence — to his apartment, to…
Renata's. Maybe Tomiko hadn't even put together that
"hacker bitch" was Renata, *until* she'd been in her
apartment.

Sitting up in the bed, he rubbed his temples. If
Tomiko worked for Lucas… maybe she'd been
working on behalf of Wolfe as well. If Lucas had told
enough before his death, Wolfe knew that he and
Naomi were working on his demise. Maybe he'd given
Tomiko carte blanche to take care of it, since there was
a personal history there?

But… then again… Wolfe shared a personal
history with Renata as well. The thought of *that* made
Quentin swing his feet out of the bed, handle his
morning hygiene routine, then make his way down to
the empty gym.

He always had it to himself at this time of the
morning — four a.m. — and today, Quentin decided to
visit Naomi's usual equipment of choice — the heavy
bag — to work out his wrath. At Tomiko, for violating
Renata's sense of home, and security, and her role in
the hole through her shoulder. At Wolfe for stealing her
innocence, for the emotional violence he'd waged in
her life over the years, and his continued terrorization
now, of withholding her child from her.

And… at himself.

For doubting her loyalties, for treating her
harshly, for not stepping back sooner, to see things
through her lens so he could find some compassion, and
most of all… for *not fucking realizing what Wolfe had
done.*

That pissed him off most of all.

He'd looked *right at* the date when Taylor was born. Looked *right at* Renata's birthdate — another clue that told him she was painted_pixel. He'd gone over all of the available information a dozen times, knew that Renata was only sixteen, and Wolfe was in his thirties. And yet, in his anger at the perceived betrayal, he hadn't allowed himself to see her as exactly what she was — exactly what Naomi had *called her*, if only he'd picked up that clue before — a *victim.*

He hadn't even been upset when he found out Naomi knew before he did. It wasn't Naomi's story to tell. The snide comments he'd made, the bullshit about Renata "making a choice to be connected to the devil"… *he'd* done that, and the guilt for it belonged to him. *All* of the fault for how he'd acted laid with him, and he accepted it, with the knowledge — and the *promise* — that while he had to "play nicely" for now, to ensure Taylor's safe return, he would never hurt her again, and he would never, *ever*, allow Wolfe to do so either.

By the time he aimed one last blow at the heavy bag, an hour had passed and he was soaked with sweat. The ache in his back told him that he'd overdone it, but it was more than worth it. He felt better — *lighter*— as he headed back up the stairs to take a shower.

Shaking his head, he chuckled a little as he remembered the way Inez had wagged her eyebrows upon informing him that she was putting he and Renata on this end of the house, away from everyone else, and that they would have to share a bathroom. As much as he may have wanted to share a shower with the adorably sexy Special Agent Parker when they first met, those same thoughts felt… inappropriate now, knowing what she was going through.

But… at the same time, the kiss he'd given her three days ago, and the subsequent innocent pecks on the forehead or cheek he'd snuck since then, had *nothing* to do with his lust for the "new girl" on the team, who was his *dream* girl. *That* was all about fifteen years of pent-up feelings for his "anonymous" friend.

And goddamn, she'd been *so* sweet.

He had feelings for her, had since they were kids, so that wasn't really something that needed to be established. She was smart, funny, and interesting enough that she kept him engaged, without him ever seeing her face, or even hearing her voice. More than once, — many times, in fact — he'd passed up going out to spend time talking with her instead, and he never felt "lame" or "nerdy" because of it. Yeah, he liked to kick back, party, club, drink, and so forth, just as much as the next man. And he *loved* women — their bodies, their company, their attention — but none of them offered the same thing painted_pixel — Renata — did. *Nobody*, not even Naomi, came close to giving the same type of easy connection he had with her. Not a sexual, physical link, but an intellectual, emotional bond that nobody else touched. Hell, *they* hadn't even touched.

But now they had. And damned if he didn't want to do it again. He'd imagined what she looked like before, but it *definitely* hadn't been the quiet, curvy, braided goddess who walked into his office at the gym with Marcus and Kendall that day. She was beautiful, yeah. But… Quentin wasn't new to beautiful women, not by a stretch. It was that brain of hers, working double-time under her long, jet black braids that sent blood rushing away from *his* brain, to other places. Lush, pretty lips that opened to speak words that showed a sweet personality. Big brown eyes, that were bright and expressive, that he now knew hid an abundance of pain —old and new.

So, although he would love to take secret sexy showers with Renata, while they were stuck in this house together, working to return her daughter, it just… didn't seem appropriate to even think about something like that. Knowing she was stressed and upset about her daughter, knowing she'd been violated in the worst way… she didn't deserve his *lust*… she deserved his respect.

He was up the stairs, bypassing the bathroom to grab a change of clothes before he doubled back for a shower when the door swung open, and the object of his thoughts stepped out. Quentin tried to avoid her, but they ended up colliding anyway, and dismay filled his chest when she yelped and reached for her injured shoulder, while trying to keep her towel pressed to her body.

"*Ouchhh, shit,*" she groaned, closing her eyes as she sucked in a calming breath. "*Jesus.*"

"Dammit, my bad. I think that may have pulled at your stitches a little. You're bleeding," he said, cringing at the red stain — blood mixed with the water from her skin — forming at the top of her towel.

Renata pulled her hand away, lifting it up to look it before she closed her eyes a little, like she was dizzy from the pain. Her grip on her towel moved from tenuous to non-existent, and Quentin — grudgingly —

126

caught it as it slipped down, holding it closed against her body.

"Let's sit you down, and get you bandaged up, huh?" Not wanting to find out if she was steady enough to walk, Quentin reached past her to push the bathroom door back open, then backed her in.

In the bathroom, he sat her down on a padded bench in front of the sink, set away from the toilet and shower, then washed his hands. Under the sink, he found an extensive first aid kit, and sat it on the bench beside her. He moved quickly, washing and bandaging the exit wound — which was worse — first, then moving in front of her, and kneeling down to tend to the entry wound.

"Hey," he said, noticing that she still had her eyes squeezed shut. "When did you last take anything for the pain?"

She opened one eye, then gave him the sheepish grin of a child caught misbehaving. "Um… yesterday…*morning.*"

"Come on now, *cher.*" He gave her a playful, gentle smack on the thigh, an action he immediately regretted once his palm came in contact with her warm, still slightly damp flesh. She pulled in a sharp breath, and *both* of her eyes opened then, focusing on his.

Move it. Stop touching her, a little voice in the back of his head demanded. But… louder, *stronger*, was the little voice telling him to move a little higher, to see how she reacted to *that.*

He kept it where it was.

"Ain't you supposed to be wearin' a sling?"

She swallowed hard, letting her gaze drift down to his lips before she finally answered, with a nod. "But not all day. I took it off to shower."

"Mmhm," Quentin grunted, as he reluctantly moved his hand from her thigh to carefully clean the stitches keeping her shoulder closed. "What's your excuse for not takin' your pain meds like you should?"

She winced as he gently pressed a clean, soft cloth against her wound to stop the last of the bleeding, but... the tension he felt emanating from her was more than just a reaction to the pain. This was something... different.

Renata gave her head a slight shake before lifting her gaze to meet his. "They make me all loopy, and dizzy. Makes it hard to think... and I'm finding that hard enough as it is."

She glanced away immediately after those words left her lips, as if she'd given away a secret. He noticed then that she was trembling.

"You cold?" he asked, then looked around the bathroom for another towel to drape over her shoulders. Before she could respond, he was already on his feet, grabbing a towel, and then back in front of her, covering her bare arms. "That better?"

The corners of those soft, plush lips turned up in a smile. "Yeah. Thank you."

"My pleasure."

She blushed a little at that, then turned her gaze away again as he pushed the towel back enough to resume his task. He moved a few of her braids out of the way, but they fell right back in place, and she gave a quiet laugh. Quentin sat back as she used her left hand to gather her braids, pulling them out of the way over

128

her left shoulder. When she was done, she looked up at him and smiled.

"Better?"

Damn she's beautiful.

Quentin hadn't known Renata long enough — in person — yet to know that he loved her hair pulled over her shoulder like that, hanging nearly to her waist. Sitting there in nothing but her towel, hair hanging over her face, skin still slightly wet... she kinda took his breath away, and for a moment, he couldn't do anything but stare.

With a little chuckle, he finally nodded as he moved closer to her again. "Yeah. Thank you." He pulled a tube of antiseptic from the first aid kit, then used a gauze pad to carefully apply it to her stitches. He rested his hand on top of her thigh, and when he touched her, pressing the pad to her shoulder, he quickly realized she was trembling... *again.*

So... she's not cold.

But if it wasn't that... what? Quentin lifted his eyes in an attempt to meet hers, but she had her head turned, focused on something else. He kept his gaze trained on her face as he tightened his grip on her thigh, and the way she briefly closed her eyes, lowering her brow into a slight frown made him wonder... was she... *nervous*? Was he making her uncomfortable?

Shit.

"Sorry, *cher,*" he said, moving his hand away from her thigh.

Renata looked at him then, lifting an eyebrow. "For what?"

"Making you feel uncomfortable."

Her eyebrows dropped as her eyes narrowed in confusion. "Quentin… I've never felt uncomfortable around you."

…Oh.

So… if she wasn't cold… or uncomfortable… what the hell was she trembling for? He covered the wound on her shoulder with clean, dry gauze, then held it in place as he reached for the tape, accidentally brushing a hand over one of her firm, ripe breasts through the towel. She inhaled deep in response, letting out the tiniest, almost imperceptible little sound, halfway between a sigh and a whimper. He froze for just a moment, and then… clarity came.

Been stuck in the house too damned long. Losing my common sense.

She wasn't cold, or nervous, or uncomfortable… she was…excited. *Horny.*

Just the prospect of a horny Ren made blood rush to his groin. Trying to focus elsewhere, he retrieved the tape and quickly finished the bandaging of her arm and sat back on his heels.

Bad idea. Goddamn she's sexy.

"Thank you," she said, the soft, sultry rasp of her voice filling the silence in the room. "It always takes me forever to do that myself."

"You're welcome." He didn't move to get up. He wasn't even sure *why* he was still there, other than a sudden desire not to pull himself away from the citrusy vanilla scent of whatever she'd showered with. It reminded him of that first day she'd come up from the medical room… the first time they'd kissed. The memory of her sweetness made him want to do it again.

He drew closer to her, and she didn't pull away. Her lips were parted, chest heaving, and from his formerly innocent place between her legs, he could feel the heat of her arousal, like it was *calling* to him. So… he answered.

She let out a trembling breath as Quentin cupped her face in his hands, then pressed his lips to hers. That first touch sent another wave of heat rushing to his groin, and what felt like straight electricity rushing to his chest. She opened her mouth for him eagerly, and he obliged her by delving his tongue inside as she lifted her hand to the back of his head. Gently, trying not to jostle her too hard while she wasn't wearing her sling, he drew her as close as he could, groaning at the feeling of the hot apex of her thighs pressed against him.

Just as sweet as the first time, Quentin thought as he lowered his hands to her legs, running them up the silky skin of her supple thighs, and underneath her towel to touch more of her velvety flesh. He withdrew a little, just enough to gently nibble her bottom lip, sucking it into his mouth to soothe it before he pushed his tongue in again. He moved his hands over her hips, and the sexy little whimper she let out almost took away his restraint.

She wasn't just sitting there, being kissed. Renata was sucking, licking, kissing him back with an intense urgency that surprised him — but pleased him as well. If she was down… so was he, and he was already *right* there between her thighs, and… *so much for lust vs respect.*

Shit.

With *much* reluctance, Quentin ended the kiss, sitting back on his heels again. Looking slightly flustered, Renata pulled her bottom lip into her mouth, blushing as she met his gaze.

"You good?" he asked, looking away as he stood, putting some distance between them before he gave in and hauled her into his arms and sucked on that bottom lip again himself.

"Yeah. Thank you again, for bandaging my arm."

When he looked back, he avoided her eyes, knowing his chances of not being drawn back in were slim. "No problem, Ren. Make sure you put on that sling, please."

He got out of there quickly, not looking back, not stopping until he was behind the door to his room. He leaned into the wall, then let out a loud groan.

Never.

Never.

Never had Quentin been *that* close with a beautiful, consenting woman, and not taken things as far as she was willing to go. He wasn't the type to over-analyze whether a woman was *really* ready or not — he preferred women that said it, and *meant* it. But... Renata wasn't just *any* woman, and their current situation was far from typical. Their friendship still felt... fragile. The last thing he wanted to do was complicate their newly-forged bond with sex, which might later make her feel taken advantage of, but... *goddamn.*

As he sighed, that overheard conversation between Tomiko and Naomi came once again to Quentin's mind. *Somebody already has his heart...*

132

hacker girl who he's been talking to for years. Had Naomi seen, all the way back then, what he was just now starting to realize?

Quentin adjusted himself in his sweats, trying to ease some of the discomfort of being painfully hard with no outlet. A few moments passed before he finally heard the faint open and close of one door, then another, letting him know that Renata had left the bathroom.

He quickly grabbed shorts and a tee shirt, then hurried into the bathroom to take his own much-needed shower.

A *cold* one.

nine.

For the first time since being confined to Inez's house... Renata wished she had something else to wear. In the mirror, she surveyed the charcoal grey yoga pants and bright yellow tee shirt she wore.

Not good enough.

Not since this morning, not since Quentin had kissed her, *again*, and run those big, strong hands up her thighs, and... *Jesus*... made her feel things from a simple touch that she'd only ever made *herself* feel—with a whole lot more effort. Now, the simple, comfortable clothes she'd been given, since everything she owned before had been destroyed, just seemed... *ugh*.

You sound like Taylor.

She laughed at that. She *did* sound like her teenage daughter, whining about her clothes not being cute enough. The only difference was, Taylor was a child. Besides her grades, she didn't have other, more important things to be concerned about.

Renata did.

But... she was doing all she could to get Taylor back — everyone was. Unfortunately, what they were doing would take time and patience. They *would* take King Pharmaceuticals down, and they *would* get Taylor back... and in the interim, Renata would just have to take that sexual frustration and... bottle it.

Right?

With a heavy sigh, she sat down on the edge of the bed, raising her fingers to her still tingling lips. Closing her eyes, she drew in a deep breath then let it go. Maybe... maybe she was overthinking this. She was an adult... a grown, healthy woman. Who said that even in the middle of a stressful situation, she couldn't find some sort of light in the darkness? Being attracted to — *turned on by* — a handsome man was just... human.

The way Quentin could make her feel light-headed and giddy with just a smile, the electricity he ignited in her body, the heat he kindled between her thighs... *that* was the normal reaction she should have to a man. Not the discomfort, ranging from mild to extreme, which she usually experienced. Not the nausea, and creepy-crawly sensation from being touched. Not the overwhelming sense of embarrassment and shame when she took off her clothes for someone else's gaze.

She'd actually felt *sexy* under Quentin's attention — wanted to show him more. Nearly lost it at the heat of his touch. And more than anything, felt safe, and protected, and calm in his presence. It was just... different. And sitting there on the edge of the bed, it honestly felt foolish to look for reasons to push him away.

But then again.... She *hadn't* pushed him away. He'd left on his own.

So what was up with *that*?

What was the deal with kissing her the way he had, pulling her close like that? Close enough that she could tell that — physically, at least — he wanted her just as badly as she wanted him.

Ugh.

She didn't know *nearly* enough about men to determine why he would back down, but... she knew someone — *two* someones — who probably did. Renata adjusted her arm more comfortably in her sling, then left her room, forcing herself not to linger at the bathroom door, where she still heard the shower running. It took her a few minutes, but she found Naomi and Inez sitting on the balcony off the kitchen, sharing a pot of coffee as the sun rose.

When she stepped outside, Inez smiled up at her from her seat, but Naomi barely reacted. She grunted a "hello", then just kept staring at some unknown point in the distant trees. That cold reception made Renata hesitate before closing the door, but Inez shook her head, beckoning her to come on out.

"Don't mind Mimi. She's been like this all morning, just one of *those* days. Everything okay with you?"

"Umm...," Renata started, taking a seat at the table with them, "I... yeah. Yeah, I guess. As "okay" as it *can* be."

Beside her, Naomi snorted, breaking herself from her reverie to return her mug to the table. "You don't sound very convincing. What's up? Is it about Taylor?"

"Yes and no."

When Renata didn't say anything further, Inez waved her hand in a circle, urging her on. "Out with it, girly. We have to get to work soon."

Renata looked back and forth between the two women, both of whom were giving her expectant looks. With a deep breath, she turned her gaze to her hands.

"Well, I'm having these feelings… *sexual* feelings, for Quentin. And… I don't really know what to do."

Naomi, who was across the table from her, lifted an eyebrow. "So… have sex with him. Use a condom." She shrugged, then looked to Inez, who was wearing a similar expression of confusion.

"Yeah… I don't see the problem," Inez said, tipping her head to the side.

Renata groaned, then pushed out another sigh. "It's just… I guess it's not really that simple for me. I mean, we're only in such close proximity because Wolfe has my daughter. I feel like I should be worried about *that*."

"Wrong," Naomi said, finally seeming fully engaged as she sat up. "Good sex is *exactly* what you need, to burn off some of that stress. I can't tell you how many times I've been in the middle of plans for a really stressful job and had to just take a break and get *taken care of*. It *always* worked. My mind would be clear, joints loose, great attitude… trust me. Sex during times like this is a *magical* thing."

Inez nodded. "Naomi is right. Some of my *best* work happened after getting tossed around all night. Don't you… I don't know, *hack* better after great sex?"

Swallowing hard, Renata quickly found something else to look at as she searched her mind for an answer to the question that had caught her completely off guard. She could feel Inez and Naomi both staring at her, so she reluctantly turned her attention back to them.

"Renata…Have you never…?"

Naomi didn't even have to finish her question before Renata knew what was being asked, and began shaking her head to respond.

"Like... *never*?" Inez asked.

Renata shook her head again.

Nope.

Like... *never*.

Unless you counted the experience with Wolfe, which she *didn't*. Her memory of the events leading up to her assault were clear in her mind, but she — blissfully — had no memory of the act itself. Even so... the trauma of that experience had lived with her, guiding her through every interaction she had with a man moving forward. No, they couldn't buy her a drink. No, they couldn't pick her up for a date. No, she couldn't come to his house to "chill".

Eventually, she lightened a little on that, and allowed herself to date. Never the complete strangers who asked her out though. Always, *always* men who she saw with some regularity, the guy at the bank, or the grocery store, or the gym. Places where she could find out a real name, then run him through every legal or illegal background check she could, finding out every connection, every blip on his criminal record, every parking ticket or fine, *everything* before she allowed herself to be alone with him, especially in a position where her safety could be compromised. And even then... she never felt quite comfortable, so it rarely got past a kiss.

There was *one* guy though. A police officer she'd worked with who asked her out. He was handsome, and smart, and just a *good* guy. And patient. They dated longer than she'd ever dated anyone, and there came a point where she thought she trusted him enough for sex... until her clothes were off. Then, she felt so uneasy and distressed that even *he* felt it. He was sweet to her about it, but after that it just... fizzled out.

"So... you're basically a virgin?"

Naomi's words brought Renata out of her memories, and she shook her head. "No. I mean... I have a kid. I don't really know that I can call myself a virgin."

"Uh-uh." Inez wagged a finger in the air. "You have to *give* your virginity. If you didn't *give* it, you've still *got* it."

"And she wants to *give* it to Quentin," Naomi chimed in, giggling as she turned to Renata. "Consider yourself lucky. You're gonna get what most women *don't*. A virginity loss experience that's actually *good*."

Renata knew that statement was supposed to be encouraging, but coming from Naomi, it only highlighted *another* fear she had. She ran her tongue over her lips to wet them, then looked right at Naomi.

"So... you and Quentin... is there anything....?"

At first, Naomi just lifted an eyebrow, but then her eyes went wide, and she shook her head. "Like, romantically? *No*. I mean..." Naomi paused for a moment, brushing her hair back from her face, and Renata could tell she was carefully considering her words. "I'm going to move forward with the assumption that you already know there was *something*, or else you wouldn't ask, but I promise you, you have *nothing* to be concerned about. Q and I are very good friends, absolutely, but anything beyond that was purely... fucking," she said bluntly, shrugging afterwards.

140

Renata tipped her head to the side. "So, no romantic feelings?"

Naomi scoffed. "*Never.* I've known Quentin damn near all my life, and I've only ever known him to have *that* kind of feelings for one person."

Who?

Renata bit her lip to keep herself from asking that question, although she desperately wanted to know. She quickly realized she must have been showing her curiosity on her face, because Inez started laughing, shaking her head.

"Ay dios mío, Ren. She's talking about *you,* don't look so concerned."

"*Me?*" Renata gave a dry laugh. "I… I'm not so sure Quentin is checking for me like that."

Naomi and Inez looked at each other, then both broke into laughter.

"*Chiquita,* after that day Wolfe called, and you went into that little funk for a few days? Q was down there peeking his head in the door to check on you every hour on the hour. Has been up all hours of the night, working double time to find out every little detail about King and Wolfe, to help you. And the man looks at you like *you* hung the moon in the sky. What more evidence do you need that he's *feeling* you?"

Leaning forward, Naomi chimed in. "And not to mention, Marcus told me he walked in on you two sucking face."

Heat rushed to Renata's cheeks as Inez's mouth spread into a smile.

"He *kissed* you?"

Renata gave her a subtle nod, then held up two fingers.

"He's kissed you *twice?*" Inez rolled her eyes. "What planet are you from, Ren? *How* do you doubt that he likes you "like that" when he's *kissed* you? *Twice.*"

Groaning, Renata reached up to sweep her braids over her shoulder. "The planet of 30 year olds who have *no* real experience with men. Marcus and Kendall are the longest, closest "real life" relationships I've ever had with a man, and the most either of them has ever given me is a *hug.* I've *tried* romantic stuff, and it just... doesn't seem to work. There was *one* guy where we got far enough to take off clothes, and I freaked out."

"Why did you freak out?" Naomi asked, absently swirling her spoon in her cold coffee.

Renata shrugged. "I guess... I was only really doing it because I felt like I *should.* It was two years ago, and Wolfe hadn't bothered me in a while, so... I started trying to build some normalcy. So... I met a guy, and he was nice, and sweet, so I guess I figured that was enough, but looking back I can see that I was forcing it. Which is probably why when we tried to have sex, I clammed up. We didn't have any chemistry. Not like..."

"Not like what you feel with Quentin?"

With a wry smile, Renata nodded. "But... I don't understand how you guys can be so sure he likes me, when the times that we've been alone... he pulled away."

"*Because* he likes you," Inez said, covering Renata's hand with hers. "Knowing the things that you've been through, knowing what you're *still* going through now... he probably just wants to give you some breathing room. You probably *need* some breathing room."

Across the table, Naomi agreed. "I know we were encouraging you to go for it, and do it, but... just take it easy. I don't mean to sound like I'm giving advice to a teenager, but... it'll happen when it's the right time." Just then, Naomi's phone chimed, effectively ending their conversation. She smirked at the screen, then stood, pushing in her chair.

Inez patted Renata's hand. "So, do you feel any better?

"I do, actually. Thanks guys."

The three women headed inside, where Naomi took off for another part of the house, Inez began searching the refrigerator for breakfast, and Renata headed for the "war room", which had become her and Quentin's preferred workspace.

She powered on her laptop, started the basic programs she used nearly every day, and then... did nothing.

She couldn't focus.

After the stream of new information and advice she'd just gotten from Naomi and Inez, her head was swimming with possibilities.

— & —

"You rang?" Naomi asked, stepping into Quentin's room as he pulled his shirt over his head. He nodded, then grabbed his phone from the dresser, tossing it to her.

She caught it, but the catch was so clumsy that it made Quentin do a double take as he sat down at the desk. Naomi didn't *do* clumsy.

"You a'ight?"

Naomi responded to his question with a dismissive nod of her head as she turned on the screen of his phone. "What am I looking at?"

"The first text message," he said, tipping his head to the side. He knew from many long years of experience that his question had just been ignored, but he also knew better than to press it. If he mentioned that she seemed a little clumsy, that he'd been concerned about her energy level even before the attack, and that she just frankly looked *tired*... her response wouldn't be pretty, and the conversation wouldn't turn into anything productive. He'd just mention it to Marcus instead, since the two of them seemed to get off on that arguing shit.

"Heard about all those... holes in your car. Should probably leave hacker bitch alone. Hope she liked the work at her apartment." After reading the message aloud, Naomi closed her eyes, squeezing her hand into a fist. *"Hacker bitch?* This is Royale," she said, tapping her finger against the phone.

"Tell me somethin' I don't know, *cher.*" Quentin leaned back in the swiveling chair, propping his hands behind his head. "What I'm trying to figure out is where this all fits? Was she just finishing what Lucas started with you, or is this her own agenda?"

Naomi shook her head. "Probably both. I knew this bitch was crazy, but not *this* crazy. At the house, she was talking about keeping you alive, now she's sending out hitmen?"

144

"Hold up… at the house?"

"Yeah," Naomi nodded, tossing his phone back to him. "Lucas's house. She mentioned seeing if she could get permission to keep you… as her personal boy toy."

Quentin lifted an eyebrow. "Is *that* right?"

"That's right." Shaking her head, Naomi laughed. "She is… for real gone in the head. If the circumstances were different I would laugh, but this chick is dangerous. What are we going to do about her?"

Shrugging, Quentin leaned forward, balancing his elbows on the tops of his thighs as he propped his chin in his hands. "Well… gotta find her first. After that… I say snatch and grab. Bring her here, see what she knows, then turn her over to the FBI with that video of her cutting Rochas' throat in Barbados."

"That's *it*?" Naomi whined. "No… creative interrogation? Beating her to the white meat? Perhaps a bullet to the head?"

Quentin chuckled. "Well… we probably shouldn't involve any bullets, but you and Inez can be as inventive as you want with getting information out of her. I know that "enhanced fact finding" bullshit is right up her alley."

"Damn straight." Naomi smiled, then a flicker of… *something* crossed her eyes, and she placed a hand on her stomach briefly before dropping it away. "So… who'll do the actual grabbing?"

"I would think," he started, carefully watching her face for reactions, "You'd be ready to kick my ass if I suggested anybody but you, so… what's up? Scared you'll kill her on sight?"

145

Naomi gave him a dry smile. "Well, *that*, yeah. But, I also just … think I should sit this one out."

She went quiet after that, and Quentin couldn't get over the weird, overly cautious vibe she was putting off now that it was time to make a plan.

"Mimi... this ain't the time to bullshit me... spit it out. The hell is going on?"

After a deep breath, Naomi looked up at him, bringing her hand to her stomach again. "Q... I'm... pregnant."

What?

His eyes dropped to her hand, covering her still-flat belly, — which let him know it couldn't be his, she would have to be *much* further along— as the air expelled from his lungs.

Pregnant?

"*Wow*... uh, does Marcus know yet?" He asked, moving his gaze up to her face.

Naomi tipped her head to the side, expression drawn into a scowl before she rolled her eyes. "I like your roundabout way of asking if it's yours, asshole. Yes, Marcus knows, and to ease your mind, I'm only six weeks. Congrats, you're not a daddy."

Quentin groaned. "Come on, Mimi, don't be like that. You know— "

"Yeah, yeah," she said, her scowl shifting into a grin as she waved a hand to dismiss his words. "I'm messing with you, fool. I know you wouldn't have played me like that."

His shoulders sagged in relief. He would have — eventually — warmed to the idea of a baby, but Naomi was his friend. He loved her as such, but she was *not* who he imagined as the mother of his kids. And

146

as sacred as the idea of a family was to Naomi, he knew he wasn't her ideal father either.

"Good," he said, scrubbing a hand over his face. "Women have me confused enough this week. How are you feeling?"

She shrugged. "I feel okay. But let's go back to you and this confusion for a second... trouble in hacker romance paradise?"

"You could say that."

Nodding, Naomi made her way over to the bed, and sat down opposite Quentin's place at the desk. "So... spill it."

Quentin tossed his head back and laughed. "So you're really gonna change the subject here?"

Naomi smiled. "Sure am. What's up with you and Ren?"

"I...," Quentin sighed, then leaned back in his chair again. "I don't know."

"Bullshit, you know." Naomi shook her head, then leaned back on her elbows. "You've known her *all* these years. You two have talked, flirted, shared secrets... yeah, you've dated people, she's dated people, but... she's never been far from your mind. And I'm pretty sure *you've* probably never been far from hers. And now you're finally together, finally in each other's space... misunderstandings out of the way, and you just... don't know?"

Quentin held up his hands, in a questioning gesture. "I don't know what you wanna hear Mimi. Shit is... complicated."

"What's complicated about it?" Naomi asked, pulling herself back into a seated position on the bed.

"She's goin' through a lot right now. She doesn't need me clouding her head, takin' her mind off the goal."

Eyebrow lifted, Naomi smirked. "I beg to differ. I talked to Renata this morning — something to take her mind off things is *exactly* what that girl needs. She's stressed out."

Quentin narrowed his eyes. Just how much *talking* had Renata done?

"So what are you suggestin'?"

Naomi's smirk grew into a full on grin. "I'm suggesting you screw her stress away. You know you want to. You've *been* wanting to, even before you knew who she really was."

"Says who?"

"Says your reaction whenever the girl walked into the room. You were hanging on her words, mouth dropped open, drooling—"

"Okay, you're exaggerating."

"*Barely*," Naomi agreed, laughing. "In any case, like I said...Renata needs to decompress. It's been a stressful week, and I just think if she's willing, and you're willing, the hell are you waiting on?"

Quentin groaned, clapping a hand to his forehead. "I'm *waiting* to not feel like a fuckin' creep. She's..." He hesitated for a moment, then remembered that this was *Naomi* he was talking to. He didn't have to downplay anything for her. "Ren is... important to me. *Really* important. I feel like there's a chance for something to happen there, and... I don't wanna mess it up."

Tipping her head to the side, Naomi gave him a little smile. "I know. And I know you're trying to be

148

all... gentlemanly, and respectful, and all of that. *But...* even with everything going on... Renata is still a woman. I'm not suggesting you should try to seduce her or anything, but... follow *her* lead. On the surface, it may seem like she's fragile, or weak, but... that's not really the case at all, is it? Look at all she's endured, *alone.* She had you, from a distance, but who else? Nobody except her child. And she's been out here living her life, kicking ass at her job, wearing a smile on her face... in spite of stuff that would have torn a *lot* of people down. I think that... when you bottle so much up, just so you can *function*, it weighs on you."

Naomi stopped for a moment, staring down at her hands before she shook her head. "Ren and I share a... unique type of pain. A rare sort of *fear*, a constant, unmoving shadow over our lives, put there by Damien Wolfe. And it's... a really lonely place. Renata doesn't need a "friend", Q. She needs her soul pulled out of a *really* dark place that "friends" can't reach. She needs somebody to make love to her, and hold her, and make her feel... human again. Somebody to wake her spirit up, and love it back to life."

She raised a hand to her belly again, smiling a little before she looked back up at Quentin. "Marcus... he did that for me. He's *doing* that for me. I think you're probably the right person to do it for Renata."

For several minutes, neither of them said anything. Naomi seemed to be lost in her own thoughts, and Quentin was running over everything she'd said, trying to make it all fit. Eventually, he realized that just *thinking* through it wasn't going to help anything or anyone. He wasn't sure about the philosophical, soul-mate stuff Naomi was talking about, but... he *was* sure

149

that he cared about Ren. Following her lead... that was something he could definitely do.

"A'ight, back to *you*, Mama Mimi. Now that you've played psychologist... my turn. I wanna know how you're feeling about this baby."

As he suspected, Naomi's expression changed. Not to anger, or annoyance, more like... apprehension. She chewed at her bottom lip for a few seconds before she lifted her gaze to his, shuffling her feet on the carpet. "I... am not sure what I feel about this baby. Mostly because I haven't decided if I'm keeping it or not."

Quentin nodded. That answer didn't shock him. He'd known Naomi long enough to know that as much as she wanted a family of her own, she wanted Wolfe eliminated more. It was hard to get around, difficult to plot takedowns with a baby bump in the way. And besides that, a kid was leverage for their enemies — leverage they couldn't afford.

"How does Marcus feel about that?"

She lifted her shoulders. "He... wants me to keep it. *Really* wants me to keep it."

"And what do *you* wanna do, cher?"

Dropping her gaze, she ran her tongue over her lips, then brushed her mass of hair back from her face. When she looked up again, her eyes were glossy as she shook her head. "I'm so confused, Q. I don't want to bring a child into all of this mess, but... I wanna keep my baby. I mean... anything could happen. What if I never get another chance?"

Quentin stood up, then took a seat beside Naomi on the bed. "I can't give you an answer on what you should do," he said, pulling her into an embrace against his chest. "But... I wanna encourage you *not* to make your decision based on fear. If you *want* this... don't let it become another thing, another happy experience that Wolfe has taken from you. Okay?"

With a deep sigh, Naomi pulled back to look at Quentin's face, then nodded. "Yeah."

"Good," Quentin said, planting a quick kiss on Naomi's forehead before he stood, grabbing his phone from where he'd left it on the desk. "I need to get down to the war room, get started on running through these files again. I guess at the briefing this afternoon, we can tell everybody about Royale."

Naomi rolled her eyes. "That *bitch*. Yeah. The sooner we get her brought in, the better. She's always been unstable, but there's no telling what her crazy ass might be up to now."

Following her to the door, Quentin opened it for her to step out first. "Yeah, I'm thinking maybe once we figure out where she is, we send Inez and Kendall. They can—."

Just as Quentin and Naomi exited his room, Renata appeared at the top of the stairs. She glanced back and forth between he and Naomi, and Quentin could practically *see* the wrong impression forming in her eyes.

"G'Morning cher," he said with a smile, hoping that his warm greeting would help show he wasn't hiding anything. Naomi laughed, shook her head, then walked up to Renata and spoke something Quentin couldn't make out into her ear.

Renata blushed as her lips parted, but Naomi just smiled, turning to shoot a wink at Quentin before she disappeared into another part of the house.

ten.

"Bets on who gets hands on her first?"

Kendall's deep baritone, edged slightly with a musical Caribbean accent, broke through the silence in the car, pulling Inez from her thoughts.

Two days had passed since Quentin and Naomi informed the team that their old friend Tomiko was claiming responsibility for the attacks. This was Kendall and Inez's second day of staking out the hip, semi-luxury apartment in the newly rebuilt part of the city Q and Ren had tracked Tomiko to, and Inez was sick of watching and waiting — she wanted action.

They'd spotted their target the day before, dressed in all black and apparently in charge of the rotation of people she kept with her. That day, Tomiko looked to be handing out orders before climbing into a black SUV. Inez wanted to grab her then, but Kendall had been more cautious.

Patience, he warned. So they waited, all day in the car, armed with enough weapons and ammo to outfit a small army until Q and Ren had successfully gotten into the security system and surveillance cameras so they wouldn't be going in blind. They were skilled, but not crazy — neither had a death wish.

With that resource — the camera feeds — in hand, they were able to see who had been coming and going, and determine who would be in the apartment and when. Tonight, they'd seen Tomiko come in, but hadn't seen her leave.

It was time.

Inez looked up, right into Kendall's dark eyes, and had to catch her breath.

Damn he's fine.

"I don't make unfair bets." She winked at him, then cast her gaze downward, pretending she needed to check the gun strapped to her calf, even though she'd already done so three times. It wasn't that Kendall made her nervous, not at all. It was the *other* sensation he set off that made her avoid his eyes.

It had been a long time since anyone had set off the insane, wild level of desire in Inez that Kendall did. In another time, or perhaps just different circumstances, she would have used that towering, powerful body of his as her own personal playground. Kendall was — to Inez — absolute male perfection. At first, second, and third glance, everything about him screamed danger. Smooth, deep mahogany skin, punctuated here and there by unexplained scars, some ugly, all sexy as hell. Piercing onyx eyes, harshly — but still *handsomely* — chiseled features, and an unnerving affinity for intense stares, quiet contemplation, and sudden, confident action. But... Inez knew that behind the dangerous exterior, he was a man who enjoyed and cared about his friends, and looked for fun. He knew how to flirt. And he had that damned *accent.* And he was... a fellow federal agent, albeit from a different agency.

No.

Nope.

Not at all.

Never again.

The last time she'd taken it there with a colleague, she ended up wishing she'd just killed him instead. Eventually...she did.

Probably shouldn't count on getting away with that twice.

Perhaps it wasn't fair to draw such a comparison between Kendall and he-who-didn't-deserve-a-name, but... that was her prerogative. She'd been misled by a handsome face, a big dick, and a badge before. Not again.

"What do you mean, unfair? You say that as if you know you could beat me."

Inez looked up with a smirk. "Well..."

"Oh," Kendall laughed. "Cocky, are we? What, you think I can't handle you?"

Again, Inez had to bite her lip. As much as she may have wanted to, she couldn't ignore or deny the heat his little innuendo created between her thighs. But... She knew how to create heat of her own.

"I don't doubt that," she said, dropping her voice to a lower, sexier timbre as she leaned over him, practically into his lap to retrieve the entry keycard to the building from the pocket where she'd seen him place it earlier. When she drew back, Inez let her hand drag over his lap, lingering for just a moment at the bulge in his pants before she sat up again. "Too bad you'll never get that chance. Let's go."

Before Kendall could respond, Inez opened her door and climbed out of the delivery van they were using as a cover vehicle. She took a second to take a deep lungful of the cool night air before she pulled on her mask to obscure her face.

155

That's what you get for trying to play, she scolded herself silently. Now she was just more turned on. She hadn't expected his bulge to be so... *bulging.*

Dios mío.

"Ready?" Kendall asked, from right beside her, making her flinch. She was always surprised by how such a large, powerful man like him could move around so deftly, without making a sound.

"Yeah." She took another deep breath, then unholstered her gun, bringing it in front of her in a two handed grip as she followed Kendall to the back door of the building. Silently, they made their way into the building and up three flights of stairs, stopping on either side of the door that would lead them to where Tomiko was.

Inez pressed her ear to the wall, listening for sounds on the other side as Kendall carefully slid a tiny, wired camera under the door. He moved it around carefully, watching the screen connected to it for any signs of movement. When he found none, he pulled the camera out and pulled it away, silently caught Inez's attention, then nodded.

She dropped to her knees in front of the door, swiftly picked the lock, then stood and placed a high-powered magnet on the door. Little by little, she inched it up, right, just slightly down, until she had it in the right place. Slowly, she turned the magnet, allowing herself the indulgence of a smile for *just* a moment when the tumblers of the deadbolt slid out of place, settling with a quiet click as the door unlocked.

With a nod to Kendall, she stepped back, stored the lock-picking kit in one of her pockets, then waited. In her ear, she faintly heard the tapping of keys from

Quentin and Renata as they did... whatever they were doing. A few seconds later, a low but firm *go* made Kendall reach for the doorknob, look up at Inez for confirmation, then soundlessly open the door.

Inez went in first, weapon pointed, sharp eyed, even in the semi-darkness, as she scanned the room for armed targets. They only needed to bring Royale in alive. Anybody else — especially if she saw a gun — was fair game. She didn't have to look back to know that Kendall was behind her, providing cover and doing his own room clearing as they made their way through the large apartment, room by room, finding... no one.

The apartment was unnaturally cold, a sharp contrast against the summer heat that awaited them outside. Although her sleeves were long, they were thin, and Inez shivered as they skillfully made their way through the apartment. By the time they made it to the last room — the main bedroom — an uneasy feeling had settled into Inez's stomach. Where the hell was everybody? Another cursory glance at Kendall, and she opened the door.

She went left, Kendall went right, moving through the room with precision. The first thing she noticed was that the bed, along with the rest of the room, was empty— so again...where the hell was everyone? They quickly checked the closets, and then with an unspoken agreement, made their way to the attached bathroom.

As soon as the door was open, and the lights attached to the ends of their guns fell upon the tiled bathtub, the reason for the temperature in the apartment, as well as the loud, steady hum of the bathroom exhaust vent became clear. From where she was, Inez counted at least four bodies piled into the tub. She recognized the faces from the two days she and Kendall had been staked out, but... no Tomiko.

Inez started to take another step closer to the tub, just to be sure, but Kendall snatched her back, lifting her feet off the floor.

"*Qué carajo, Ken?! What the hell are you doing?*" she hissed, struggling against him.

She may as well have been fighting a brick wall for all the good her tussling did, but Kendall drew her into his body, lowering his mouth to her ear. "*Stop.* You were about to trip something."

Reluctantly, Inez went still, then looked down at the floor to see the razor thin wire, set just about an inch off the ground, that had gone completely unnoticed by her. Kendall lowered her to the ground, then met her eyes with his. Without looking away from her, he raised his gun in the direction of the bathtub and emptied his clip with silenced shots.

"Just in case," he said, seamlessly loaded a new clip, then turned out of the bathroom, taking care to shine his light on the floor, checking for other tripwires as he went.

She had no idea what would've happened if she'd touched that wire, but she was pretty sure it wouldn't have been glitter falling from the sky. Was the trap intended for *them*, or just whoever found the bodies? Based on the cold temperature, and bodies stored in the bathroom, obviously there was some attempt to conceal their presence, and prolong the time before someone noticed the inevitable smell of decaying human flesh... but to what end? She felt safe in assuming that Tomiko had committed the murders herself, keeping some of her team to help with whatever her plan was.

What was the plan?

And why hadn't they seen her leave the apartment?

Inez blew out a deep breath as she watched Kendall's imposing figure travel through the bedroom. She hadn't stepped out of the bathroom yet, but a flash of something in the corner of the room caught her eye. Easing back so that she was out of sight, she watched as the closet door crept open, then raised her weapon as the barrel of a gun came into view on the other side.

Kendall!

Without giving it a second thought, Inez fired once, then a second time through the closet door. The resounding thump of a body hitting the floor provided no comfort to Inez as she swiftly moved out of the bathroom. The zip of her silenced gunshots had caught Kendall's attention as well, and he was right beside her when she came to rest against the wall where the closet was.

"Where did he come from?" Kendall mumbled, gesturing toward the dark figure bleeding onto the hardwood floors.

Inez shook her head. *"No idea. We cleared this closet already. Nobody was in there."*

"What's goin' on?" Quentin's drawl rang in their ears, reminding them he was there. "We don't have eyes in the apartment. If you need help, you've gotta let us know."

"Do you have the blueprints pulled up? We're in the back bedroom, beside the closet. Tell me what's

on the other side of this wall, Q." Kendall glanced at Inez, who nodded. They were thinking the same thing.

There were a few moments of intense silence as they waited. Before Quentin could give them an answer, Inez felt rather than heard something heavy move against the floor of the empty closet. As if by some prior agreement, she and Kendall both switched off the lights on their guns, and held their breath as they waited for what would happen when the newcomer discovered the dead body on the floor.

There was no gasp, or scream, even a sharp intake of breath, but Inez could sense the shift in energy. A moment later, gloved hands, holding up a gun came into view through the hinged crack of the door. Inez raised her own weapon, but froze for a moment as cold, piercing blue eyes met hers through that crack. They narrowed, and he turned to her, but before he or Inez could fire, the air behind her crackled with force. The following second, intruder #2 hit the ground.

"Nez, Ken, the apartment on the other side of the wall you're on is occupied by an elderly couple, and you're separated by a foot of concrete. The apartment *behind* this one though… the closet wall is shared, and there's no concrete separation."

Inez looked back, exchanging a glance with Kendall. The new information confirmed her suspicion. A nod of corroboration was their only discussion before Inez pulled the closet door all the way back to the wall, giving them a full view of the dead assailants. They stepped deftly over the bodies and into the closet, switching their lights on again to see in the dark.

160

This time, because they were looking for it, they noticed the fine crack in the back wall of the closet. The hinges were probably on the other side, out of view. Heart racing, veins pumping with adrenaline, Inez pressed her back into the wall, then turned to Kendall.

"Guess we're gonna get some action after all, partner." Her whispered words were further muffled by the mask over her face, but Kendall gave a low chuckle in response.

He pushed a finger through one of the belt loops of her dark jeans, dragging her a little closer. *"So this is what it takes to get you hot and bothered? Guns and danger?"*

Inez shrugged, willing herself not to tremble or moan at the feeling of being pressed into his broad chest. *"Is that a problem?"*

"Not at all, Sexy. Just... something to keep in mind."

She couldn't see his mouth, but she could tell he was probably smiling behind his mask as she pulled away. Inez pushed her aroused state into the shadows of her mind, allowing the job to take the forefront again as Kendall moved in front of her.

Raising her weapon, she watched as Kendall lifted his foot, pressed it against the wall, and pushed hard to reveal the opening the assailants had used. Kendall went through first, clearing the closet, then moving into the bedroom as Inez stepped through as well.

She was just stepping out of the closet when Kendall fired his first shot, which was followed by the distinctive thump of someone hitting the floor. They both stayed quiet, waiting to see if they would hear

161

footsteps, or if someone else would pop out of the woodwork. When nothing happened, they finished clearing the room, then headed for the door that led to the main area of the apartment.

They moved through the apartment silently, methodically, eliminating armed attackers as they went. When they made it to the front, they did another sweep, then checked the other apartment again as well, but there was still no sign of Tomiko.

Nostrils flared, Inez stomped angrily back into the kitchen of the apartment, where a lone attacker sat, tied to a chair. "Where is she?" Inez asked, kneeling in front of him. The man fought violently against his restraints, but Inez didn't flinch.

First of all, there was no way he could break through the plastic roping she'd used to tie him up — he'd cut his wrists and ankles beyond repair against her impeccable, secure knotting. Kendall had his gun aimed for a shot right between the man's eyes, and even if he somehow made it through *all* of that... Inez was trained in six different international hand to hand combat styles, and armed with seven different ways to kill him in one move — not including her hands. She had nothing to worry about.

"You can fight against that rope all you want. You're not going anywhere, *doing* anything, *seeing* anyone until you *answer my question.* Where. Is. Tomiko?"

"Kiss my ass, bitch!" the man snapped back, his eyes cold and narrowed as he stared at Inez. Behind her mask, she smiled.

"*Besar el culo*, huh?" She giggled as she paced back and forth in front of him. "*Besar... el... culo...*

162

that's so rude, you know? I really can't stand it when people are rude to me. It just makes me so... *ugh!*" She sucked her teeth. "*Besar el culo.* Do you talk to your mother like that, with that filthy mouth?"

She went over to the sink, grabbing a bottle of dishwashing liquid.

"Such a dirty, *dirty* mouth to talk to a lady. Let's work on that before we move along, huh?"

Standing behind him, Inez grabbed a handful of the prisoner's hair and yanked it back. While his mouth was open in protest, she poured a long squeeze of the dishwashing liquid down his throat, then stepped back as he spit out what he could, coughing and sputtering.

"What the fuck is wrong with you?" he asked, choking.

Standing well out of range of his spitting, Inez propped her hands on her hips. "What's wrong? *What's wrong* is that you still haven't told me where Tomiko is. I really, *really* think you should. You see... that itching and burning in your throat and chest now, the way your lungs feel like they're on fire from ingesting that soap... I was just *playing* with you. That was just me having a little fun, because you disrespected me. I haven't even *started* doing my job yet, and trust me... *that's* going to hurt a whole lot more."

Instead of doing what Inez would have preferred — simply spilling what he knew, the man shook his head. "I'm not scared of you, and I'm not saying shit."

Across the room, Kendall laughed, a deep, throaty, rich sound that made heat settle between Inez's legs. "Trust me, brother. You *should* be scared."

Smiling, Inez turned back to the prisoner as she pulled a knife from the holster at her belt. She lifted it, hesitated just long enough to make him give her the sardonic grin of someone who *really* thought they shouldn't be scared.

Hmph.

With precision, Inez brought broke the knife down, straight through the bones in his knee, flicking it to separate the muscles. The man screamed, until Incz covered his mouth and nose with her hand and squeezed tight.

"You should have listened to the man. He's right. You should *absolutely* be scared."

eleven.

Shit.

Quentin dropped his head into his hands, groaning as he closed his eyes. Several days had gone by since the failed attempt to snatch Tomiko, and still... no sign of her. On one hand, it was good. No more near death experiences, no more destruction. But on the other hand...

What the fuck are you up to, crazy ass girl?

Inez's interrogation of Tomiko's henchman at the apartment had led them to a small townhouse near Naomi's, which currently sat empty while they figured everything out. They could see Tomiko had indeed been there, from the fire accelerants, weapons, ammo, and blueprints from the buildings where they lived and worked. Naomi came to the quick conclusion that since she couldn't get to them — Naomi, Quentin, or now Renata — the next best thing was going after the gym. In any case, by the time they found the townhouse, she was gone, and hadn't been back.

They had nothing.

Raising his head, Quentin sat back and propped his hands behind his head, staring at his computer screen. Tomiko occupied one side, Terry King occupied the other. Two targets that he couldn't seem to get any closer to than where he was.

Shit!

Frustration had driven Renata up to her room, without her laptop, nearly an hour before. The stress of it all seemed to be weighing on her heavier now, especially since the video call with Wolfe the day before, where Taylor had excitedly shown her new clothes, a computer, school supplies, all preparations for her to start school hundreds of miles away, *"since mommy was so behind on her work."*

And the bastard had offered — insisted — on setting her up in a new apartment, which she refused to even go look at. Who knew what kind of surveillance he would put on her, what kind of favors he would feel like she owed, if she accepted such a thing provided by him? The call ended with him feigning offense at Renata's refusal of his gesture, and as soon as the line was closed, she broke down in tears.

Nothing would have given Quentin more satisfaction than putting a fist through Wolfe's face, but that wouldn't have been helpful at this stage, unrealistic or not.

Get Taylor back. Then, Wolfe was fair game.

Recognizing that his focus was shot for the day, Quentin pushed himself out of his seat, shut down his computer, then headed upstairs. As he passed the door to Renata's room, the faint thump of music caught his attention. He glanced down at his watch for the time. It was past late at night, but music playing meant she was probably awake... probably up worrying.

He knocked lightly on the door, and when she didn't answer, knocked a little louder to be heard over the music. When he still got no response, he turned the knob and eased the door open. The lights were off, but

166

she'd lit what appeared to be at least a dozen candles to illuminate the room.

Quentin's first glance was toward the bed, and when he found that to be empty, he pushed the door a little a further to seek her out in the room, expecting to see her at the desk.

Instead, she was standing in front of a canvas propped on an easel against the wall. A counter-height table had replaced the desk, and it was covered with tubes of oil paint she'd requested of Kendall and Marcus a few days before. She had the window open, and a fan going to pull any fumes out of the room and into the night air. She had a paintbrush in her left hand, moving deftly across the canvas to create highlights and shadows for what, as far as he could tell, was a striking image of two people, just their torso area, a man and a woman, pressed together.

Quentin grinned.

Oh that's *how she's feeling right now, huh?*

Neo soul playing, lights low, candles lit, her chosen creative outlet on hand... She was *vibing*. And he...was interrupting.

"You don't have to leave," she said, just as he was turning to leave her to her project. When he looked back, she was turning to face him, and the sight stopped him cold.

From the back, the oversized tee shirt she wore dipped low, low enough that she was well covered. But in the front, it rode high, high enough that juicy, dark brown sugar colored thighs were on full display, and... *goddamn* was that a peek of sapphire-blue boy short panties? He brought his eyes up to her face, a little smile crossing his mouth at the sight of a streak of paint across her cheek.

He was still wondering how the hell she could look so sexy in a sling when she put the paintbrush down and took a step toward him.

"Q... what's up?"

"Huh?"

Renata smiled, shaking her head a little as she took yet another step. "What's. Up?" she repeated, tipping her head to the side. "You came into my room.... You must have wanted something?"

He pushed his hands into his pockets. "Um... yeah. I just wanted to check on you... you were pretty upset earlier, so..."

She nodded. "Yeah. It's... a lot happening, you know? And then finding out that Wolfe is buying Taylor school supplies, like he's not even planning to let her come back, even if we *can* pull off this thing with King any earlier.... I already know what he's gonna say, that's it not fair to pull her out of school in the middle of the semester, and I... does it make me crazy that I thought about that too? Knowing what he did to me, when I was just a little older than she is now, how he's tortured me over the years, I actually considered if I should have her stay to finish out the semester. What kind of parent does that make me?"

"One who got put into a shitty situation, but also wants the best for her child. Wolfe is being daddy of the year right now. He's not harming Taylor, he's providin' for her, being kind to her... all the things that good parents do. So... I don't think it's abnormal that, because you see her being well taken care of, you wonder if *you're* fallin' short. He's setting you up, Ren.

168

Wants you to feel guilty, like you're the bad guy. Taylor is a teenager. She doesn't see Wolfe for what he is, she sees him as her elusive, magical father, who comes bearing gifts. It turns *you* into the villain, for taking her away from her new friends, disrupting her school year, etc, when it's time to get her back. Now... I'm not a parent, but... I'm pretty sure you do things all the time that Taylor may not necessarily like, or understand... but it's still what's best for her. Don't let the fact that *Wolfe* is on the other side change what you've been doin' for years."

Twirling a braid around her finger, Renata shrugged. "I guess. But really, if I wasn't moving so slow with this King Pharma thing, this wouldn't even be a problem. If I could use both hands, this wouldn't even be a problem right now."

"That's not true and you know it." Quentin took a step closer, closing the distance between them as he reached for her hand. "This isn't a quick job. We have to finesse it, if we want it done right. It's not enough to just put a scandal into the news, we have to make sure the backstory checks out, alter records from clinical trials, all kinds of stuff that we can't do *quickly,* some things that we have to wait on paperwork to go through, so we establish a proper trail. We're working as fast as we can."

Renata shook her head. "*I'm* not. Even with the voice recognition, I'm just... slow. And then... this crazy bitch Tomiko trying to kill me, and burning down apartments, and we don't know where the hell she is, or what she's capable of. What if *she* goes after Taylor because of *me*? I'm failing right now. Failing my daughter, failing the team, fail—"

"*Stop*," Quentin urged quietly, bringing her fingers up to his mouth to kiss her hand. "You're *not* failing anybody... you're doing what you can."

"You're just saying that to make me feel better."

"I'm saying it because I *mean* it."

He kissed her fingers again, then moved so that he was behind her, and wrapped his arms around her waist, pulling her close. "Talk to me about something else," he murmured against her ear, before planting a kiss there. "Tell me about what you're doing right now. Tell me about your painting."

For a long moment, she didn't answer or move, and almost seemed to not even be breathing, until Quentin kissed the spot behind her ear again. Then, she sucked in a breath, which she exhaled in a stream before she finally began to speak.

"This is the other thing I can't get off my mind," she said, settling back against Quentin's chest. "So... I set this mood, with the music, and the candles, and ... painted what I was feeling."

Quentin cast his eyes upward to look at the painting again. A golden-brown man and deeper brown woman, neither clothed, faces hidden, pressed together in an obviously intimate embrace. It wasn't lewd, or erotic, but the sensual nature of it practically oozed off the canvas, making Quentin wonder just how much she was "feeling" this.

"Is this me and you?" he asked, tipping his head over her shoulder to see her face.

She cast her gaze upward to meet his eyes, then wet her lips with her tongue. "This is weird, isn't it? I'm being... weird, and inappropriate... right? I'm not

170

supposed to be feeling like this, thinking of me and you like this, when I should be concerned about Taylor."

"I think you're being too hard on yourself. It's okay for you to relax sometimes, *cher*. What, exactly, is piling yourself with worry and guilt going to accomplish?"

She shook her head. "Nothing."

"Exactly. Nothin'. So why do it? You're a grown woman, Ren. Nothing wrong with not wanting to think about all the messed up shit happenin' around you. It's called taking care of yourself." Quentin reached up, sweeping Renata's braids over her shoulder so that he could press a kiss against the exposed back of her neck. Her soft whimper made him pull her closer, trailing more kisses up to her ear. "You've gotta be good to yourself sometimes too, *cher*."

He placed a final kiss against her cheek, then released her from his embrace. "I'm gonna leave, so you can chill out to your music, paint, enjoy yourself without feeling bad about it, okay?"

"Wait a minute," Renata said, catching his hand as he turned for the door. "*This* isn't what I want to do." She paused for a second, chewing nervously at her bottom lip before she returned her gaze to his. "This is…. the substitute."

Quentin reached up to brush her hair back from her face. "So what do you *want* to do?"

"I want you to stay." She released his hand to point at the canvas. "I don't wanna *paint* that. I wanna *do* that. With you."

— & —

Renata's words hung in the air for a moment before she reached for him, grabbing a handful of his shirt and yanking it upwards, trying — and failing — to pull it up further than his chest with one hand. And then... she panicked. Just a little.

I don't know what the hell I'm doing.

She didn't have any experience initiating sex. Or... *having* sex really, but... she didn't think that really mattered. She'd watched movies, and read books... she knew what the experience *should* be like.

Kinda.

Quentin grinned, then grabbed a handful of *her* shirt, using it to drag her closer. He pressed his lips against hers in a soft kiss. "Ren... you sure this is what you wanna do?" he asked, his lips brushing hers.

"Yes."

Their eyes met, and Renata saw the hesitation in his. Her heart dropped a little, remembering the conversation with Naomi and Inez. Was he... concerned about taking advantage of her? Was that the reason behind his reluctance?

"Q," she said, cupping his chin in her hand. "You *just* got finished encouraging me to practice some self-care. This — you and me — is what I want. Don't deny me that."

For a moment, neither said anything, but then Quentin moved his hands to her waist to pull her closer. Renata pushed herself up on her toes, meeting him halfway. Their kiss started off slow, sweet, the soft press of lips as they tried to gauge each other. At first, Renata could still feel a bit of hesitation from Quentin, but she draped her arm over his shoulder, pressing her hand to the back of his head to keep him close.

172

That little movement seemed to be the confirmation he needed that she *really* wanted to take it further. He ran his tongue along the seam of her lips, requesting entry, and she granted it hungrily. Slipping his tongue into her mouth, Quentin tasted and teased, deepening the kiss to a point that she became lightheaded, high off him, wanting so badly for him to touch other places that they throbbed.

He lowered his hands, and Renata shivered as his strong fingers gripped handfuls of her butt, kneading and caressing until finally, he picked her up and carried her to the table, where he shoved aside the painting supplies that covered the surface before sitting her down.

Quentin pulled his shirt over his head, tossing it to floor. Renata's eyes traveled hungrily over his newly revealed, ink-covered golden skin, admiring the ridges and planes of his chest and abs illuminated by the candlelight.

"I put you up here, instead of the bed, so we don't forget and put too much weight or anything on your arm. Is that cool?" he asked, positioning himself between her legs.

What arm?

In that moment, Renata couldn't have chosen her arm out of a lineup, but she nodded, because she wanted to feel his lips again. He lowered his mouth to her neck, nibbling, sucking, kissing his way down to her collarbone as his hands slipped under her shirt. The first touch of his fingers on her breasts made her gasp, and made her nipples peak into hard beads against his skin.

Quentin drew back, to carefully remove her arm from the sling, then even more carefully pulled her shirt over her head and tossed it aside. He lowered his mouth to kiss her again, and she moaned as he drew her lip between his teeth, sucked it, then pushed his tongue back into her mouth to deepen the kiss.

Pressed into his hard, muscled chest, Renata's breasts ached for his attention. A moment later, she got her wish as he pulled away from her mouth to trail kisses down her neck. His lips traveled, across her collarbone, then down to her nipples; first one side, then the other. With him between her legs, she could feel the power of his erection pressed against her, making her hot, and dizzy, and light-headed, and it was… *wonderful*.

She'd been kissed before, touched before, but… it never felt like *this*.

"*Cher*," Quentin murmured, raising himself up to speak into her ear. His hand swept gently over her breasts, down her stomach, stopping to touch the apex of her thighs, through her panties. "Can I touch you here? Is that okay?"

He seemed so… *concerned*, so focused on making it a good experience for her that tears pricked Renata's eyes as she bit her lip. "*Please*," she whispered, nodding her permission as he pressed his lips to hers again. A moment later, he slipped a hand into her panties, spreading her folds as his thumb danced over her clit. Her brain, it just… wouldn't fire right, not with Quentin touching her like that. Her vision blurred, thoughts went fuzzy as pressure built in her core, and his mouth was on one of her nipples again, gently teasing it with his teeth, rolling it with his tongue, and she had to squeeze her eyes shut to handle the intensity of pleasure it caused.

She opened her eyes at the sound of the chair that previously went with the desk being rolled into place in front of her. At first, she was confused, but then Quentin sat down between her legs and pulled her panties down her legs and dropped them to the floor. He draped her thighs over his shoulder, and then up at her with a sexy smirk.

He didn't give her a chance to say anything before he covered her with his mouth, pulling a whimper of pleasure from her throat. Pulling her closer to the edge of the table, he buried his face between her legs, licking, and kissing, and sucking, and nipping, and driving her right to the brink of ecstasy as he devoured her.

Renata gripped the edge of the table with one hand, trying to keep herself upright when he pushed a finger inside her. His finger and tongue moved in unison, building a type of pressure that was… different, hotter, stronger, more… *powerful* than any orgasm she'd ever given herself. And *still* she felt uninhibited, and free, and *sexy*, as Quentin worked his mouth on her most intimate places, making sounds of pleasure as he consumed her, like she had sugar between her thighs.

She threw her head back, biting her lip to keep herself from screaming out loud as that coil of pressure tightened too far, then burst as she climaxed. Pleasure hit her in waves as Quentin continued, planting open-mouthed kisses on her sensitive flesh until her breathing finally calmed. He kissed his way up her stomach, over her breasts, then finally back up to her mouth, where he kissed her deep, massaging her tongue with his before he pulled back.

"That was *beautiful*, chérie," he said, gazing into her eyes for a long moment before he drew her into another kiss. "Watching you come like that... and you taste *so good*." After that, he gave her that look again, filled with such adoration that it made heat rush to her cheeks.

"You called me... chérie, instead of cher... is there a difference?"

Quentin grinned as his hand drifted down between her legs again. "Yeah," he said softly, just before he pressed his lips to hers again. "*Cher* is something I call female friends. *Chérie* is something I call *you*. Only you. Do you understand?"

Nodding, Renata let out a gasp as he pushed a finger into her again. His mouth covered hers, swallowing her moan of pleasure with a kiss as he slipped in a second finger and began stroking her.

He dropped his mouth to her neck, trailing gentle bites, followed by soothing kisses as he made his way back up to her ear. "You are *so* damned sexy," he whispered against her ear, before sucking her earlobe into his mouth. She whimpered as he dragged his thumbs over her clit, teasing and massaging as he stroked her. "*So* wet... nice and tight... *perfect*."

Wait... no.

Something in his words triggered... *something*. A memory... a flashback... Renata squeezed her eyes shut.

— & —

"Nice and tight," he groaned. "Perfect. Let's go."

176

Her vision went black as someone dragged her up from her seat. Faintly, she heard Stacy's giggly voice asking what was going on, but soon her hearing was as muffled as her vision. Shortly after, there was nothing.

She didn't know how much later it was that a faint sense of consciousness returned to her. She couldn't see, couldn't hear, couldn't smell anything, but something... somebody... was touching her, and pain was emanating from between her legs. The distant memory of being carried out of the club tugged at her mind as something... someone... moved inside of her.

She tried to open her mouth, tried to say something, but her lips wouldn't move. She just wanted him to stop touching her.

Don't touch me. Please, don't touch me.

— & —

"Please stop touching me!"

Quentin's fingers stilled, then withdrew, and he looked up, confused by Renata's sudden demand. "I'm...sorry. What happened, did I hurt you?"

"Get away from me!" She yelled again, her eyes frantic as she looked around her on the table for... something.

Baffled by what was happening, Quentin stepped back, raising his hands in midair. "I'm *sorry*, Ren...did I *do* something?"

Renata snatched her tee-shirt from the end of the table where Quentin had thrown it, yanking it over her head. "Just... get out. Get the hell away from me."

"*Cherie*... I'll leave if that's what you want me to do, but can you tell me what's going on?" Not

177

thinking, he reached forward, placing a hand on her knee, and she immediately snatched away.

"*I said don't touch me!*" she shrieked, snatching up a palette knife from the table beside her.

"Ren, what the fuck is happening?"

"That's a good damned question."

Quentin turned to the door to see Inez standing there, weapon drawn. He glanced back at Renata, wielding that tiny little knife, looking terrified of him, and he sighed.

This looks so bad.

"So you already know, right?" Inez asked, not lowering her gun. "I'm coming down the hall, hear her screaming *don't touch me*... I come in here and she's half naked, with a knife... I need you to explain this shit quickly, *por favor*."

Scrubbing a hand over his face, Quentin took a step toward Inez, but she raised her weapon a little higher, moving her finger to the trigger. "Uh-uh. You're the homey, Q, but no sudden movements, and keep your ass where you are until I know what's going on. Ren... you alright chiquita?"

When he looked at her, she was sitting all the way on the table, knees drawn into her chest as she nodded.

What the fuck just happened? He thought. He still had Renata's taste in his mouth, her scent on his fingers... what the hell had changed? One second, they were sharing a moment, and the next... Inez's crazy side had a gun pointed in his face.

Nez kept the barrel of the gun trained on him as she stepped into the room, then moved so that she was between he and Renata.

178

"Did he hurt you?" Inez asked over her shoulder.

"No."

"You just want him to leave?"

Behind Inez, Renata nodded, her voice trembling as she delivered a shaky "Yes."

With that, Inez gave Quentin a pointed look, then made a "shoo" gesture with her gun. "You heard her, Q. Come on."

Only because he was still confused did he go quietly to the door, but as soon as he was there, he faced Inez, keeping his voice low.

"The fuck is this, Nez? Pointin' a *gun* at me?"

Inez's face dropped from her tough girl expression as she lowered the gun, pulling the door closed behind them. "I'm *sorry*, Q! But you *see* her, don't you? The girl is traumatized, and I'm trying to make her feel safe! What the fuck did you do?"

"What did *I* do? Exactly what she asked me for! We're having a *good* goddamn time, then all of a sudden, she flips on me!"

Inez groaned. "Maybe... maybe you triggered something, Q. Remember, you *know* what she's been through. You know better than any of us."

"So she thinks *I* did something to her?" Quentin stepped back, swiping a hand over the back of his head. This was *all* messed up.

"No," Inez said, leaning back against the wall. "If she thought that, she probably would have had me shoot you. I think she knows what happened, and just had a moment. I'm gonna go in here and talk to her, see if I can figure it out."

Quentin pushed out a breath, then shoved his hands in his pockets. "Please do, cause… shit, I thought she was okay with it. She *said* she was okay with it. You know I wouldn't do anything to hurt her, right?"

Inez nodded, then tipped her head to the side with a sympathetic smile. "Q… I know that, and *Ren* knows too. Trust me. She probably *thought* she was okay with it, until it was actually… happening. I'm gonna talk to her. Chin up, chico, we know you're a gentleman."

"I'm not worried about that, I'm worried about *her*."

"I *know*. *Dios mio*, are you gonna let me go talk to her or not?"

"Please, go."

Inez shot him another little smile before she went back in the room and closed the door, and Quentin shook his head. He still didn't really understand how his stopping, just to *check* on Renata had turned into him getting kicked out of her room at gunpoint.

Shirtless.

At three in the morning.

Sucking his teeth, he bypassed his room for the bathroom, taking a quick shower before he climbed into bed. Thirty minutes, then an hour passed with him tossing and turning, unable to sleep while wondering what was going on with Ren. Was she okay… was she mad at him?

Realizing that trying to sleep was futile, he got out of bed and set up his laptop at the desk. In front of it, he spent some time working on breaking the encryption on Terry King's private files, but he still couldn't focus. The only thing on his mind was Renata.

180

Quentin lifted an eyebrow when a chat box popped up on his screen, but smiled when he saw the username.

[painted_pixel: hey... are you awake?

CrawDaddy: yeah. couldn't sleep. guessing you couldn't either... why didn't you just text me?

painted_pixel: didn't want to bother you if you were sleeping.

....

....

painted_pixel: can we talk?]

Quentin pushed out a heavy sigh, then scratched at his chin. Then, he shook his head, at himself, because he didn't know why he was stalling.

[CrawDaddy: of course.

....

....

painted_pixel: ......can you come over here?

CrawDaddy: uh... yeah. Be there in a sec.]

Quentin didn't bother shutting down the chat, just closed the lid on his laptop, then sat back in his chair. Swiping a hand over his face, he chuckled at himself. When had he become *this* guy, who was willing to, just a few hours after being kicked out, go *back* to a woman?

But... then again... he'd *always* been willing to go above and beyond for Renata, since they were kids. He'd ignored it for a long time, but when he thought back over the years of their friendship, something had shifted, very early on. Only for a short time, when they *first* met in that teenage hacker chat room, and Renata shut *everything* down had they been simple friends. It had almost always been something … different. Never sexual because they didn't have the chance, but if he was *very* honest with himself… Renata was the reason no other girl — and later, *woman* — had ever stood a chance.

He pulled on a tee shirt and shorts over his boxers, then left his room to travel the few feet to Renata's door. He leaned against the doorframe as he knocked, and a couple of seconds later, the door swung open to reveal Renata's pretty face.

Her arm was back in the sling, and she was in shorts and a tank top this time. Her braids were pulled back from her face, and her eyes… it was obvious that she'd been crying.

If Quentin had even a little bit of indignation left over from earlier, it was quickly swept away by her subdued expression. She stepped back so he could come in, then closed the door behind him, and they stood there for moment in silence, giving Quentin the distinct impression that *neither* of them really knew what to say.

Finally, Renata cleared her throat, then looked up to meet his gaze. "I… I am *so* sorry, about earlier. I'm completely mortified about what happened, and I think I would understand if you wanted to just pretend I wasn't even here anymore, but…. I hope you don't wanna do that."

"I don't," Quentin said, shaking his head. "Just wanna know… what the hell happened?"

182

She dropped her eyes, and her expression shifted to one of such intense discomfort that Quentin wished he hadn't asked. He was struck by an overwhelming need to hug her, touch her, *something*, but... he kept his distance.

When she looked up again, her eyes were glossy, but she gave him a weak smile. "Can we sit down?"

Quentin nodded, taking a seat in the desk chair while she sat on the end of the bed. Not wanting to rush her, he waited patiently while she collected herself, then finally spoke.

"Um... for a long time... since it happened, really... I... always thought that I was completely out of it while Wolfe um... did what he did to me, all those years ago. I didn't remember any of it. And... I never talked to a professional. Or... anybody at all about it. I just... told myself I was okay. But I wasn't. All this time, I've tried to date people, tried to be intimate, and it just... didn't work. I think that some of that has had to do with my feelings for you. You... filled a void for me emotionally, so I didn't really need anyone else there. So... I've never gotten... as close as you and I got... with anyone else before."

Eyes wide, Quentin sat forward in his chair. Had he heard that right? "Are you telling me... you've never...?"

She shook her head. "The night that Taylor was conceived is the only time."

Guilt sucker-punched Quentin in the chest as he processed her words... realized the magnitude of what tonight *could* have meant for her.

"*Chérie*," he said, sliding out his seat to kneel in front of her, cupping her face in his hands. "I am *so* sorry."

Her eyes narrowed in confusion. "For *what*? Q… you didn't do anything wrong. I just… something you said to me, reminded me of something *he* said to me that night, and it triggered a memory. A really *ugly* memory, and I freaked out. That's not your fault."

"But I'm still sorry. Sorry that you even have to deal with something like this."

She shrugged. "I guess… I maybe should have expected it. But everything felt so… natural, and so right with you. Nobody has ever come *close* to making me feel taken care of like that. You have *no* idea how much I appreciate you." She smiled, then closed her eyes as Quentin reached up, using his thumbs to wipe away the stray tears that escaped down her cheeks. "I'm *so* sorry," she whispered when she opened her eyes, and Quentin pulled her into an embrace as she broke into sobs.

"Stop apologizin'," he said, kissing her forehead. "You've been through a *lot*… what kind of person would I be to hold that shit against you? I just wanna see you happy."

Pulling back, Renata nodded. "I'm… gonna talk to somebody. A *professional* somebody. Inez actually suggested it to me earlier, and… I think I need that."

Quentin smiled. "And *I* think you should do whatever you need to find peace."

"Thank you," she said, returning his smile. "So… you don't hate me?"

With a scowl, Quentin tipped his head to the side. "Come on, now. Hate you? That's about… as far as you can get from how I feel about you, Ren."

"Really?"

Chuckling, he nodded his head. "*Really*." He leaned forward, intending to kiss her on the mouth, but stopped short, drawing back. He regretted that as soon as he saw the hurt on her face. "Wait a minute, now," he said, covering her hand with his. "*Don't* get the wrong idea about that. I just… is it okay to kiss you? I don't wanna overstep."

Her shoulder sagged in relief. "Oh. *Oh.* Yes, it's okay for you to kiss me. I *want* you to kiss me, I want you to touch me. I want you to want me. Because… that's how I feel about you. We don't have to be awkward with each other… we like each other… *like that*… right?"

"Yeah."

"Well… then… we can show that. But… before we try to take things… *there* again… I should…"

Quentin nodded. "Yeah."

Before she could say anything else, Quentin cupped her chin and kissed her, then drew back with a grin. She smiled back, and relief flooded his chest, with the knowledge that he would be leaving her in a better mood than she'd been in when he came in.

He stood up, intending to leave, but she reached out, grabbing his hand. "Wait," she said, standing with him. "This… could be really awkward, with what we just established but… I don't wanna be by myself right now. Could you… stay?"

"Uhh…" Quentin lifted an eyebrow, then used his free hand to rub the back of his neck. When she pulled her lip between her teeth and started gnawing at it, he started chuckling. "I'm just playin' with you, chérie. Of course I'll stay."

Renata sighed, then laughed a little too as she switched off the light, then led him to the bed. They climbed in together, and Quentin couldn't help smiling in the dark as she settled against his chest, propping her leg over his. Reaching down, Quentin gently stroked her back, and she was asleep in no time.

At first... it felt a little strange to be sleeping with her like this, but then the overwhelming *rightness* of it settled in. He kissed the top of her head, then lowered his head to whisper something in her ear before closing his eyes. A few moments later, Renata stirred, lifting her head enough to press a soft kiss to his lips.

"I love you too."

twelve.

Naomi took a deep breath, then stared up at the building she was about to enter.

You can do this, Mimi. It's a good decision.
A healthy decision.
The right decision.

But that didn't make it feel any easier. She took another deep breath, then ran a hand over her hair, smoothing her bun in the rear view mirror.

Like anybody in there cared what her hair looked like.

Hands shaking, she climbed out of the car, telling herself to just put one foot in front of the other. Left, right, left, right, just to keep herself distracted enough to actually make it to the front door.

Inside, breathing got a little harder. It was decorated in plush furniture and warm tones, probably to give the people coming in a sense of home. Naomi suddenly wished she'd asked Marcus to come with her, but imagining his expression, what he might say, if she asked him to come here with her... She shook her head. Maybe Inez would have been better... But she still hadn't told her,

One foot in front of the other. Don't have all day.

She started moving again, and the pretty, perky woman at the front gave her a sympathetic smile. "Are you okay, honey?" she asked, and Naomi nodded, giving her a tight smile in return as she walked past her, to the rooms in the back.

She'd already read the available information on their website, and had already decided what she wanted. Naomi had even called ahead... this place called it a reservation.

She closed the door behind her in the tiny room, taking several deep breaths to pull much needed air into her lungs. It was bad enough that she was off-grid, after Marcus had insisted on protection for her, but to risk it to come *here*... He wasn't gonna be pleased. But Naomi had to do what felt good for her, what was best for her — just like he'd said. And even though her stomach was in knots, brain on overdrive, heart stuck somewhere around her throat...this felt good.

Standing, she slipped out of the simple, gauzy sundress she'd worn, for ease of removal, and its ability to conceal weapons. She unstrapped a gun from one thigh, and a knife from the other, hiding them under her dress before she turned to face herself in the mirror.

Six weeks pregnant had turned into eight far too soon. Naomi ran a hand over her flat stomach... still too early to see anything. She probably could've waited another month to do this. More time to think about it... more time to decide... but, she'd already known what she was going to do.

From the rack across the room, she pulled out a garment and pulled it over her head, forcing her eyes to the mirror and she straightened and pulled it into the proper draping on her body. Then she turned to the side.

188

Nothing.

She arched her back, trying to poke her belly out further, with no luck. A heavy sigh, with a poked out bottom lip made a stray curl from her bun float away from her face, and that action drew her eyes back to the bench where she'd laid her dress. Without a second thought, she picked it up, rolled it into a ball, and stuck it under the maternity dress she was trying on. Turning to the side again, she let out a shuddering breath at what she saw.

Me... With a baby bump...?

She laughed at herself, a real, deep laugh from the soul, until her eyes began to water. A few moments later, those tears of laughter turned to tears of relief. And... release.

She was having a baby.

A *baby*.

And... It was okay. It would be okay. The other bullshit was just that... bullshit. She could live a normal life, do the normal, crazy things that other pregnant women did... Like making an appointment at a luxury maternity shop to try on a ridiculously expensive dress she had no intention of buying.

Or... Maybe she *would* buy it. Why not?

Someone knocked at the door, and before she could remove her improvised bump, a smiling salesperson walked in. Feigning embarrassment, Naomi quickly removed it, tossing the dress on the bench to cover her weapons before the woman saw them.

"You know," the saleslady said, grinning, "We *do* have belly forms, if you'd like to get a visual on how certain things would look as you progress in your pregnancy. Would you like to try one on?"

189

As you progress in your pregnancy.

Progression… in the pregnancy. That was going to happen…like… for real. She was actually having a baby.

With a deep breath, Naomi glanced at herself in the mirror one last time before looking up at the saleslady again. "Yes. I'd like to try one."

— & —

About an hour later, Naomi exited the maternity shop, bags in hand. She was positively giddy, a feeling that was strange, and unfamiliar, and… made her even more giddy. She glanced down at her bags, wondering if she left them out, would Marcus recognize the logo? That was what *normal* women did right, thought of a cute way to reveal to their partner they were having a baby?

Or, in their case… *keeping* a baby.

She slipped her cell phone from her pocket and turned it on, knowing that Marcus would probably track her as soon as her signal was available again. But that was fine. She was going to wherever he was anyway. She unlocked her screen, navigated to his number, and pressed the call button as she stepped off the sidewalk, into the parking garage.

"A *maternity* store, Mimi? I never, ever would have thought."

Ice rushed through Naomi's veins at the sound of Tomiko's voice, and the feeling of something hard pressed against her head. She didn't have to look to know it was a gun. Slowly, she drew the phone away from her ear.

190

"Tomiko... what a disappointment it is to see you," Naomi said, as Tomiko moved so that she was in front of her.

Shit. Another mantra fail.

If she'd been diligent about her surroundings... this wouldn't be happening. If she'd been focused on something other than cute maternity dresses... this wouldn't be happening. If she'd listened to Marcus, accepted a bodyguard... this wouldn't be happening.

Her agility... right now that wasn't even a factor. She couldn't *fight* Tomiko, not with the knowledge that it would very likely put the baby in danger. As subtly as she could, she maneuvered her phone with one hand so that her fingers could reach the button on the edge of the case Quentin had modified specifically for her. She pressed it, and held down.

One. two. Three. Four. Five. Six—

"Watch the smart mouth, *bitch*." Tomiko pressed the barrel of the gun into Naomi's chest, hard enough that she stumbled backward, and her finger slipped off the button.

Shit.

Swallowing hard, Naomi tucked the hand with the phone behind her, hoping that Tomiko wouldn't notice. Looking into her former friend's face, Naomi noticed that while she was still pretty as ever, Tomiko's eyes looked vacant, and cold. She moved her finger back to the button and pressed it in again.

"Tomiko, what do you want?" she asked, trying to distract her long enough for the distress signal to go through.

Come on, just four more seconds.

Naomi's nostrils flared, and her fingers slipped from the button *again* as Tomiko grabbed her by the front of her dress, pressing the gun to her head.

"I *want* you and your fucking sidekick to stop messing things up for me. We had a good life, taking what we wanted, but you and nerd-ass Q just *had* to "give back to the needy"," she said, in a mocking voice. "*Messing shit up.* So I leave. I get away from you, I live my life, and things are fine. I *finally* get in with a man with some real money, and then here you come again. Next thing I know, Vick is dead, and my whole lifestyle is thrown out the window. Because of *you* and *him.* You're in my way, and I'm tired of it."

"Victor Lucas's death wasn't my fault, Miko." Naomi kept her voice strong, confident. She wasn't scared *of* Tomiko, but she was scared *for* herself, and the baby. *Especially* the baby, with Tomiko wielding a gun. "Damien Wolfe did that, in retaliation for what Lucas did."

Tomiko sucked her teeth. "He's your uncle, *bitch.* And you wouldn't have even been on Vick's radar if you hadn't *broken into his house.* Do you know I'm gonna have a *scar* under here?" Tomiko asked, pointing under her chin.

Naomi suppressed a smile, remembering the way she'd kicked Tomiko there that night at Lucas's house. But, this wasn't the time for fond memories. While Tomiko ranted, Naomi found the distress button again and pushed down. She had to hold it for a full ten seconds to activate it, to keep it from accidentally going off in her pocket, or purse when she carried one. She made a mental note though, to talk to Quentin about it taking so long.

"— care about who your family ties are, or anything else. Your ass is *mine*, and when I'm done with you, pretty boy and hacker bitch are next. Might throw *Agent Calloway* in there too, just for fun. All of you are responsible for me losing nearly everything I had, so I want you tell me again how this isn't your fault."

Seven. Eight. Nine —

"Answer me, bitch!"

Naomi cringed as Tomiko grabbed a handful of her hair, wrapping it around her fist as she snatched it from her bun. Cold metal bit into her skin as Tomiko pressed the gun to her cheek, and the phone, along with her bags, slipped from Naomi's hands.

"*Ohh*, we're gonna have so much fun. I've got a room set up, just for you."

In one smooth motion, Naomi brought her hand up, using her fist to jab the gun away from her face before Tomiko could react. While Tomiko was still surprised from the attack, Naomi hit her wrist, with enough force to send the gun flying out of her hand and onto the asphalt.

"I'm *not* going anywhere with you," Naomi said, aiming a fist for Tomiko's jaw. Now aware of what was happening, Tomiko released Naomi's hair to dodge the blow, then stepped back.

From the corners of her eyes, Naomi saw that Tomiko had assistance. Men dressed in black, armed with guns. Outnumbered or not, she *wasn't going anywhere with Tomiko*. They'd have to kill her first. Moving swiftly, Naomi reached under her short dress and drew her own gun, pointing it at Tomiko.

193

"Stay back," she demanded. "Or your boss dies."

Tomiko smirked. "If I die, so do you."

"Then I guess there will be new funeral announcements in the paper because *please* believe I will pull this trigger."

On the ground, Naomi's phone started ringing, and the second she took to glance at the screen was all it took for Tomiko to pull a knife and send it flying at her, before Naomi could even think to pull the trigger.

Pain erupted in her mid-section, and Naomi dropped to the ground on her knees, clutching at the knife embedded in her abdomen.

No. No, please. Please.

Hearing Tomiko begin to chuckle, Naomi looked up through tear-soaked eyes to see the other woman standing over her, grinning.

"Pregnancy has made you lose your touch, Mimi. Too bad."

With tears streaming down her face, Naomi reached for the gun she'd dropped, but Tomiko kicked it out of the way. "Uh-uh-uh," she said, leaning into Naomi's face. "You lost, Black Swan, Arabesque... Madame Mimi, whatever it is you go by these days. Your ass is *mine* now, but don't worry. I'll make sure to keep you alive long enough to find out if the baby survives."

Naomi saw Tomiko raise her fist, but was too weak to react before pain exploded against the side of her head, and everything faded to black.

— & —

Shit.

Harrison cursed again under his breath as the SUV pulled to a hurried stop in the parking garage. The other men were out of the vehicle before he was, easily picking off Tomiko's armed guards before they could reach where she was, kneeling over Naomi.

Wolfe wasn't gonna be happy about this shit, not at all. *Livid* was more like it, but Harrison would be damned if *he* was gonna be the one to catch that wrath. He'd found himself on the receiving end of Wolfe's anger exactly *once,* and had the scars across his back to prove it. Harrison had stood up for himself then to prove himself, so he wouldn't get blamed for shit like this *now.*

They'd been tracking Tomiko for the last few weeks, ever since they figured out she was the one behind the car attack, and the fire. She was using Lucas's people, which were basically Wolfe's people, since he owned Lucas too. It hadn't been hard to figure out.

It was easy enough to sit back and wait, trying to see what she was up to before they figured out a plan, but once he got word that they were going after Naomi… all bets were off. There were few things in the world that Damien Wolfe cared seriously about. One of them was his family

Nah, Tomiko would have to pay the fine for fucking with Wolfe's kin today.

He snapped his fingers at one of his armed guards, then motioned toward Tomiko, who seemed too paralyzed by fear to take off and run.

Always run, dummy.

While they collected her, he jogged up to where Naomi lay, passed out. He dialed a number on his phone for an EMT they kept available for such things, holding it up to his ear while he scanned her for injuries. There was the bruise developing on her head, where he'd seen Tomiko punch her, and then there was the knife still embedded in her stomach.

That made things quite a bit more complicated.

When he finally heard a raspy "hello?" on the other end of the line, he rattled off the address for where they were and a demand to "hurry the fuck up" before hanging up, and glancing around the nearly empty parking garage.

Beside her on the ground, Naomi's phone was ringing. Harrison picked it up, glancing at the screen before he looked over at the large yellow and white shopping bags that had spilled onto the asphalt. A *maternity* store.

Shit!

When the EMT arrived, Harrison stood back to let him work, while he pulled Naomi's phone from his pocket. If he had to guess, her team was on their way, but he planned to be long gone before they arrived. The phone started ringing again, and he grinned at the screen. Marcus Calloway, aka Mike Lowery, calling for the third time.

"Mike! What's up, man?" He answered, turning his back as the EMTs loaded Naomi onto a stretcher to put in the back of the ambulance. He pulled the phone away from his ear as Marcus launched into a "*who the fuck is this, where the fuck are you, you better not fucking touch her*" rant on the other end of the line.

196

"Would you relax, Mr. FBI? Naomi is... *indisposed* right now, but Mr. Wolfe wants you to know... he'll make sure she's well taken care of."

Without waiting for Marcus to say anything else, Harrison ended the call, then walked up to the ambulance just as they were getting ready to close the door. He quickly counted off a wad of cash from his pocket and handed it, along with Naomi's phone and bags to the EMTs.

"You know what to do."

— & —

Heart pounding, Marcus rushed through the halls of the hospital, not caring about the people he almost ran over as he tried to get to Naomi. The only thing overshadowing the intensity of his anger was a desire to see for himself that she was alive. He already knew "well" was out of the question.

He and Kendall had been on their way to her way before Harrison answered her phone, from the moment Quentin called him to inform that she'd pushed that distress. They all knew Naomi well enough to know it was no accident.

Marcus was aware enough of the details of Naomi and Quentin's "friendship" that he knew they'd slept together, and the idea still made him cringe, even now. But today... He was glad Quentin knew Naomi well enough to track her phone, glad he had enough foresight that, knowing she was pregnant, and may not be on her usual "diligence, focus, agility" grind, he had reset her panic button to notify them at first press, instead of a delayed response.

He was already *beyond* furious that she'd dodged the body guard he assigned, although he'd honestly expected that of her. Learning that something had actually happened to her, and that Wolfe was involved... that was a feeling beyond simple anger. *That* feeling was closer to rage, wrapped in apprehension, topped with a need to rip something in half when he'd heard Harrison's voice on the line.

Simply put, Marcus was sick to death of them both — Harrison with his smart-assed mouth, and his punk ass boss, Wolfe. They were preying on two women that he cared about deeply.

When they got to the location that she'd sent her signal from, the only thing they found was bloodstained concrete and a mostly empty parking deck, with Naomi's car still there. Without any leads, Marcus followed the only option he felt he had. He went back to Inez's house, down to the war room with her and the rest of the team to work out their plan to show up at Wolfe's door and blow his brains out. The only thing that stopped them was the second call, nearly an hour later, from a nurse at the local hospital.

Naomi had been dropped off, and left in their care, which was all the nurse would say. As happy as he was that she wasn't kidnapped, or *worse*... the fact that Naomi hadn't been the one to call, that a nurse had to do it... Marcus considered that a clear indicator that she wasn't okay.

And what about the baby?

The thought of that made him rush a little faster.

198

Naomi hadn't been exactly open to talking about, or making plans for a pregnancy, a birth... a nursery. To Marcus, that said she was either unsure about what she would do, or that she was *very* sure what she would do, and the decision wasn't in his favor. If she decided not to keep the baby... that was something he could process. Having the choice taken away from her... he didn't think he could handle that.

He slowed down as the numbers on the doors neared the one they'd given him for Naomi's room. A quick glance told him hers was the one at the end of the hall, in a corner, and he was pleased to see that the guard he'd sent ahead was indeed posted at her door, looking sufficiently menacing with his hand on his weapon.

The guard inclined his head in greeting, stepping aside so that Marcus could get in. He stopped just inside the door, taking a deep, cleansing breath before he ventured further, preparing himself for what he might see.

Naomi had her eyes closed, and she was curled into a ball underneath the hospital bed covers. She always slept that way, so *that* wasn't a surprise, but seeing her like that, in this setting — an oxygen mask over her face, IV stuck in her arm even though she was buried under the covers — was... *painful*. He'd been *so* enraged that she "got herself into this situation", but all that anger melted into concern as he approached the bed.

Pulling one of the wooden visitor chairs up to the bed, he slipped a hand underneath the covers to find hers. As soon as they touched, her fingers tightened around his palm, but she still didn't open her eyes. He pulled her hand forward, kissing it as he leaned down, resting his chin on the bed. They stayed that way for a while, neither saying anything until finally she opened her eyes, moving her hand to stroke his face. Marcus caught it, keeping it secure between his as he kissed her fingers again.

"I'm scared to ask if the baby's okay," she said, her voice cracking as tears filled her eyes. "I'd decided we were gonna keep it. Marcus, I was *so happy*. I was getting excited, I bought clothes, I… I don't know if I'll be able to handle it, if—"

"*Stop*." Marcus reached up, cupping her face in his hands. "We don't know yet, so… for now… just tell me what happened. Can you do that?"

Sniffling, she nodded, and Marcus pulled several Kleenex from the box beside the bed and cleaned her face.

"Um…," she started, chewing at her lip. "I was leaving Bitty Buns, to—"

"Bitty Buns?"

She nodded again. "Yeah. You know, like… an itty bitty bun in the oven? It's a maternity store, here in town."

"Oh…" Marcus lifted an eyebrow. "So you're telling me you skipped out on your protection detail to… go shopping?"

A fresh wave of anger began rising in his chest, and he sat back, creating distance between them. But… the distressed look on her face was like a bucket of ice poured over his ire.

"I know it was stupid, Marcus, but… it was more than just shopping. I wanted privacy, because I was still trying to work my feelings out."

200

Marcus scoffed. "And look where privacy has you now."

He regretted those words before they were even past his lips, but Naomi's reaction to them, recoiling as if he'd hit her, made him feel even worse. Being upset with her was one thing, but being *worried* at the same time, especially now that even though he hadn't verbalized it, he recognized that he *loved* Naomi... it was a fucked up mixture of emotion that made his head hurt. Marcus scrubbed a hand over his face, then leaned forward, taking her hand again.

"I'm sorry, Beautiful. Finish telling me."

Naomi wiped her eyes, then cleared her throat. "Um... I was heading back to my car, and... Tomiko snuck up on me, and pulled out a gun. I didn't want to risk the baby getting hurt, so I tried not to antagonize her. But she tried to get me to go somewhere, and I knew if she took me somewhere it was over. So I fought, and I had the upper hand, but I got distracted. And... she threw a knife at me, because she saw the maternity store bags, and she *knew*."

Marcus climbed onto the bed beside her as she broke into sobs, the sudden movements sending the vital monitors into a frenzy, but he didn't care. He pulled her against his chest, folding her into his arms as she cried.

"I don't really know what happened after that," she choked out through her tears. "I think she hit me in the head, but then I woke up here."

Marcus frowned. "So you didn't see Harrison at all?"

"No," she said, sniffling as she looked up. "I don't think Wolfe did this. It was messy, in broad daylight... this was all Tomiko."

"But Harrison answered your phone, Baby. Said something about Wolfe making sure you were well taken care of."

Naomi shrugged, wiping her face with the back of her hand. "I don't know, Marcus. I was—"

"Um, *excuse me!*"

They both looked up at the sound of a woman's voice in the doorway. Marcus wasn't surprised to see Quentin and Kendall lurking behind her, but the woman — a doctor, guessing from the white coat she wore over her scrubs didn't seem pleased about their presence or *his*.

"I'm glad to see my patient has some support, but if you don't get off that bed, messing up her stitches, you're gonna need some yourself."

Marcus scowled at her, and she scowled right back, propping her hands on her hips. Indignant, Marcus climbed down from the bed, pulling out his badge as he approached the doctor.

"Special Agent Marcus Calloway, FBI. This woman is under our protection."

The doctor lifted an eyebrow. "Portia Morris, MD. PhD. OB-GYN. This *patient* is under *my* protection as well, and seeing as I have the authority here, you can put your little badge away."

Tipping his head to one side, Marcus glanced at Kendall and Quentin, but both looked away, scratching their heads. Dr. Morris side-stepped him, walking up to Naomi.

202

"Let me look at your stitches, sweetie," she said, and Naomi nodded, covering her mouth with her hand. Marcus sucked his teeth, shoving his hands in his pockets as Dr. Morris pulled the covers back, lifting Naomi's gown just enough to peek underneath the bandage to check her wound. "Still looks good, but I need you taking it *very* easy. I'm gonna stop *just* short of assigning bed rest, but if you don't have a doctor yet for your pregnancy, I want you to come to me. I understand that the situation is... delicate."

Marcus put his hand on his weapon. What the hell did she know about the "delicacy" of their situation? "You care to explain what you mean by that?"

Turning to Marcus, Dr. Morris lifted an eyebrow. "Well... she's pregnant, and was brought in here with a knife in her stomach and fuzzy circumstances. *You* just said she's under FBI protection. So... the obvious conclusion would be that it's a situation that requires some discretion."

"I think I'd like that, Dr. Morris," Naomi said, before Marcus could interject. He rolled his eyes, crossing his arms over his chest. "But... talking about the pregnancy... that means the baby is okay?"

Her voice was filled with so much hope that Marcus forgot his anger as he approached the other side of the bed to grab her hand.

"Yes, the baby is perfectly fine." Dr. Morris shook her head, smiling. "You're actually incredibly lucky. Incredibly *blessed*. If that knife had gone an inch deeper, it would have pierced your amniotic sac. Now... with that said, Naomi you *have* to take it easy. This time, you were fine, but the stress that your body

has been through, with the surgery and everything...
I've seen miscarriages happen under *much* less trauma."
With a pat on the hand, she turned to leave. "I'm gonna
go get you some information."

When she was gone, Marcus leaned forward,
kissing Naomi on the head. "Really?" he asked. "This
lady, as the doctor for our baby?"

Naomi laughed. "Yes, *her*. She's feisty. I like
her."

"You like her because she was mean to me."

"I like her because she wasn't taking any shit
from you. Flashing your badge at her Marcus, really?
What were you doing?"

"I was...." He stopped, with a heavy sigh. He
really didn't know *what* he thought he was going to
accomplish by flashing his badge in her face, but he
knew he didn't like her demanding he get away from
his woman.

His woman.

Shit.

When he thought about how close he'd been to
losing his woman, it made heaviness settle over his
chest. Dr. Morris said Naomi had been "brought in",
presumably by Harrison, who worked for Wolfe. So...
what was Wolfe's end game? If *he* wanted Naomi
eliminated, he could have easily let her bleed out on the
ground, or let Tomiko do whatever. Instead, he'd...
brought her to the hospital.

What the hell did that *mean*?

Before he could come up with a response for
what he'd been trying to prove to Dr. Morris, she was
back, carrying a huge bouquet of pink and white roses.

204

"Looks like someone is thinking of you," she said, smiling as she placed the bouquet on the table beside the bed.

Eyes narrowed, Naomi reached for the attached card, opened it, then read it aloud. "Tell the hacker to check his email…"

Dr. Morris looked confused, but everybody else looked at Quentin, who immediately drew his phone from his pocket.

"Dr. Morris, can you excuse us?" Marcus asked. "Official business."

This time, she glanced at Marcus's hand on his weapon, the serious expression on Naomi's face, and Kendall's menacing posture as she leaned against the wall beside the door. She seemed to make a quick calculation that it wasn't a problem she wanted, handed Naomi the paperwork she'd originally gone to get, then hurried out of the room.

Marcus turned to Quentin, whose face held a somber glare as he stared at his phone. Apprehension prickled his skin as Quentin looked up, shaking his head.

"It's from Wolfe."

At the sound of that name, anger blossomed forth again. Quentin seemed in no particular hurry to get to them, so Marcus knew whatever was on that screen must be bad. Without a word, Quentin handed him the phone, and Marcus held it up in front of he and Naomi, pressing play on the video on the screen.

Naomi gasped, and Marcus's stomach clenched at the sight of Tomiko, in what appeared to be some type of dark basement room. Her pretty face, normally the color of brown sugar, was decorated in purple and black bruises. One eye was completely swollen shut, but a steady stream of tears flowed from the other as she screamed against the gag tied to her mouth, seemingly oblivious that a camera was there.

She wore a tank top and pants, but they there were bloody and dirty as well, and what was visible of her body was just as bruised as her face. Marcus tried to find a little more sympathy for her, from somewhere, but... she'd caused too much trouble for that. The only reason he felt even the *tiniest* bit bad for her was because it was Wolfe who had her.

A moment later, the man himself came onto the screen, dressed in nice slacks, suspenders, and what was probably an expensive button-up — complete with cufflinks — and blood splattered across the front. He looked right at the camera, cleared his throat, then opened his mouth to speak just as Tomiko launched into another round of muffled screams.

"Shut her up," he said, to someone, without taking his eyes off the camera. He held up a finger in a "wait a second" motion, while an armed guard pressed a knife to Tomiko's face, then bent to whisper something in her ear. Her eye went wide, and she immediately stopped screaming, settling instead for quiet sobs.

Wolfe smiled.

"Now. Mimi, Baby Girl... if you're watching this, I want to tell you something I'm not sure if you know or not — I *love* you. You're family," he shrugged, then smiled again. "Because of that, I want you to understand that I feel a certain... obligation to protect you. It's what your mother has asked me to do, and... you know how I feel about Noelle. Whatever the

206

lady wants." Wolfe stopped to chuckle a little, running his thumb over the patch of hair under his lip. "But I digress. In any case, it *pained* me to find out that Lucas's whore was causing trouble for you and your little friends, especially since I have an um… *vested* interest in making sure that you all stay alive — I need that job completed. So I'm taking care of this little problem for you, because *that's* what family does. This little girl won't be picking on you anymore, okay Princess?"

Wolfe nodded at the screen, then turned, walking toward where Tomiko was still quietly sobbing. He removed the gag from her mouth, then bent low to speak into her ear, loudly enough that the camera caught it. "Now … remember we talked about this, right? I want you to apologize to Naomi."

"I-I..s-s-s-sorry," Tomiko managed to choke out, her bottom lip trembling as she eyed Wolfe with trepidation.

His nostrils flared, and he shook his head. "No, you can do better than that. Your mouth was *so* slick when Harrison brought you to me. You had so much *irresponsible* confidence, you were *so* sure that because you were beautiful, and had a pussy, I was just gonna roll right over and let you do what you wanted, but you were *wrong about that today*. I should have had your ass taken care of when I got rid of Lucas, but *no*. I showed you *mercy*. And you repay my excessive kindness by laying hands on *her*? On Naomi. My family, my blood, you *know* this. You fucked up. You fucked with the wrong one, so I want you to apologize to my blood like you want me to spare your despicable little life, do you understand me?"

Trembling with fear, Tomiko nodded, then shakily lifted her head toward the camera. "N-naomi. I'm s-sorry."

"Say it again."

"N-naomi, I'm s-sorry."

"Louder."

"Naomi, I'm s-sorry."

"Again!"

"N-naomi, I'm sorry!"

Naomi's hand flew to her mouth as a loud crack sounded from the phone, and Tomiko's lifeless body slumped to the side. Marcus swallowed, covering his mouth with his hand as well as Wolfe simply stood there, his face lined with contempt as he stared down at the hole he'd blown in Tomiko's head. And then... he smiled.

"Oh this motherfucker is *crazy*," Marcus said aloud, glancing at Naomi, who looked *horrified.*

On screen, someone had handed Wolfe a towel, and he wiped the blood from his face and hands before turning back to the camera.

"Baby Girl, now... I know you probably think I'm a monster for that, but please understand that was something I had to do. I promised you she wouldn't bother you again, and I'm a man of my word, if nothing else. I promised Noelle that I would protect her baby girl, and I intend to do that. I will not abide by any physical harm coming to you. This *trash*," — he tipped his head to where Tomiko still sat — "crossed a line. Especially now that I know about your delicate state. Harrison tells me that congratulations, to you and Agent Calloway are in order, for the news of your pregnancy.

So… congratulations. I hope to meet your child one day."

After that, the video cut to black, with a message that it was being removed from the server. Marcus tossed it to Quentin, then immediately turned to Naomi, whose eyes were already welling with anxious tears.

"No," he said, cupping her face in his hands. "*Never*. That will *never* happen, do you understand?"

"Marcus, I can't—"

"Mimi, Baby listen to me. Wolfe will never *see*, will never *hear*, will never *touch* our child. Trust me on that. We *will* figure it out. I need you as stress free as possible, baby. For *our* baby, okay?"

Averting her eyes, Naomi broke into sobs again, and Marcus sat down on the edge of the bed, mindful of her stitches this time as he pulled her into his arms.

"It's gonna be okay," he whispered into her hair as he held her close.

"I just… don't understand." Naomi looked up, wiping her face with the back of her hand. "After what he did, *why* is he so protective of me? He sounded obsessed!"

"Because he is *insane*. That's all there is to it.

Naomi nodded, then rested her head against Marcus's chest. He looked up as Quentin nodded to Marcus in an unspoken communication to see if he could do anything to get the video back. On-camera murder had to be worth *something*.

Kendall and Quentin slipped out, leaving Naomi and Marcus alone in the room. For a long time, neither said anything. Marcus hoped beyond hope that she wasn't second-guessing the baby again, after she'd *just* made up her mind to keep it.

"Marcus…," she said, resting her head against his shoulder as she looked at him with tearful, red-rimmed eyes.

He took a deep breath, steeling himself for what she might say. "Yeah?"

"Why was he talking about my mother in present tense?"

thirteen.

"So… don't you think it's time you said it out loud?"

Looking up from her hands, Renata turned her attention back to Layla, as she insisted on being called. *None of that stuffy Dr. Alexander stuff please*, she'd said.

A smile tipped the corners of Renata's mouth as she thought about their first session, almost three weeks before, and her great first impression of the therapist held true.

Layla Alexander looked more like somebody's fly auntie than what Renata pictured in her head for a therapist. She was a beautiful older woman, with skin the color of honey, and long, regal, chocolate brown locs tipped in blonde, occasionally flecked with grey. She exuded a quiet confidence that Renata envied, and that, paired with the fact that talking to her felt more like talking to a *friend* than a *professional* had kept Renata rooted in her chair for the last three weeks in a row, in Layla's warm, homey office.

"Say… *what* out loud?" Renata asked, tipping her head in confusion.

"That you were raped. I mean… that *is* what happened, isn't it? You keep referring to it as "what he did", and "what happened to me", and "that terrible night". Why do you keep absolving this man of guilt by minimizing the way he violated you?"

Renata lifted an eyebrow. "I didn't realize I was doing that."

Layla nodded. "Every time you use prettier words to soften it, you're allowing him an out he doesn't deserve. Call it what it was, Ren."

"I... I don't really want to... can we skip this?"

With a sympathetic smile, Layla shook her head. "I'm afraid not, sweetheart. In previous sessions, you've told me that you want to move forward. You want to *heal*. But... how exactly do you heal if you won't accept that you've been wounded?"

Running her tongue over her lips, Renata shrugged. "I don't know the answer to that, but I *do* know that I don't want to say that word out loud. I don't *want* to be a victim."

"But you already are. You weren't given a choice. You were *absolutely* a victim of a crime. So... let's explore why you're having a hard time with that *fact*."

Nostrils flared, Renata turned her gaze out the window, swallowing hard before she spoke. "Um... it's just such an *ugly* thing, you know? Being violated, having something *stolen* from you like that, when you aren't even old enough to *vote*, barely old enough to drive, it's just... it's hard. I would love to just forget that it happened to me. I've googled, and watched documentaries, and I see these strong, powerful women who retook control of their lives, and found love, and they're stable... they're *thriving* after what happened to them, and I'm... not. I'm not strong like that. I don't

212

know that I can handle, or accept the reality that I was... the reality of what happened to me."

"Not strong enough?" Layla raised an eyebrow, her expression incredulous as she shook her head. "My dear, you were date raped and impregnated at sixteen years old, put out of the house by your emotionally and verbally abusive mother, still graduated high school, graduated college, went to the FBI, and raised a smart, healthy child, all while her father popped up sporadically to harass you. And despite all that, you have one of the *sweetest* spirits I've ever had the pleasure of coming in contact with. I would venture to say... you're a lot stronger than you think. So... just give it a shot for me. Please?"

Shifting in her seat, Renata reached up to run her hand through her braids, sweeping them over her shoulder. After a long moment, she nodded, and Layla smiled.

"Okay. Repeat after me: I was raped."

Renata let out a heavy sigh. "I... was raped."

"I was raped... and that's not okay."

"I was raped... and that's not okay."

Again, Layla smiled, with a little encouraging nod. "I was raped, and that's not okay... but *I* will thrive anyway."

"I was raped, and that's not okay," Renata started, then paused to clear her suddenly tight throat. "But I will thrive anyway."

"I was raped, and that's not okay. But I will thrive anyway, because I *am* strong."

Tears welled in Renata's eyes as she repeated Layla's words. "I was raped, and that's not okay. But I will thrive anyway, because I *am* strong."

"And powerful."

"And powerful."

"And I not only *can*, but *will* retake control of my life."

"I can, and will, take control of my life."

"And I will reach stability."

"I'll reach stability."

"That's *right*," Layla said, clapping. "And find a big strong man who makes me feel beautiful, and is patient with me, and makes me wanna have his little big-headed babies."

At that, Renata broke into laughter through her tears, and Layla handed her a box of tissues to clean her face.

"Tell me how those words make you feel, Renata."

Swiping her face with one of the tissues, Renata nodded. "They make me feel good. But… it can't be that easy, can it?"

"Unfortunately… no. But it's your first real step in the right direction. The fact that you were raped takes nothing from *you*. It doesn't minimize *you*. It doesn't devalue *your* humanity, it devalues the person who violated you. It makes *them* less than. There is no magic pill, or exercise that I can take you through that will ever make your rape okay. But, there are things that we can do to help you move forward, help you feel strong, make sure that *most* days are good days, and make sure that the bad ones aren't *so* bad."

"Thank you." Renata gave her a grateful smile, then went silent. After a moment, she took a deep breath. "Um… something in particular that I wanted to ask was about… sex. What happened to — I mean…

the rape… happened more than fifteen years ago. I feel like I should be past this part by now, and able to… let go, and be free, and… enjoy someone. I have the *urges*, that's not a problem. And I know how to please *myself*, and I *do*, but… I'd like to be share the experience with someone else without freaking out."

Layla smiled. "Well, self-exploration, and self-pleasure are both really, really important for your healing process, so if you've already mastered that step, you should feel very proud of yourself. Healthy, consensual sex can really hold transformative power. You're thirty years old, Renata — entering your sexual prime. Wanting sexual gratification is completely normal, regardless of your history. Tell me… is there a particular gentleman you have in mind?"

Blushing, Renata buried her face in her hands for a moment before she looked up again. "Yes. His name is … Q."

"And does this *Q* know about your history?"

"He does," Renata replied. "He knows about these sessions… asks me how they went. He's even researched things he can do to help me move past it. He's very *sweet* with me. Patient, respectful. I'm *just now* getting him to stop asking my permission before he touches me, or … kisses me."

Renata bit her lip, squeezing her thighs together as she remembered just the day before, in the kitchen at Inez's compound. There was plenty of room in the huge kitchen, but Quentin still found it necessary to brush past her as she stood at the sink washing a handful of strawberries. And it wasn't just that he brushed past her, he *lingered*, and when she turned around, he was right there behind her.

"What, Q?" she'd asked, heat building between her thighs under the warmth of his gaze. He'd put his hands on the sink at either side of her, boxing her in as he stepped closer. *"What, I can't look at you now?"* had been his answer, to which she'd responded by shaking her head, with a coy smile. Before she could offer a verbal retort, he'd leaned in closer, enough that the cool sweetness of his breath tickled her lips. *"I wanna kiss you right now. Would that be okay?"* And those words made her lungs constrict. She swallowed hard, and somehow found the capability to give a flirtatious answer. *"I told you, you don't have to ask..."* Quentin grinned, cupped her face, and right there in the kitchen, in the middle of the day, gave her a kiss that made her toes curl in her fuzzy socks.

"Must have been *some* kiss," Layla chuckled, scribbling something down on her pad.

Blushing again, Renata dropped her head. "It *was*. And... I wanted to do more, *much more*, than kiss."

"So why didn't you?"

Renata sighed. "Well... we've *tried*. And it was incredible. He made me feel things I've *definitely* never made myself feel. But then I had a flashback, and like... I guess a panic attack or something, and I wasn't very good to him. But... I want to try again."

Layla shrugged. "So try again. As I said before... there's no magic cure, except a partner who cares for and respects you, is willing, and kind, and patient, and... just happy to be invited into the room, despite what some may consider flaws, or baggage. The two of you could do an exact repeat of that failed encounter, and this time... it might not fail. Or, maybe

216

it will. The only thing that really works is an understanding and acceptance of what could happen — terrible, or terribly good — and a willingness to try again."

Tipping her head to the side, Renata lifted an eyebrow. "That's it? Just… try again?"

"Yes ma'am," Layla nodded. "Just… try again."

— & —

"Mmmm, *huele delicioso aquí!*"

Renata smiled as Inez slowed her steps, taking a deep inhale of the aroma coming from the kitchen. They'd just walked into the house, and the smell of Andouille sausage and green peppers had filled their nostrils as soon as they got up the stairs.

"It *does* smell good in here," Renata agreed with Inez, following her toward the source of the heavenly aroma. They found Quentin in the kitchen, bobbing his head and rapping along to whatever was playing in the headphones that covered his ears as he stirred the contents of a pan.

Quentin cooking had been mentioned before, but for the last six weeks, the team had been living on takeout and bagged salad mixes, because they were focused on the job. But they'd come to a place with the King Pharma job that they couldn't hack — time. Programs had to run for hours on end to lay the foundation for the emails they'd created that "proved" the newest drug wasn't safe for public consumption, and that King knew that. They had to wait for the quarterly reports, and answers from investors, because King wouldn't announce the new drug until then.

So, with a little more spare time on their hands, Renata deduced that Quentin must have found himself tired of eating out, and wanting something homemade and fresh. She just wasn't prepared for how damned sexy he would look while doing it. Dark gray sweats, and a black tank that molded to his body, showing off the results of his daily five a.m. workouts, and those inky-black tattoos that popped in high contrast against his skin...

Damn he's fine.

"Put your tongue back in your mouth, *querida*," Inez giggled in her ear, pulling Renata out of the kitchen door and off to the side. "Unless you're planning to do something to *him* with it."

"*Inez.*"

Inez pulled Renata into a little sideways hug. "I'm joking with you... but I have noticed that you two have been hot and heavy... I'm not going to have to threaten him again, am I?"

Renata shook her head. "I... I think we'll be okay. The sessions with Layla have been going really well... making good progress."

"Good," Inez said, pulling her into a hug. "At least *one* of my girls is doing okay."

"Is Naomi still...?"

Inez nodded. "Yeah, still trying to figure out what Wolfe meant about her mom. The emotional warfare that man wages is repulsive. I don't understand why he does what he does." She stopped, then patted Renata on the arm. "Anyway, I'm sure you and lover boy probably want some alone time. I'm gonna go check on Mimi."

218

"Okay Nez. And... thank you, for driving me to these appointments. I appreciate it."

Smiling, Inez pulled Renata into a quick hug. "Anytime. I wanna see you happy." With a wink, Inez left her standing alone near the doorway, and Renata took a moment to collect herself before she ventured into the kitchen. Quentin was still lost in his music, but this time he was turned toward the island, pulling seasonings from the spice rack Inez kept there.

As Renata moved closer, he looked up, smiling when he realized it was her. He pulled his headphones down, letting them rest around his neck. "Hey, you're back. How'd it go today?"

That smile of his... *Jesus, help.* His gaze rested on her face, then skipped down, lingering on her body, making her lightweight sweater dress feel like a good decision.

"Great, actually. I feel really good."

He tipped his head to the side. "*Great.* Alright now, the time before that was "good", and the one before that was "okay", but now you're up to *great.* That's whassup. I'm happy for you."

"Thank you," Renata said as she closed the last few steps between them. There was no hesitation on Quentin's part as he emptied his hands to accept Renata into his arms. She snuggled close to him, closing her eyes as he pressed his lips to her forehead.

After a few seconds passed, he drew back, then used a finger under her chin to tip her head up to face him. "You hungry?"

"Well, I *wasn't* until I smelled whatever heavenly thing you've created in that skillet over there. That's andouille, right?"

Quentin grinned. "Yes it is. And chicken, and shrimp, and…"

"Let me guess," Renata said, smiling as she held up a finger. "*Crawfish.*"

"*Oooh.*" Quentin narrowed his eyes, biting his lip as he bent to press his forehead to hers. "You know me so well. You know I love it when you say sexy shit like that, right? Talk dirty to me baby, say it again."

Lifting an eyebrow, Renata lowered her voice to a sultry whisper. "*Craw. Fish.*"

She giggled as Quentin pressed his lips to hers, then shrieked as he lifted her off the floor, wrapped tightly in his arms. When he put her down, he planted a kiss on her cheek, then grabbed his seasonings from the counter. "Jambalaya will be ready shortly, chérie. Just adding some finishin' touches."

"Hey," Renata said, raising her hand in mid-air as she took a seat at the island. "No rush from me, I'm just glad to hear I get a bowl."

"*First* bowl, *bien-aimé.*"

Quentin winked at her, then turned back to the stove as Renata blushed. She wasn't just glad to get a bowl, she was *glad*, period. Quentin was just so… extremely… *everything*, and if he gave her another sweet nickname — *my beloved*, this time — she might melt.

"So you're breaking out the *proper* French on me now, huh? No more Creole patois?"

He glanced back, with his mouth twisted in a little scowl. "I'll have you know, our patois *is* proper French. Just wit' a lil bit of extra seasonin' on it. And what, you didn't think I could speak French? *Je parle*

220

beaucoup de langues ... peut-être plus que vous, douce fleur."

Renata laughed, shaking her head. "You don't know how many languages I speak… but point taken."

When he was done cooking, everyone was invited to the table, but as promised, Renata *did* get the first bowl. She was happy to see their entire team, people who she was starting to think of as family, all gathered around the table to talk, eat, and laugh. She did more observing than speaking, since that was what she preferred anyway, and even had a glass of wine. Guilt stirred in her chest for indulging in such enjoyment, while her daughter was being kept from her, but… she tucked it away. As *batshit* crazy as he was, logic held that Taylor was actually *safe* with Wolfe. He'd proven himself to be fiercely protective of those he considered family. Taylor was happy, well-taken care of… so Renata relaxed into the moment of normalcy.

It felt *good*.

Not just the wine, the entire atmosphere, surrounded by friends — people who cared enough about her daughter to risk their lives. Even though the importance of the job loomed over their heads, in *this* moment, there was peace. Even for Naomi, who still held a haunted look in her eyes, but smiled with real joy when she looked at Marcus. At Inez, who was on her third drink of the night, and seemed to be accepting a lot more flirting than usual from Kendall

And… there was Quentin.

Charming, sexy Quentin who kept leaning over to murmur sweet things to her. Who just that morning, had come up behind her chair while she was working,

221

just to kiss her cheek and whisper *I love you* into her ear before returning to his work in his own seat.

It felt *so* good.

Later, when everyone else was cleaning up, Quentin grabbed Renata's hand, pulling her out of the room. He'd slipped away a while before, but with so much activity happening in the kitchen, she'd been too distracted to wonder where he'd gone. Now, as he pulled her onto the screened porch, with the fire pit roaring in the dark, she knew.

"Just for us?" she asked, smiling as he sat down on the outdoor sectional, then pulled her onto his lap. Renata snuggled against his chest, being mindful of her still-healing shoulder.

Quentin kissed the side of her head, then her cheek, then her neck, before bringing his mouth up to her ear. "Just for us. No company."

Renata smiled, and closed her eyes, soaking in the tranquil moment where they could be intimately alone. These times were much rarer than she would have thought, with them essentially living under the same roof. There had been so many things to do, so much to hack, so much to handle, and then... the incident between Tomiko and Naomi. Things had been hectic, and then she started therapy... so time by themselves — when neither was tired, or stressed, or cranky because of faulty code or stubborn firewalls — was precious.

"I should probably start looking for a place," Renata said, speaking the words aloud as soon as the thought entered her mind. "We move forward with the takedown of King Pharma in two weeks. I've been here because it's convenient for us all to be together while

222

we work on this job, but… I need a place for my baby to come home to."

For a long moment, Quentin didn't say anything, just kept stroking Renata's back. "Well," he said finally, clearing his throat. "You know… *my* place is pretty big."

Tightness and warmth bloomed in Renata's chest at the same time, and she smiled as she kicked off her shoes, then slid out of his lap, just enough that her butt was on the couch, but her legs were still draped across his. Now that she could see his face in the flickering light of the dancing fire, she reached up, running her hand across his chin.

"That is *very* generous of you. And if it were just me, I'd accept in a heartbeat, but… it's not."

"You know I was invitin' Taylor too, right?"

She nodded. "I do. But… with everything that's happened, it's important to me to make sure that once this is all over, Taylor feels safe, and protected. *I* know you, but *she* doesn't. She's only fourteen, and I haven't done much dating, so can you imagine how uncomfortable it would be for her to *move in* with a guy she's never even heard me mention? I *so* appreciate your offer, but Taylor's comfort is paramount."

"I *cannot* argue with that. You let me know what you want, and I'll help you find a place," he said, brushing his lips over hers.

"I knew you'd say that."

Quentin lifted an eyebrow, then kissed her again. "How?"

"Because you've always gone out of your way to help me… Remember? You actually helped me get

223

the *first* place for me and Taylor, before she was even born. It's like déjà vu."

He chuckled. "I *do* remember that."

"We were *so* young. *Teenagers*. How does a teenage boy come to the decision to help a girl he only knows through dial-up internet, and on *that* level? Why did you do that for me?"

"Because it was the right thing to do. I cared about you. We were friends. I don't think I recognized it then, but... I *loved* you."

Renata swallowed hard as a lump built in her throat. "You'd never even seen me before."

"Which is a blessin'," he laughed, pressing his head against the cushions. "If you looked anything *then* like you do *now*, my sixteen-year-old heart wouldn't have been able to take it. I woulda said all kinds of nasty shit to ya'."

Renata giggled. "Like *what*, Q?"

"Man... *je veux vous sentir sur mon corps* — I wanna smell you on my body... I'd eat you like a praline."

"Are you serious?!" Renata clapped a hand over her mouth. "You were saying that kind of stuff to high school girls?"

Quentin scoffed. "I was sayin' that kinda stuff to *college* girls."

"That's terrible."

"I know," he said, running a hand over her thigh. "That's why I'm grateful for the way things went between us, as far as getting' to know each other. I got to know and love you here first," — he touched her forehead — "then here," — he placed his hand over her

224

heart — "and now that I see the physical package... I just feel fortunate as hell."

Renata's breath hitched as he tipped his head forward, pressing his lips to hers with a gentle urgency that made her scoot closer to him. "You know I could say the same about you, right?" she asked.

"You think I'm a catch, huh?"

She nodded. "I do." Renata lifted a hand, running it over his head, then down to his ear. "I feel... kinda like the luckiest woman in the world right now."

Or maybe it wasn't luck. Maybe more like... divine intervention that had brought them together, even if the circumstances were... chaotic and unconventional.

Moving into the corner of the sectional, Quentin sat all the way back and opened his legs, for Renata to settle between them, with her back to his chest. The late night temperature began to drop, so he unfurled the blanket he'd brought out, draping it over them.

"You wanna talk about your session today?" Quentin asked, and Renata shook her head. "Wanna talk about apartments, or houses?" Renata gave him a no to that as well. "What about... figuring out how to get into those old emails we found, between King and Wolfe. They've gotta be decrypted so we can read them, and—"

"Nope." Renata shifted a little, settling into a more comfortable position. "I don't want to talk about *any* of that. We don't have to talk about anything at all."

Quentin chuckled, then tucked his chin over her head, but said nothing. They stayed like that for a long while, just staring into the fire. Renata closed her eyes, and was close to drifting off to sleep when Quentin moved, lowering his head to place a kiss on her neck.

Renata kept her eyes closed, but her body responded, tipping her head to one side to grant him more access. He kept going… kissing, biting, sucking her neck until she whimpered.

He'd kept his hands wrapped respectfully at her waist, but now, Renata covered them with hers, pushing his fingertips down to her thighs. It wasn't until she parted her legs, guiding one of his hands between them that he resisted.

"You sure, *chérie?*" he asked. His voice was different now, roughened with arousal, and she could feel him growing hard against her back.

Eyes still closed, without turning around, she nodded, and a moment later, he'd slipped a hand under her panties. She moaned as his fingers slipped and slid through her slick wetness, bringing her to the edge of frenzied with in what felt like no time, with what seemed to be minimal effort. He pushed two fingers inside her, keeping his palm pressed to her clit as she pushed her body against his hand. His mouth was still on her neck, lavishing attention from one side to the other, finding hot spots she'd never even known she had as her body grew tense.

With his other hand, he cupped her chin, urging her to turn her head so that when he tipped his head forward, over her shoulder, they could kiss as he kept working his fingers between her thighs. She had her legs spread wide underneath the blanket, but she didn't feel nervous, or ashamed. She felt… *amazing* then, and even better after she came, with a powerful rush of sensation that made her skin tingle.

226

Renata deflated against Quentin's chest, panting from the intensity of her climax. He chuckled against her ear, then kissed her there. "Let's go inside."

"Uh-uh." She took a deep breath, then turned to face him, straddling his lap as she shook her head. "Let's stay here. Nobody can see us... right?"

"Right. Disabled the security camera myself," he said, dragging her closer, so that the heat of his erection pressed between her legs.

She lowered her mouth to his, whimpering as he palmed handfuls of her butt and squeezed. He pressed his tongue to the seam of her lips, searching for hers, and she eagerly opened for his exploration. She began to rock her hips against him, creating a pleasurable friction between them, and he groaned into her mouth. Knowing *she* was doing something that made *him* feel good made her feel bolder... *sexier*.

Reaching between them, she slipped a hand under the waistband of his sweats and down into his boxers, her fingers brushing over the smooth skin of his penis. There was a fleeting moment where she wanted to snatch her hand away, not because she was scared, but because... yeah, she was a little scared. This was *happening*, like... for real happening, and while she knew how to please *herself*, none of that expertise extended to pleasing a man.

But... something had changed. His lips were still pressed to the hint of cleavage that showed above the neckline of her dress, and he was waiting.

To see what she would do next.

What the hell do I do next?

She knew what *fictional* women did, but seeing a love scene played out on a screen, or visualizing the

227

words in a book was much, *much* different than a very real, very hot, heavy penis against your fingers. She sucked in a deep breath, then covered him with her hand, curling her palm around him. She moved her hand in one gentle, cautious stroke, and finally he exhaled.

Or... maybe *she* had been the one holding her breath. Because when their eyes met in the glowing light from the fire, as she carefully stroked him, there was no apprehension, no hesitation in his, only desire. He *wanted* her. Knowing things that no one, not even her therapist knew, things that had made her feel dirty, and ashamed for so long. And he wanted her anyway.

Suddenly, having him in her hands wasn't enough. She moved out of his arms, out of his lap, and onto her feet, letting the blanket fall to the concrete as she stood. She grabbed the hem of her dress, but Quentin quickly sat forward, covering her hands with his.

"Hold on," he urged, scooting to the edge of the seat. "You're supposed to be careful about over-extending this arm, remember? Your shoulder's still healing."

Renata bit her lip, taking a step back as he stood, then carefully helped her out of the dress. Standing in front of him in just her underwear, she trembled at his touch as he ran his fingers over her body, then sat down in front of her. The air held a chill, but between the fire, and the heat radiating from Quentin, she didn't feel cold at all, and was confused for a second when he picked the blanket up, lifting it to drape across her shoulders.

228

She held it around herself willing, but purposely kept the front view exposed as Quentin brought his hands to the waistband of her panties. He hooked his fingers in them on either side, then slowly dragged them down over her hips, instructing her to step out. She did, and a moment later he tugged her forward, propped her foot on the seat beside him, and covered her with his mouth. Her back arched in immediate pleasure, and she forgot about holding the blanket, reaching instead to hold onto his shirt to keep her balance.

He hooked his arm under her leg to keep her open, using his fingers to spread her feminine flower wide as he devoured her, nibbling and teasing and licking until she climaxed again, with violent trembles that made her knees give out. She collapsed into his lap, high off passion, but still eager to explore.

Renata helped him out of his shirt, and he helped her out of her bra, moving them deep into the corner of the sectional and pulling the blanket back over her shoulders before he touched her again. Quentin slid his hands up her thighs and butt, over her stomach to reach her breasts. Squeezing them in his hands, he looked up at her with a smile.

"*Vous êtes magnifique, bien-aimé.*"

She blushed at his compliment — telling her she was gorgeous —, then pulled her lip between her teeth as he covered her nipple with his mouth, keeping his gaze focused on hers. She closed her eyes as he sucked hard, drawing a gasp of pleasure. He repeated that on the other side, then flicked his tongue over her nipple before taking it in his mouth again.

Renata moved her hands between them, removing him from the confines of his sweats and boxers this time. With no preamble, she lifted herself up, intending to lower herself onto him, but he caught her by the hips.

"Whoa dere," he chuckled. "Unless you're trying to make a baby chérie... hold on."

Averting her gaze, she watched from the corner of her eyes as he pulled his wallet from the pocket of his sweats, then handed her a condom from inside. She simply... stared at the little foil packet as he eased off his boxers and sweats, and toed off his shoes. When he was done, he looked at her, and she looked at him, wondering if her confusion — and lack of experience — showed on her face.

He lifted his hand, burying his fingers in her freshly redone braids as he pulled her into a kiss, then gently pulled the condom from her hands. She watched with interest while he tore it open, then deftly covered himself with the flimsy film. He sat back then, tipping his head to the side with an expectant grin.

"You comin'?"

She lifted her eyebrows. "Oh... I thought you would want me to like... lay down."

"Nope," he said, gripping her thighs to pull her into position. "If we do it like this... you get to be in control. The pace you want, the rhythm you want... however deep you want me."

Excited heat rushed through her, followed quickly by a mild sense of panic. "But... I don't know what I'm doing."

"Just do what feels good."

230

The smile on Quentin's face served as a soothing balm for her apprehension. With a deep breath, she raised herself up, and onto him.

She almost expected her body to clamp down and reject him, refusing entry. Instead it *welcomed* him, and she gasped as it did, spreading and stretching to accommodate his size. She wrapped her arms around his neck, holding onto him, not moving, just… *feeling* him. Focusing in on the way her body contracted around him, relishing in the foreign sensation of having a man inside of her.

Foreign, but… good.

Better than good.

He'd groaned, kneading her butt cheeks as she lowered herself onto him, but he hadn't moved since, hadn't shown any signs of impatience. He was waiting for her. Waiting for her to *do what felt good*. So she did.

Her body moved instinctively, just a soft, subtle rock as she got used to feeling him inside of her. She loosened her grip around his neck, moving back so he could palm her breasts, and his gentle, encouraging squeezes made her rock her hips harder, moving up and down, raising and lowering herself onto him again.

She didn't know what she was doing, she was just doing what felt good, but more than good. Much, *much* more than good as he lowered his mouth to her breasts again as she rode him. It felt *great* then, moving into incredible as he kissed and sucked her nipples, then brought his hands up to caress her butt and thighs. And even better when he slipped a hand between them, using his fingers to stimulate her as she began to move faster, spurred on by the chase of *what felt good*.

He brought his mouth back to hers as a heavy, but somehow... *freeing* sense of pressure began to build at her core. Her movements were frenzied, frantic, and she kissed him hungrily, *desperately*, because ... hell yes, *this* was what felt good. Quentin put his hands at her hips to steady her, but not slow her down, lowering his mouth to her neck, finding one of those hot spots again and sucking *hard*. Hard enough that Renata knew she would have a mark, but she didn't care, because she'd found *what felt good*, and she wasn't letting it go, not for anything in the... *world*.

Renata squeezed her eyes tight, gasping as tremors shook her body, and a kaleidoscope of colors exploded in her mind, and she couldn't breathe, or think, but she could feel, and it felt *magnificent*, and liberating, and she felt... different.

Free.

She clung to him for a long time, and didn't realize she was crying until her mind cleared enough to realize that the muffled sounds in her ear were soothing words from Quentin as he rubbed her back. His shoulder was soaking wet, and when she drew back, the concern in his eyes made pain stab at her chest.

"I'm *fine* Q," she assured him, smiling as he reached up to wipe away her tears.

He brushed a handful of braids away from her face. "Your mouth is sayin' one thing, but these tears say somethin' else, Beautiful."

"Happy tears." She smiled again, then leaned forward to press her lips to his. He didn't let it end at a simple peck, he cupped her face and held her close, pulling her bottom lip between his.

232

When he finally let her draw away from the kiss, she buried her face in his neck. He was still inside her, but she felt no inclination to separate herself from him.

"Q?"

"Yeah baby?" he asked, pulling the blanket up, yet again, to cover them from the chill of the night air.

Renata lifted her head, pressing her lips to his.

"Thank you."

fourteen.

"Are you awake?"

Eyes still closed, Quentin smirked. He *was* awake, but he briefly considered pretending not to be, just to see what Renata would do. As he suspected, a moment later, she climbed on top of him, lowering herself onto his chest.

"I *know* you're not sleeping," she whispered, tracing the outline of his face with her fingers, then pressing a soft kiss to his jaw.

Bringing a hand up to palm her butt, Quentin kept his eyes shut. "I *am* sleep. Don't you see me sleepin' right now?"

"*He's* not asleep." She moved her hand down between them, running it over the erection straining his boxers. "I think *he's* wide awake."

Quentin chuckled. "*Insomnia*. Because you won't let him have a break."

Since *that* night, three nights ago now, Renata had been eager to explore her newfound sexuality. Not that Quentin was complaining. He definitely didn't mind being her chosen partner, and making love to Renata was... an experience. She was curious, and responsive, and vocal, and *beautiful*. But more than anything, he loved how much more *free* she seemed, like she was relieved to have broken through a barrier. She'd even been more productive on the job lately — it was *her* hacking that had finally gotten them into an email stack they'd been working on all week, and planned to start going through today.

Whenever she let them out of the bed.

"You don't need a *break*," she teased, slipping her hand into his boxers. "It's *not* like I'm tiring you out. You've been gentle with me, I can tell. Holding back."

She turned her face up towards his, waiting for a response, which *really* wasn't very fair, not when those soft, sweet hands of hers had him hard as steel.

After a deep breath through his nose, he spoke. "I *have* been gentle with you, because... you're... I don't want to hurt you."

"Hurt me?" she asked, lifting an eyebrow. "Hurt me how?"

She sat up, pulled him free of his boxers, then licked her hands before she touched him again, using the moisture to stroke him harder.

Goddamn.

He forced himself to look up at her face. "If we get too... vigorous, you might be sore after."

"And you've gotten that complaint?"

He grinned, then sucked in a hiss of air, nostrils flared as she gave him a gentle squeeze. "Not exactly a *complaint*. Just the reality of what happens."

"I wanna do it."

"You wanna do what?"

"I wanna do *vigorous*. I want you to stop "going easy" on me. Stop treating me like I'm fragile, or... *weak*."

Something in her voice made him look up to meet her eyes, and he was disappointed to see a trace of

236

sadness there. He sat up, moving her hands away from him before cupping her face in his.

"I don't think you're weak, *chérie*. Not at all. Just want you to feel well taken care of, so I'm followin' your lead, workin' at your pace. Whatever makes you feel comfortable."

She smiled, then leaned forward, pressing a gentle kiss to his lips. "I don't know what I'm doing though, Q. I *just* learned how to touch you, what, *yesterday*? I'm willingly *giving* you my body, because I love you, and you love me. But… that's all I know, when it comes to this. I'm still learning…. I need you to teach me. I trust you to take care of me."

I'm such a goner.

Quentin kissed Renata's forehead, then her nose, cheeks, and finally, her lips. He laughed at the condom she produced from underneath her pillow, then gently pushed her down onto the bed. Positioning himself between her legs, he propped them around his waist, then used his hands to pin her wrists above her head as he pushed inside of her in a swift, confident stroke that made her gasp, and attempt to scoot away.

Grinning, he pulled back, then stroked her the same way again, pulling a whimper of pleasure from her throat as she tightened her legs. Lowering his mouth to hers, he slipped his tongue between her lips as he continued moving inside of her. He knew it felt good to her, from her moans and facial expression, but still… she kept moving away.

He released her wrists, using his arms to lift her body from the bed, so she couldn't get any leverage. He kissed her again, then moved his mouth to her ear. "Am I hurting you?"

"I can't tell," She said, letting out a breathless moan as he pushed into her again. "It's like… it *almost* hurts, but then it feels *amazing*."

He chuckled, then nodded, driving into her again as he kissed her ear.

"So… lesson one: don't run from it."

— & —

An hour and a half later, Quentin practically bounced down into the war room to set up his laptop for the day, freshly showered and feeling *great*. Renata was still soundly asleep in bed, where he suspected she'd be for a while after the morning session they'd just had.

He was working slowly through Terry King's old emails, scouring them for names, places, *anything* that might tell him anything. Quentin shook his head. His first thought was that it was *stupid* to talk about some of the things discussed, but then he reminded himself that these correspondences were from the late nineties. They didn't have the technology innovations then that were available now.

Which is probably why we had to work so hard to get into them.

King *had* to recognize the sensitivity of this information, for all parties involved. Quentin guessed that the only reason they weren't destroyed *now* was because King was holding on to incriminating information as leverage. But… email didn't gain real popularity until the nineties. King, Wolfe, and their other peers didn't suddenly stop being legit then, so it

238

begged the question... was he harboring *other* evidence of misdeeds?

Instead of reading them, Quentin sat back in his chair, running a query through the database of emails, searching for mentions of Damien Wolfe's name. While that ran, he stroked his chin with his thumb... if King was saving correspondences as potential power... other than the emails, what else.... What else.... What else?

Phone calls!

Quentin clapped his palms together, then sat up again, fingers clicking away as he pulled up a folder of audio files he'd originally dismissed as irrelevant. They were *marked* as music, but Quentin realized with disgust what an *amateur* evasion tactic he'd fallen for. The folder was filled with files not marked with song names, but with dates, and a person's name.

Most of them were marked with Damien Wolfe, dating back before Quentin was born — or even *conceived*. Those would have had to be wire taps, converted later to audio.

Damn.

Terry King was *calculated*. He was bad... but he was *good*.

The earliest of the files were from the very early eighties, so Quentin started there, pulling on his headphones to listen to them as background noise while he completed other tasks.

Wolfe and King — Williams, back then — were only in their twenties, just out of college, trying to make a name for themselves doing something different in the drug trade. The first few audio files didn't hold anything of much interest, but then suddenly, Quentin

239

stopped what he was doing on the screen to focus on the audio.

"King: So that's why you've been MIA, chasing pussy?

Wolfe: Noelle ain't just pussy, I might marry this girl.

King: And what are you gonna do about your brother? Isn't Noelle his lady?

Wolfe: Half-brother. And I saw her first. I had her first. He only went after her because he knew she was important to me. She's just scared of the lifestyle, and Nelson's punk-ass seems "safe". I oughta tell her about how he kicked his last old lady's ass, and that's how he ended up in New Orleans in the first place. Can't go back to Texas.

King: You serious?

Wolfe: Hell yeah. Nelson will hit a bitch in a heartbeat, but won't step up to a man. That's how I punked his ass into working for me in the first place. I've got him making my money, while I screw his lady.

King: So she's screwing both of you... and you're okay with that?

Wolfe: I didn't say I was okay with it, but she thinks he's the safer option. I'm content with her figuring her shit out while I figure out mine. When the time comes... I'll have her."

"What are you listening to?"

Naomi's voice rang out in the room, drowning out the voices in Quentin's ears. He stopped the playback, then took a deep breath as he pulled the headphones off and sat them on the edge of the table.

"What you doin' up so early this mornin' Mimi?"

240

She shrugged, her hand resting on her stomach as she moved out of the doorway, and further into the room. "Couldn't sleep, I guess. Where's Ren?"

"Sleeping."

Naomi grinned. "Mmhm. You tiring her out yet?"

"No idea what you're talkin' bout, *cher.*"

"Oh *please*," Naomi said, taking a seat in the chair beside him. "You two have been humping like teenagers for the last three days, and we *all* know it. I *saw* you in the hall closet, and you should be glad it wasn't Inez, she probably would have shot both of you for sexing near her ammo."

Quentin lifted an eyebrow. "Ammo?"

"Yeah… you know *that* closet is where she keeps the extra stuff from the armory downstairs, you know how she is. But *anyway*, my point is that I'm actually happy for you and Ren. Her whole mood is changed, and outside of the times when she gets into her feelings about Taylor, Marcus says that she's back to the Ren he knew before all this happened."

"Is that right?" Quentin asked, sitting back in his chair and turning toward Naomi.

"Yep."

He nodded, then sat forward. "So… what is it going to take to get *you* back? I mean yeah… it feels like we've *always* been after Wolfe, but it's different this time. You seem … defeated now What's going on?"

Naomi took a deep breath. "It's not just *me* this time. I have to think about the baby, and what it's going to be like bringing him or her into a world with Wolfe. Look at what he's doing to Ren. How he's manipulating *us* to get to Ren. I'm *afraid* of that." She stopped, shaking her head. "You know… in a lot of ways, Ren and I have a lot in common. Both sixteen when Wolfe left our lives in ruins. Both haunted by the shadow of what he did. Neither of us able to… do what *all* women who want a family should be able to do: enjoy their pregnancy. It's like he gets off on terrorizing women, and I don't understand why. I mean… that stuff at the hospital, about my mom… why would he even say that to me?"

Quentin placed his hands over Naomi's on the tabletop. "To fuck with your head. That's all he does."

"Well it's working," she scoffed. "Has me second-guessing everything I thought I knew. I mean… I didn't *see* her body when she committed suicide. The funeral was closed casket. I don't *really* know where she was, or what happened to her when she was supposedly kidnapped by Wolfe. I didn't see it. *She* didn't tell me. I'm just going by what my father said, and if we're being completely honest here… *he* was a criminal too. Maybe all of it was a lie, you know? Even the story about how he and my mom ended up together. Maybe Wolfe did have her first."

Quentin turned away, unable to help a scowl of derision from crossing his face.

"What?" Naomi said, grabbing the arm of his chair to turn him back around. "What is it? Why that face?"

Shaking his head, Quentin gazed up at his screen, where the conversation with King and Wolfe was still up. He quickly weighed his options between telling Naomi about the tapes and *not*. If he didn't… it was kinda the same thing as telling her a lie, and

242

Quentin had exhausted his ability to lie to her when he was keeping the secret of painted_pixel being in trouble. His lack of focus, and overlooked information, could've honestly gotten her killed. He *really* wasn't up for a repeat of that.

But on the other hand… what would Naomi gain, hearing her parents talked about that way? Her mother as an adulteress, her father as an abuser… but those little tidbits *did* raise questions. What if… things really *weren't* as they seemed? They'd hinged their lives not only on what they *knew* Wolfe had done, but also on what they *thought* he'd done, as reported by Naomi's father. If Nelson Prescott really was abusive… it wasn't exactly a stretch that he could have been a liar as well.

And where did that leave *them*?

It hadn't really hit him while he was listening to it, but it did now. What if their entire plan for vengeance… wasn't really what it seemed?

"Q, are you gonna answer me?"

With a heavy sigh, Quentin picked up the headphones, and put them on Naomi's head, positioning them over her ears. He skipped the audio file back a bit, then hit play, watching the emotions play over her face as she listened.

"What the fuck was this?" she asked, snatching the headphones off when the audio file ended. "Was this Wolfe, and Terry King, talking about my parents?"

Quentin nodded. "I'm afraid so, *cher*."

Naomi shook her head, tossing the headphones onto the table. "What… so, I'm supposed to believe that Wolfe was… *waiting* on my mother? That he loved her or something?"

"I know as much as you do, Mimi. *Less*, actually. You lived with them. Does anything ring a bell for you?"

She stood, her hand clutched to her stomach as she walked back and forth. "*No*. My parents were like the perfect couple. I mean... I was little, so I saw what a little girl sees. Always stealing kisses, and holding hands, and they wouldn't even fight... in front of me." She stopped where she was, covering her mouth with her hand.

"What is it?" Quentin asked, turning his chair to face where she stood. "You said they wouldn't fight... in front of you. What does that mean? Did you ever see them fighting?"

Absently, Naomi nodded. "Uhh... yeah. It wasn't a lot, but... it was always about Wolfe. They thought I was sleeping. And umm... there was actually a *really* bad one... a few nights before she disappeared. Oh my God." Her voice broke as tears filled her eyes, and Quentin stood, pulling her into an embrace.

"I don't know why I never remembered this, but..." she stopped, wiping her face with the back of her hands. "But... that next day, after that fight... she brought me into our little home dance studio, and she had her arms and legs covered. Q, mama *never* covered her arms and legs when we danced. But that day, she *did*. And now... I'm wondering, did my father *hit* her? Was she covered in bruises, is that why...?"

Shit!

"Mimi, *stop*," Quentin said, cupping her face in his hands. "Dr. Morris said as little stress as possible, you don't need to be getting upset like this. I should've

244

thought about that before I even let you listen to that shit."

Naomi shook her head. "No. *No*. I needed to know this, because... Quentin, when she came back from *wherever* she'd been, my mother was *different*. Like she was dead inside. My dad told me Wolfe had taken her, so I believed it. My dad told me Wolfe's men left her beat up on our doorstep once he was done using her body for whatever, and I *believed* him. But... my mother wouldn't let my dad touch her. Every time I was able to get her to come out of that shell, and talk to me, if my dad walked in the room, she was done. And *I* thought it was just the trauma of what happened to her, but looking back on it now, as an adult? She was *scared* of him."

Quentin scrubbed a hand over his face as Naomi started pacing again. "Please, don't do this to yourself. This isn't—"

"*No!* You're listening to me! The nightmare that I have, that awful memory of the night our fathers died... the *ugly* things that Wolfe said to my father, taunting him about my mother... yeah, they were ugly. But what if I misunderstood?"

"What? Naomi, we *know*, for a fact, violating a woman isn't outside of the shit that Wolfe is willin' to do, for whatever his twisted ass reasons are. You told me he threatened your father, with doing to you, what he did to Renata. You're telling me you don't think he could've done it to your mother too?"

Naomi shook her head. "No, I'm not saying that at all, I'm just saying that... with new stuff coming to light, I'm just not sure he *did*. Not that he's not *capable*. When I think about what he said... *giving Noelle to me*

245

when I asked for her, he mentioned my father taking so much time to *retaliate about Noelle* — which I *always* thought was strange. He talked about her misbehaving, he called her out of her name. I mean… he could have been talking about what Wolfe is talking about in this recording. If the brothers got into it, fought about my mom…"

"The audio is from *thirty years ago*. This is a wire-tap, that Terry King paid to get converted into digital, so he would have something to hold over his enemy's head."

"I *know*. What I'm saying is, if Wolfe and my father were doing this back and forth over my mom, for all this time, that explains why they hated each other. If she's sleeping with both of them, I'm not saying it's *right*, but… I can see Wolfe being angry about that, calling her a bitch, calling her a slut. He said something along the lines of *I can't believe it took you three years to get back at me about Noelle.* Three years before that night, that's when my mother disappeared. I've always thought that Wolfe was taunting my father about taking my mother, and abusing her the way he did."

With a heavy sigh, Quentin lifted his hands in mid-air. "What else could he have meant?"

"What if… my mother wasn't *taken* by Wolfe at all? What if she *ran*?"

Quentin narrowed his eyes, prepared to offer a rebuttal, but… he really didn't have one. The more he thought about it… the more it made sense. He couldn't imagine not wanting to put a bullet through the head of any man who violated his wife — hell, he wanted to put a bullet through Wolfe's head over Renata. Waiting *three* years to exact his revenge? It *did* seem odd. But if the situation was adjusted, just a little, so your problem was that your wife had left you for another man... that would take a little more finesse. A little more *time*. A little more patience, to ensure maximum suffering time, and maybe even time to let your victim think you forgot. With *that* scenario... three years actually made sense.

But what, in the grand scheme of *all* of this... did it even mean?

Naomi turned to him, hands propped on her hips, head held high.

"I think my mother faked her death. I think she's with Wolfe. He *has* her. She's alive."

Quentin's eyes went wide, but before he could open his mouth to respond, the door to the war room swung open, and Supervisory Special Agent Barnes walked in, his expression somber. "We've got a *big* problem."

— & —

"So you're saying... the drug that King Pharma is putting out, that we've spent months preparing to prove is dangerous... really *is* dangerous?" Renata pushed out a heavy sigh, crossing her arms over her chest. "How did we miss this?"

"Because Terry King is a *smart* man. None of this has a paper trail," Inez said. "Quentin arranged a *sudden* cross-country move for his previous secretary, so I took her place. I've been noticing a lot of last minute meetings with people on the FDA review board, so I snuck a listening device into his office. Well... today I heard money being discussed, *with* the people from the FDA.

He's paying them off to make sure the drug passes approval. What we were gonna *fake* is exactly what he's doing."

Naomi shook her head. "But what happens when people die? Won't the FDA get clocked for it?"

"Unfortunately not," Agent Barnes said from the head of the table. "He's giving them two mil each. They just don't give a shit. And when people die, he's just gonna pay out the settlements. It's still a *fraction* of the billions he'll make off the drug."

"Or maybe the drug *isn't* dangerous? Maybe he's just *ensuring* approval?"

Inez smiled at Renata's attempt to make it not *so* bad. "No, chica. Sorry. After I heard that, I snuck into R&D, and was able to the get the chemical profile. Quentin plugged it into a simulator, and it estimates that at least ten percent of the millions of people who end up using it will start experiencing organ failure within the first year. It's *bad*."

Renata sighed. "So... What do we do?"

"We gather evidence," Barnes said, nodding. "We gather *real* evidence. And we take this bastard down."

fifteen.

"Don't you dare scream."

Inez barely had time to process what was
happening before Kendall muttered those words into
her face, his normally cool expression twisted with
anger.

A second ago, she'd been opening the door to
exit her private bath after a much needed shower. Now,
she was pressed roughly into the wall, and Kendall had
the front of her towel twisted tight around his hand,
using the leverage to pull her off her feet. The other
hand was clamped over her mouth, so she couldn't have
screamed if she wanted.

She *didn't* want to.

Inez didn't scare easily, but she was scared now.
Not that Kendall would hurt her, because she greatly
doubted it. If she thought *that*, she would've driven her
thumbs into his eyes while both of his hands were
occupied, then sent her knee full force into his groin.
She *could* have gotten away from him, but she stayed
where she was, reminding herself to stay calm. She
was only scared because *he* was scared, and scared men
were unpredictable.

"Are you gonna scream?"

Inez shook her head.

Nostrils flared, Kendall swallowed, then moved his hand away from her mouth, but kept her pressed against the wall, with her feet dangling in the air.

"Why did I get notified that you pulled my wife's medical records?"

Mierda. I paid that clerk to keep quiet!

Inez kept her eyes on his, didn't blink. "Because I pulled your wife's medical records."

"How did you even get clearance for something like that? They were *sealed.*"

"I have clearance for lots of things."

Kendall looked away from her, running his tongue over his teeth — clear signs to Inez that he was trying to check his anger. "Inez... why the fuck are you in my business? It has *nothing* to do with you."

"Considering *my* ass has been on the line every day, I think it does. We're all supposed to be in together... a *team.* Does anybody else know *your* connection to King Pharmaceuticals?"

With a frustrated growl, Kendall smacked the wall beside her, but Inez didn't flinch, reminding herself that his annoyance wasn't with *her.* "How much do you know?"

"Enough to know that *you* didn't need a reason to hate Terry King. You already did. Not enough to understand why you haven't already killed him."

Kendall shook his head. "She made me promise... that I wouldn't do it because of her. Not on *her* conscience. I'm respecting her wishes."

"Okay." Inez lifting her hands, cupping his face between them. "Put me down, Ken."

Slowly, he lowered her. Once her feet were back in contact with the plushly carpeted floor, he took a step back, scrubbing a hand over his face. A second too late, Inez remembered that *he* had been keeping her towel secure around her body. It hit the floor, and she was quick to pick it up, covering herself, but from the new expression on Kendall's face — concern — she suspected he'd already seen.

Sure enough, he took a step forward, tugging one end of the towel free from her hand. "What is this?" he asked, lightly brushing his fingers over the blue-black discoloration that wrapped from her belly button around to her back.

"Run in with a security guard on my way out of the building... after I found out King was paying off the FDA. Saw me coming up from Research and Development, knew I wasn't supposed to be down there. So... me, him, and his steel-toed boots had a little showdown. I won, obviously, and Quentin made sure to scrub it from the security tapes, but... I can't go back."

"He *kicked* you?" Kendall asked, meeting her gaze.

Inez wished that the suddenly renewed rage, and alarm, and need for retribution that flared in his eyes surprised her, but it didn't. She wanted to wonder why he was so concerned, but... she didn't. She already *knew* why, and it was the same reason that if this situation were reversed, she'd be ready to kick ass too.

"I took care of it."

She nodded, hoping to reassure him, but he said nothing further. The towel got left behind on the floor as he took her hand and led her to her bed, where he sat down, then pulled her in front of him. Inez held her breath as his fingertips brushed over the bruised area again. Pain was the furthest thing from her mind, because Kendall was setting her nerve endings on fire with his touch. He replaced his fingers with his lips, turning her so that she faced away from him.

"Did you think I was gonna tell anybody?" she asked, closing her eyes as Kendall pressed his lips to the small of her back.

"Yes."

"What did you think would happen if I did?"

He brought his hands up, cupping and squeezing her butt. "Barnes would have removed me from the team. Told me it was too personal. Told me I was too close to be objective. I... can't risk that. This is my chance to be a part of King's destruction, without breaking the promise I made my wife."

"Ken... it's personal for *everybody*. Naomi, Quentin, Marcus, Renata... this shit that we're doing is about as personal as it *gets*. They think we're the objective ones."

Inez gasped as he gently nipped one of her butt cheeks, then immediately soothed the area with a kiss. "It's personal against *Wolfe* for them. A long established vendetta. It's *emotional*. King Pharma is just a job to them, and as far as anybody except you knows... it's just a job to me. Unless it fails."

"What happens if it fails?"

"King may have a tragic accident. Less anybody knows about how I may or may not feel about him... the better."

Inez closed her eyes again, sucking in a breath as Kendall flicked his tongue along the crease at the top of her thigh, then began sprinkling kisses over her butt.

"What are you doing?" she asked, as he nipped her again.

252

He chuckled a little — a sound that released the tension from Inez's shoulders. "Kissing your ass. I was rough with you, and you didn't deserve that. Isn't that what you do when you fuck up? Kiss the other person's ass, and hope they forgive you?"

"Literally kissing ass, Kendall? What would you do if I was a man?"

"Tell you to man the fuck up and not expect an apology," he laughed. "I would only apologize like *this* to a beautiful woman."

"So this is a habit of yours?"

"Nope. First time for everything," he said, running his hands up the backs of her thighs. He pulled her down onto the bed, then balanced himself on top her.

"How do you know I don't have a problem with you touching me like this? What makes you think I don't want you to stop?"

He lowered his mouth to her ear. "Do you have a problem with me touching you like this? Do you want me to stop?"

"No," she said, almost immediately, before her brain had ample time to even process the question. Of course her *body* didn't want him to stop, especially not when after her "no", he'd immediately taken the liberty of pushing his fingers inside of her.

No law enforcement guys, she'd told herself. Especially not former-CIA, current FBI, MMA-fighting, fucking *dangerous* Kendall. *Especially not* knowing his baggage. But then he licked and kissed her from her bikini line to the small of her back, devouring everything in between, and even the *slightest* hint of a protest died on her lips, drowned out and forgotten amidst whimpers and moans of pleasure.

There was a brief moment of clarity, while she was still weak from her orgasm, when a little voice told her to try to get out while she could. But... then Kendall stood in front of the bed, moving with that silent, lethal confidence that Inez revered as he stripped off his clothes. And... *dios mío*, he had *plenty* to be confident about.

Instead of kicking him out, like she wanted — but *didn't* want — to do, she scooted up, retrieving a fistful of condoms from her bedside table. He chose one, and Inez watched as he opened and put it on. She expected him to join her again on the bed, but instead he pulled her up, then *picked* her up, wrapping her legs around his waist to carry her to the edge of her dresser.

He pushed inside of her just as a new objection formed in her mind. The protest was buried under the exquisite pleasure of being filled with him, in a swift, sure stroke that took her breath away. He plunged into her again, and tears formed in her eyes, for no reason other than it felt *so* good, and it had been *so* long, and really... *really*, she wanted Kendall *so* bad.

"*What are we doing, Ken?*" she asked, choking out the words between strokes.

Kendall chuckled, hooking her legs over his shoulders. "Exactly what we've been wanting to do for the last five months." He leaned in to kiss her then, devouring her mouth with a hunger and passion that she gave right back. She slipped her tongue into his mouth, starving for his, ravenous for him. Inez pressed herself against his chest, not caring about the perfume bottles and other knick-knacks that fell as they shook the dresser. If they were doing this, they were *doing* it, and she drew back, pressing against the mirror as she scooted herself closer to the edge. She didn't care about falling, only cared that he went deeper.

When he finally released her legs, he wrapped his arms around her waist, tugging her close so that they were skin to skin, both slick with sweat. Inez draped her arms over his shoulders, burying her face in his neck as pressure began to mount between her legs.

"So this is just sex, right?" she whimpered in his ear as he gripped her butt, lifting her off the dresser.

"You want me to lie to you?"

Inez squeezed her eyes shut tight, digging her nails in his back as he stroked her deeper, faster, harder... "*Yes.*"

"Okay," he muttered, carrying her back to the bed. He laid her down, giving her an unexpectedly sweet, passionate kiss before moving inside her again. "Then yeah. It's just sex."

— & —

These people are completely crazy.

Renata pushed her laptop away from the edge of the table, then crossed her arms, laying her head there instead. She had headphones on, and the sounds of Terry King and his illicit deeds played in her ears. The recordings Quentin had found were proving to be a gift and a curse.

A gift, because the worst of King's misdeeds weren't in any of the emails they'd found, and apparently, Wolfe was smart enough not to put his crimes in writing — unlike some of the smaller, less organized criminals they'd uncovered through those correspondences. Wolfe's most major things were chronicled in the recordings. It was obvious that he really thought he and King were friends, because many of the things he spoke to him about were *very* personal.

And therein lied the curse.

Renata, Quentin, and Naomi had spent days listening to those recordings, and each mention of her mother fueled Naomi's belief that Noelle may still be alive. She kept emphasizing that she never saw her mother's body, and that the funeral had been closed casket, that Wolfe had referred to her in that video as if she were still alive.

And Wolfe himself wasn't helping anything.

Since that video of him killing Tomiko, he hadn't insisted on another video call, and he'd only briefly spoken to Renata. The calls were suddenly limited to her speaking with Taylor, and Renata strongly suspected that he *knew* he'd messed up by mentioning her mother, and was trying to avoid being trapped into speaking to her on the phone.

In any case, the more they listened to those recordings, the more evident it became that — at least in *his* mind — Damien Wolfe was very much in love with Noelle Prescott, and very much *hated* his half-brother, Nelson. More than once, there was mention of having him "taken care of", but apparently, Noelle's insistence always made him call it off.

Renata stopped listening to those. They made her feel badly for Wolfe, which disgusted her to no end. After what he'd done to her, sympathy was absolutely something he didn't deserve, so she decided to listen to the ones *not* marked Wolfe, to see what — if *anything* — else she could uncover instead.

Problem was, she was *tired*. Listening to these horrible people talk about horrible things was draining enough, but the night she'd had with Quentin just made her exhausted. Physically *and* emotionally.

For the first time since that incredible first night they'd shared, their attempt at sex did *not* go well. She'd had one too many glasses of wine at dinner, and they all caught up to her at once, while they were in the act. It hit her hard, reminding her of the woozy, vulnerable, unable to say no feeling of the night Wolfe violated her, and she reacted badly.

Very badly.

So badly that she'd worn long sleeves today, to hide the bruises on her wrists from Quentin having to restrain her from hurting *either* of them. So badly that she didn't even remember inflicting the ugly raised scratches across his chest, but she knew *she* was the only one that could have put them there.

And still… when they woke up the following morning, there was no regret in his eyes. No signals that he wished he'd never gotten himself involved, that he was unwilling to deal with her "baggage". He'd simply kissed her, morning breath and all, and asked her if she was hungry.

She broke down and cried, and he held and rocked her through it, and shrugged when she told him she didn't understand him. "You don't have to understand," he'd said. "Just accept it."

It being his seemingly steadfast dedication to loving her through the dark places. And apparently, feeding her through the *hungry* places, because he was upstairs now, fixing them lunch. Renata closed her eyes, allowing the sound of King speaking to someone who apparently handled some of his personal business to lull her to sleep.

Her eyes shot open at the mention of the name *Diana*. And the word *pregnant*. She'd not heard him *ever* mention any women before, but the thought triggered a memory... King was rumored to have abandoned a pregnant wife! They'd never gotten anywhere with it, because they couldn't find a marriage license, pictures, nothing to offer any clues, but Renata sat up, pulling her keyboard in front of her again.

She typed in *Diana Williams*, setting her system to query her database for the name first, and then the internet. Renata drummed her fingers on the tabletop as she waited, and waited, and waited some more, and then finally, results began to pop up on her screen.

Large monthly payments, deposited directly into a bank account, from Sean Williams to Diana Williams. The payments spanned eighteen years, then stopped. *There* was the marriage license, Diana Williams to Sean Williams, in the early eighties, and then a divorce decree, Sean Williams *from* Diana Williams, in the mid-eighties. There was nothing else, no pictures.

Rubbing her chin, Renata tried to run over it in her mind. After a moment, she ran her search again, this time adding *birth name, maiden name,* and *name change* to her query. This time, she got a little bit more, and got excited, leaning toward the screen as her eyes pored over the information. She lifted an eyebrow at Diana William's maiden surname, telling herself it was no big deal. She kept searching, sifting through data, and then, she found something with Diana's middle name — Allison. *That* made her heart race.

258

She ran a new search, and there *everything* was. Pictures, and newspaper clippings, and a birth certificate for a child, none of them mentioning Sean Williams. Renata sat back in her chair, a headache building at her temples as she processed the information in front of her. It didn't make sense... but... it made *perfect* sense. Renata felt sick. So, *so* sick.

Behind her, the door opened, and she felt rather than heard Quentin come in. He sat a plate down on the table in front of her, then a drink, but the thought of consuming anything turned her stomach. Quentin was talking about... something, but Renata understood nothing he was saying. After a moment, he seemed to realize that her mind was elsewhere, because he kneeled in front of her, concern filling his eyes.

"Ren? What's wrong *chérie*?"

Renata shook her head, unable to formulate words as tears sprang from her eyes.

"*Hey,*" he said, cupping her face in his hands. "Baby, talk to me. Why are you crying?"

His concern was almost too much to handle — made her discovery *so* much uglier than it already was. How was it that *Quentin,* who hadn't even seen her face until three months ago could love and care for her *this damn much* when... "Terry King."

Quentin lifted an eyebrow as he cocked his head to the side. "Yeah... what about him?"

Renata closed her eyes, trying to stem the flow of tears as Quentin raised his hands to her face to brush them away.

"He's my father."

Those words hung in the air for a long time, seeming to resonate through the room. When Renata opened her eyes, Quentin was staring at her with open skepticism.

"Ren... *what*? Why would you think that?"

She shook her head. "I don't think it, Q. I *know*. It's *right here*. Sean Williams, married to Diana Williams. Maiden name, Diana *Parker*. Middle name, Allison. After the divorce, while she was pregnant, she went back to her maiden name, and started going by her middle name. Making her *Allison Parker*. Allison Parker gave birth to a baby girl. *Guess what her name is?*"

Quentin pushed out a breath, running a hand over his face as he scanned the information on the screen. "He... paid her. Every month, for eighteen years."

"Yeah, I never would have known, based on how she always swore she was broke. Only enough for the basics while she drove a Mercedes. Never enough for me to get nice clothes, while she wore designer. Because she *hated* me, because I reminded her of *him*. Because he left her."

Renata tore her eyes away the screen. Suddenly it made *so* much sense. The mental and emotional abuse, the constant disdain, the unexplained bitterness... Allison Parker had placed all that hurt, and anger, and abandonment at Renata's feet. All of the emotions she wished she could take out on her deadbeat father.... In his absence, Renata had taken that abuse instead.

Nausea swept her stomach, and tension built in her shoulders as the full weight of the realization that Terry King was her father hit her like a brick wall. He *knew* she existed — he'd paid her mother thousands of

260

dollars every month for her care. And yet... there wasn't a single picture. His name was absent from her birth certificate. She'd never gotten a call, or a birthday card, *nothing* from him. Did he know she was still alive? Did he know he had a grandchild? Did he—

"*Oh my God*," Renata cried, clapping a hand over her mouth as she broke into sobs. Quentin pulled her against his chest, trying to calm her down, but she shook her head, pushing him back. "*This*! This is *why me*! All this time, I've always wondered why Wolfe chose me. Why he did this to *me*. Why he raped *me*. *This is why*! It was no coincidence that he drugged *me*, and maybe not even that I was at the club that night. He knew who I was, knew who my father was. He was cleaning up shop, against the people who betrayed him. He knew where your dad and Naomi's dad would be that night. They were trying to sell him out to the FBI, so Marcus's dad was collateral damage. And... he couldn't get to King, who screwed him out of millions of dollars... so he got to me. I asked Wolfe, why me? You know what he said? *Insurance*." Renata stopped, taking a deep breath as tears spilled down her face.

"Too bad my father didn't actually give a shit, right? Maybe this would be over by now if he did. But... I get it now, you know? As *fucked up* as it is, I understand Wolfe. This... this shit is *beautiful*. This is *poetic*. He tries to hurt my father by hurting me, but it doesn't work, because King doesn't give a damn about me. So... he regroups. Bides his time. *Ta-da*, Renata grows up to be of use in a *different* way. Now, he uses the kid that King threw away like garbage to take his business down." Renata shook her head, with a dry laugh. "I *knew* Wolfe was calculated, but... my God. Talk about poetic *fucking* justice."

She allowed Quentin to pull her into his arms again, stroking her back while she cried. She could feel from him that he didn't know what to say, and really... she appreciated that he didn't try. There was nothing to say. No *words* that would make any of this any better.

Something occurred to her, and she shrugged out of Quentin's arms, pulling herself into a stand. Pushing her chair back, she headed for the door, and Quentin caught her hand just as she reached for the handle.

"Ren, wait a second. Where are you goin'?"

Renata squared her shoulders, cleared her throat, then looked right at him. "I'm going to King Pharmaceuticals. I need to talk to my dad."

— & —

This was a deathtrap.

No matter how hard Quentin tried to think of something else, *that* thought kept running through his mind. Not only had he *driven* Renata to the King Pharmaceuticals corporate office, he'd come in with her, and now sat beside her in the reception area, waiting for King's secretary to get off the phone.

To his credit, he was feeling rather shell-shocked. Those recordings had, so far, done nothing except wreak emotional havoc in the lives of two women he cared for deeply, and he almost wished he *hadn't* found them. But... on the other side of that, Naomi and Renata were both struggling with their history, both paying — as children — for adult mistakes and misdeeds. Maybe... this was just part of moving forward, and getting past it. Just like Naomi deserved answers about who her parents really were, versus her childhood memories, Renata deserved some answers too. Difference was, *her* father was alive to ask.

The receptionist finally hung up, and looked expectantly at Quentin and Renata. "Can I help you?"

Hands shaking, Renata stood up, and Quentin stood as well, taking her hand to lead her to the desk. "We need to see Mr. King," he said simply, hoping that confidence would, by some stroke of luck, be enough to carry them through.

The receptionist lifted an eyebrow. "Mr. King doesn't have any appointments this afternoon. He's not available."

Quentin suppressed a scowl. He'd convinced Renata to slow down, so they could have at least a semblance of a plan. It was his handiwork that got them through security even though they were both armed, and neither had proper identification. But... getting into King's office would be a different story.

"You tell him someone is out here that he's gonna want to see. That he'd *better* see." Renata crossed her arms over her chest, staring the receptionist down, but the woman seemed unfazed.

"As I *said.* Mr. King is busy. You'll have to make an appointment."

Renata leaned forward over the desk, getting in the woman's face. "And as *I* said: Tell his ass his daughter is here."

The receptionist laughed. "You think I'm crazy? This may only be my third day, but I know better. They showed us what his kids look like, and *you* are not his daughter."

Renata smirked. "I'm his *other* daughter. And I'm *real close*," — she paused, removing the gun hidden at her waist, and brandishing it in the woman's face — "to shooting some shit up around here. *Tell him I wanna see him.*"

The receptionist looked down at the gun, back up at Renata, then over to the armed security guards, who were talking to each other instead of looking at her.

"I can get a bullet through your head before you even get their attention. Just pick up the phone." Renata smiled, and Quentin did too, moving his jacket back so she could see the gun at his waist as well.

The woman looked between the two of them, then swallowed hard before she picked up the phone and pressed a few buttons.

"On speaker," Quentin said.

A few seconds later, King's voice came over the line. "What is it Nicole?"

"Um… sir, there are some people here to see you. One of them says she's your daughter…"

There was silence for a moment, then King asked, "Brooke is here?"

"No, sorry," Renata chimed in, her voice bitter. "It's the *other* one."

Another few seconds of silence passed, then King said, "Send them in."

Renata wasted no time.

Quentin rushed to catch up as she shoved her way through the door the receptionist pointed them to, into King's office.

264

He rose when they entered the modernly designed office, eyeing Renata with interest as she strode to stand in front of his desk. For a long time, they just looked at each other, and Quentin looked between them, noting a previously unnoticed similarity in their features — the same wide, expressive eyes.

"I... I can't believe it," King said, his mouth spreading into a smile. "You are *beautiful*. You remind me so much of your mother. I never thought I'd get to see you, baby girl."

A coldness that Quentin had never seen swept over Renata, and her face twisted into a scowl. "You say that as if you *ever* tried."

"Sweetheart, I—"

"Don't you dare," Renata said, aiming her gun at him. "Call me *sweetheart* as if I mean anything to you. You don't get to call me that, you've never done anything for me."

"Now hold on." King's smile slipped away. "I sent your mother *good* money for you, every single month, before you were even born."

Renata snorted. "And I never saw a dime of it. You left, and she hated me, because she hated *you*. You never sent a birthday card, an email, *nothing*. You never even called!"

"If you knew the people I was in business with, you would understand *why*. They would have used you and your mother against me. I *had* to leave, to protect you!"

"Don't you *dare* pretend you were trying to protect me!" Renata screamed, jabbing her gun at him with one hand. "If you wanted to protect me you wouldn't have left me with a woman who made it her goal to make me miserable. A woman who kicked me out of the house *you* paid for, when I needed somebody most. *Don't you fucking dare* talk about protecting me. *He,*" — she jabbed her finger in Quentin's direction — "has protected me more than you ever have. I *hate* you."

King shook his head, letting out a derisive laugh. "You *hate* me? You wouldn't *be here* if it weren't for me!"

"*Ha!* So what, I owe you something?" Renata giggled, covering her face with her hand, but keeping the gun pointed firmly in his direction. "No, motherfucker, cause guess what? I covered for your ass already. *You* owe *me*. While you were hiding, or whatever the fuck you were doing, *your* enemy was busy raping and impregnating your sixteen year old daughter. You've been living your life, getting married, having kids, trying to play philanthropist of the decade to buy your way into heaven, but guess what... it's over for you. You're done."

Lifting an eyebrow, King lowered his hands. "What... what are you talking about? Raped you? Got your pregnant? *What?*"

"Yes, dear old dad. You heard me right. You were off, doing your absentee thing, after you screwed Wolfe out of that deal. He couldn't find *you*, so he took his pound of flesh from *me*. So you may want to cool it with throwing around the fact that I wouldn't *be here* if it wasn't for you. I grew up with a mother who hated me, and never let me forget it, because of you. I was violated, had my childhood snatched from me, because of you. I've been mentally and emotionally tortured, because of you. Tied up and left hungry, because of

266

you. *My child* is being kept from me, because of you. So don't act like you deserve a fucking medal."

"Renata, I didn't know about *any* of that. You have to believe me."

"Oh, I believe you," Renata scoffed. "I just can't believe you actually think that makes it any better. All of these resources... yet you couldn't even be bothered to *make sure* my mother did right by me. You disgust me."

"Tell me what I can do to make it up to you. Do you need money, do you—"

Renata threw her head back and laughed. "I don't need *anything* from you. I have everything I need, no thanks to you. I don't... I don't even know why I came here. I guess I just wanted to tell you to your face that I think you are the scum of the fucking earth. And whenever you go to hell — because you *will* go to hell — I hope the devil does to you, what Wolfe did to me, and I hope you feel *every single moment*."

"Now wait a minute, baby girl." King moved quickly around the desk to approach Renata, but Quentin was quicker.

He had his gun drawn, finger on the trigger as he pointed it at King. "Back the fuck up. You can hear the lady talkin' from where she is, bruh."

"And who the fuck are you?" King asked, frowning at Quentin. "Her bodyguard or something?"

Quentin shrugged. "You could say that. Just don't take another step."

"It's fine, Q," Renata chimed in, lowering her gun and returning it to it's place at her waist as she pulled out her phone. "I'm done here. We can go." She started toward the door, then turned around, walking until she was right in King's face. "You know… I was going to wait until I was outside of your office to do this, and let it be a surprise, but I think I want to say this to your face. Wolfe is forcing me to take your business down, if I want to see my daughter again, but really… I wish he'd just told me who you were. Told me that *your* kids were pushing Benzes for their sixteenth birthdays, while I had to literally *beg* for a computer. You know… I'd invented a story about you, that I told myself in order to make your absence okay. In my head… you were a *hero*. A fallen hero, a war vet, something like that. Something *strong*. Something *honorable*. You had some important, noble reason to not be in my life. But I find out now, that while I was daydreaming about my hero father, you were somewhere living in luxury without me, and you didn't even *care* to try to change my circumstances. If he'd just told me that… I would have destroyed this business in a heartbeat. But… better late than never."

Renata turned her eyes to her phone, tapping away at the screen, and King's eyes went wide in alarm. "What are you doing?"

She shrugged. "Oh, just sending a little juicy info — the recording of you bribing FDA officials, along with incriminating emails, other audio recordings, trade secrets, that sort of thing — to all of your competitors, the office that handles your government contracts, every major news network, and every online news outlet in the world. Nothing much."

With a grunt of rage, King dove at her, grabbing for the phone, but Quentin caught him with a swift hook to the jaw, followed by two blows to the stomach.

King dropped to the ground, and Quentin snatched him up by the collar, pushing him into his desk.

"What the fuck were you about to do, huh? Put your hands on her? You don't think you've done enough?"

"Baby girl, I'm sorry!" King choked out, struggling against Quentin's hold. "Please don't do this. I swear to you, I didn't know you weren't being taken of. I left to protect you, I swea—"

"*Save it.*" Renata shook her head. "It's already done."

King stared at her for a long moment before his nostrils flared, then he lunged at her again, trying to escape Quentin's hold. "You *stupid* little girl. Do you have any idea what—" his words were lost as Quentin aimed another blow at the side of his head, knocking him out. If he could help it, he wasn't about to stand by and let Renata be subjected to that sonofabitch's harsh words.

"We've gotta get outta here, *chérie*," he said, grabbing her hand. "Once he wakes up, everything is gonna go nuts."

Absently, Renata nodded, and Quentin wondered briefly about her emotional state. He could take care of her once they were home, but right now, they just needed to get out of the building. He strongly suspected that security was waiting on the other side of the door that led to the reception area, waiting for any type of signal from King that something was amiss.

But… he knew from the building plans that King had a private elevator that would put them right in the parking garage. He tugged Renata's hand, leading her to the elevator, then used the portable lock

269

scrambler he kept attached to his keys to access the elevator.

King's office was on the eighth floor — the top floor — and they needed to get to level B1. Quentin was getting excited as the floors counted down with no interruption... until it stopped on level two, with no explanation. He raised his gun as they came to a complete stop, easing Renata behind him. As soon as the doors opened, he quickly picked off a first, second, and third security guard, putting bullets through their legs before they could do *whatever* they'd been assigned to do to him and Renata with the automatic weapons in their hands.

He grabbed her hand, leading her to the stairwell as quickly as he could pull her. Gunfire rang over their heads just as he pushed her through the door into the parking garage in the basement. They made it quickly to their vehicle, and Quentin wasted no time getting them out of the lot, avoiding the armed guards that tried to stop them on their way. In the armored SUV they'd borrowed from Inez's collection, they blew right through the gate to get off the premises, then quickly navigated onto the highway with traffic.

It wasn't until they pulled back into Inez's garage that Quentin felt like it was safe to take a deep breath again. He looked to Renata, who'd been quiet the whole ride, and moved robotically to take off her seatbelt and climb out of the car.

He followed her into the house, where they were immediately bombarded with questions from the rest of the team, who'd apparently seen the news. Renata simply kept walking, heading up the stairs — presumably to her room — and Quentin stayed behind giving the team the quickest possible summary of what had happened in the last few hours.

Apparently, the internet was already going nuts with the information Renata had leaked. It was already going viral there, and television news was slowly catching up. SSA Barnes was especially unhappy with the impromptu reveal, but he had more important things to tend to than fussing at them. He had to get warrants granted, set up tactical teams for raids, and prepare to *actually* take Terry King down.

When they finally let Quentin out of the war room, he immediately went for the stairs, trying to get to Renata. Terry King was *finally* going down, and at a time she should have been able to be happy, since this was what they'd been working toward for months, to get her daughter back — she was taking yet another emotional beating.

He found her in the shower, letting the water stream over her face. He undressed, then silently joined her, holding her until the water ran cold. When they got out, he dried her off, lotioned her skin, then helped her dress in clothes for bed. He dressed himself in shorts and a tee shirt, then climbed into bed with her, holding her again until the fading daylight turned to dusk.

The entire time, she'd said nothing, simply submitted to being taken care of. But suddenly, she turned to him in the dark. "I don't understand... why he wouldn't have come back for me. Why he wouldn't have taken care of me. Wouldn't even come and see me. Why he still doesn't even see me now."

"Fuck him," Quentin said, holding her close. He pressed a kiss to her forehead. "It doesn't matter."

"How can it *not* matter?" Even in the dark, Quentin could tell she was looking at him. "He's my father. The *one* man I should always be able to count on to protect me, and care about me."

"It doesn't matter because *fuck him.* He don't deserve your tears, or your energy. He didn't want to know you... fine. Ren... you're amazing, *bien-aimé.* That's *his* loss. I protected you then, I'll protect you now. I cared about you then, I'll care about you now. I *saw* you then, baby. And I see you now. You don't *need* him. He doesn't deserve you."

Renata said nothing in reply to his words, but Quentin hoped like hell that she'd heard him. Even if King *hadn't* known what was happening with Renata, that didn't make it okay. He *should* have known.

"I love you, Renata," he said, because he meant it, and just because he felt like she needed to hear it. "If I can do *anything* for you... baby, just let me know."

She nodded, then buried her face in his neck as she snuggled close. "I love you too," she mumbled, her words muffled against his skin.

Quentin wrapped an arm around her, gently stroking her back. After a while, a change in her breathing pattern let him know she was asleep, and he hoped she would stay that way until morning. Morning would bring big, happy news, if Wolfe stuck to his word, which Quentin *desperately* hoped he would.

Morning would bring Taylor back.

sixteen.

"So I heard you've been running around threatening to bust caps in people, huh?"

Renata looked up from the spoon she'd been absently swirling in her coffee to see Marcus approaching her, with a paper bag from her favorite local donut shop in hand. She was outside, on the screened porch that had served as the setting for one of the best memories of her life — that beautiful first time with Quentin.

Unfortunately, she wasn't sitting out there to reminisce. She was out there searching for a reprieve from the constant barrage of negative thoughts in her head. She'd hoped that being out here, in this place with good energy, would help. And... it did, just not as much as she would have hoped.

Marcus sat beside her, extending the bag. Once she'd taken one, he tossed the closed bag onto the seat beside him, then pulled her into an embrace. "How are you feeling?" he asked, kissing the top of her head before he let her go.

Renata shook her head, then shrugged. "I... don't know how to put it into words. Quentin keeps trying to convince me that I shouldn't care about Terry King, but... he grew up with parents who loved him. He wasn't really close to his dad, because he was always traveling, doing stuff for Wolfe, but... he at least had a mom who adored him. A grandmother who was gentle, but strong, and tried to keep him in line. He got parental love, even though he was young when his parents died. I didn't get it from anyone. Hell, it wasn't until I met Q that I really, genuinely felt that somebody *loved* me. I held on to that fantasy that if my father was alive, if he knew about me... he would have loved me. He would have told me I was beautiful, and taught me to drive, and... given me my first flowers. You know? Quentin doesn't seem to get that I can't just... let that go."

"He gets it," Marcus said, chuckling as he sat forward, propping his elbows on his knees. "He just... he sees you hurting, and he wants it to stop. Homeboy has been working *hard* to get you into — and keep you in — a *good* place. Finding out about Terry King, and the entire, convoluted way all of this shit connects... it's just more stuff piling on. Nobody wants to see the woman they love going through shit like this."

Nodding, Renata leaned to the side, gently bumping Marcus's shoulder with hers. "Speaking from experience, huh?"

"Yessir," Marcus said, massaging the back of his neck. "I've been trying my best to get Naomi to chill. I mean... she's *pregnant.*" He stopped for a second, then looked up at Renata. "She's taking vitamins, and we're doing doctor's appointments. Her body is changing. She's starting to show, just a little bit, and it's... kinda fucking *amazing* to see, from day to day, you know?"

Renata nodded, then couldn't help grinning at the smile on Marcus's face. *That* was how a man was supposed to feel about his pregnant partner. Like what was happening to her was *amazing.* Like *she* was

274

amazing, and he wanted to be a part of the process. For a moment, the heat of jealousy burned her cheeks, and then she remembered that her experience compared to Naomi's were total opposites. Naomi and Marcus had conceived a child with an act of love. *Her* child had been conceived from hate.

All the more reason to love the hell out of Taylor, and despise Wolfe and King.

"Man," Marcus said, with a heavy sigh that took away his smile. "Even with all the *happy* things because of the baby, she's obsessed with this thought of her mother being alive. She's been talking about getting in touch with Harrison's bitch ass. I guess she thinks she'll have better luck with him, as if he's not cut from the same evil as Wolfe."

Shaking her head, Renata met Marcus's gaze. "He's not. Harrison runs my nerves in the ground, but... he's not the same as Wolfe. He *works* for Wolfe, but he's not the same."

Marcus lifted an eyebrow. "Explain."

"Well... a long time ago... maybe ten years, when Taylor was four or five, I tried to run away. I set up fake identities for both of us, and I *ran.* Wolfe kept calling, looking for me — I knew because I had the messages forwarded to an untraceable number. It wasn't the first time I'd run, but he always found me within a few days. Not this time. For a good... month or two, I was free. I was *happy.* And then one day, I opened the door to leave for work, take Taylor to daycare, and Wolfe was on my doorstep. He asked me why I was keeping his daughter from him, and when I didn't answer quickly enough, he just... hit me. I blacked out, and when I woke up, I was tied so tight that the ropes cut my ankles and

275

wrists. I still have scars," she said, holding her arm out for Marcus to see.

With a heavy sigh, she continued. "For two days, I screamed and cried, for anybody to help me, and nobody came. I thought I was gonna die. But then... Harrison came. He didn't have the bravado then that he does now. Wasn't nearly as high on the food chain, so he didn't have any leeway with Wolfe. And honestly he seemed kinda scared. But he untied me, gave me water, fed me, *bathed* me, because I was too weak to do it myself. And he was never inappropriate about it. I actually felt really safe. And then... Wolfe showed up, and he was... furious. I've never seen him so enraged. He snatched Harrison up, threw him into this glass cabinet thing that I had, where I kept all of Taylor's little awards and trinkets and crafts from school.

I... thought he was gonna die. Wolfe stood over him, saying all kinds of slick shit about him being a bitch like his dad, and just... talking crazy. He expected Harrison to cower, or beg, but he didn't. Harrison got up, and he... squared up. I thought he was *nuts*. Glass sticking out of your back, and you think you're about to box Damien Wolfe? But... he stood there and told Wolfe he was dead-ass wrong for what he'd done to me, and he wasn't just gonna stand by and watch. He told Wolfe he didn't get down like that. I was like... twenty. I think Harrison was maybe twenty-five, twenty-six? But... in any case, I was sure I was about to witness a murder, but.. Wolfe smiled. Told him he was proud of him. Said the men twice his age didn't have enough heart to stand up to him, but... Harrison did.

When I saw him the next day, I guess he'd gotten stitched up, and promoted, because instead of his usual hustler gear... he was wearing a designer suit when he brought Taylor back."

Reluctantly, Marcus nodded. "So maybe not *all* bad. Just annoying as fuck."

"Maybe not. I'm just wondering if he's gonna be the one to bring her back this time."

Renata smiled, thinking about seeing Taylor's face, in person, for the first time in months. She wanted to call Wolfe now, but she was trying to wait. The last thing she wanted to do was call too early, or seem too eager, or get on his nerves, or give him any arbitrary reason to go back on his promise. She'd thought long and hard about the complications of pulling Taylor out of school once the semester was already started, and decided she didn't give a shit. Taylor would get over it — she'd be going back to the friends she already knew *anyway.* Getting her away from Wolfe was much more important.

"Have you talked to Wolfe yet?"

"Not yet. Trying to be patient, but...God, I'm *so* excited! We're going to pick a new apartment together, and she'll get to redecorate her room, and... it should be fun. I *have* to make it fun for her, so she doesn't hate me for making her come back."

Marcus nodded. "She doesn't know about him, does she?"

Renata shook her head. "No more than she could find out on Google, which isn't much. He does a really good job of keeping his run-ins with the law scrubbed from the internet, and you know they've never gotten him on anything. *Not enough evidence,* supposedly."

"Too bad we couldn't save that video of him killing Tomiko."

277

"I know," Renata groaned. She and Quentin had spent long hours trying to unscramble the video, which had gone corrupt and basically self-destructed after one play. "Even if we had it though, without a body... Marcus you know he would have been free within the hour."

Marcus scrubbed a hand over his head. "Yeah, but... a kid can dream, right?"

"If you say so." Renata smiled, then patted Marcus's hand. "Come on, let's go see what everyone is doing."

They stood, and went inside, finding everyone gathered in the war room. Since Renata had jumped the gun, and released the files to the media, everyone was calling for Terry King's head. He was being dragged across social media, the internet, and it seemed every law enforcement agent had a warrant for his arrest. Problem was... nobody could find him.

"It's like he's disappeared off the face of the earth," Inez said, crossing her arms over her chest. "Every property he owns, every place he frequents... nothing there. He's probably in a bunker somewhere knocking back tequila, waiting for this all to blow over."

"But in the meantime..." Quentin grinned at Renata, grabbing her hand. "Stock is plummeting, people are resignin' from the board of directors. The government has cancelled *all* of their contracts with King Pharmaceuticals, and the president is holdin' a press conference later today, with the surgeon general present.. We've got good intel that it's about easing the American people's fears about their prescription drugs, and condemning Terry King's actions. So... it sounds like a win to me."

Beaming, Renata squeezed Quentin's hand, then blushed when he grabbed her waist to pull her close. "We did it, baby. *You* did it. You win." He pressed his lips to hers, and she eagerly kissed him back, giggling into his mouth when Inez led a series of whistles and claps.

Renata was turning to say something to them when her cell phone rang, and everyone went quiet. One look at the screen, and her heart surged.

It was Wolfe.

She looked nervously at Quentin, who gave her an encouraging nod. Renata answered the phone with the biggest smile, and perkiest hello she'd *ever* given Wolfe.

"Good morning, Agent Parker," he said, chuckling at Renata's obviously bright demeanor.

"Good morning. When is Taylor's flight? Or are you doing a road trip? Do *I* need to come get her? Just say the word."

"Right to the point, I see." Wolfe cleared his throat, then looked pointedly at the screen. "There's been a change in plans," he said, with no trace of humor. "I'll be keeping Taylor with me indefinitely."

Immediate, white hot anger swept Renata. "*What*? You son a bitch, you said if we took King Pharma down, you would give her back!"

"I *did* say that, and according to the news, you haven't quite held up your end of the bargain yet. Stocks are falling, yes. People are upset, yes. But Terry King is still walking this earth, alive and free. King Pharmaceuticals is *still* standing. You've done well Ms. Parker, but you've still got work to do. I want to see that daddy of yours *burn*."

From the way he smirked at the screen, Renata could tell he thought that last statement would be a surprise to her. But, she shook her head. He was about 12 hours too late to use that as a jab.

"I already figured out why you wanted *me* to do this, you sick, *twisted* bastard. How do even fucking sleep at night?"

Wolfe smiled. "Don't be naïve, Ms. Parker. I sleep *wonderfully*. I hope you're not taking any of this personally. I think you're a wonderful young woman, so it was never anything against you, but business is business — and family is family. Terry King fucked with my business *and* my family."

"*Your* family? *How?*" Renata asked, even though she immediately hated herself for being curious.

"*Yvette.* My beautiful baby sister, who wanted nothing to do with *any* of this shit. She got pregnant when she was sixteen. No father. I made sure she had everything she needed, made sure her little man had something to eat, and I sent her away from the city, away from trouble. She got sick, when her kid was about 20, and *that's* when I find out Terry's bitch ass was the one who got my baby sister pregnant. She told me before she passed away. He had been skinning and grinning in my fucking face for *twenty years*, knowing what he'd done, knowing he hadn't done right by her. He'd already screwed me out of that drug deal, and I hadn't gotten with him about that yet either. Then Nelson and Julian finally decided to pop off too, so I just handled *everybody*."

Renata shook her head. "And you decided to use me as your weapon."

"Unfortunately so. But I did better by you than your bitch ass father *ever* did by my sister. I didn't just send money, I checked in, made sure Taylor was taken care of. She'll be fine with me. *Taylor* has a father."

"And she needs her mother too!" Naomi chimed in, stepping beside Renata to speak to Wolfe. "I want to meet my cousin, and she *needs* her mother. Why don't you just stick to your word, and send her back?"

Wolfe smiled. "*Madame Mimi.* I appreciate your concern for Taylor, but be assured, she has a mother figure. My wife is here, and she is *loving* taking care of the girls."

Renata's anger flared again. She didn't even know Wolfe *had* a wife. How had they missed that? "Is that supposed to appease me? Some woman I don't know is taking care of my child?"

"You may not know her, but Naomi does. Naomi is *very* familiar with my wife."

When Renata glanced over at her, Naomi had her eyebrow lifted, and returned Renata's glance with a frown. "What are you talking about? Who is your wife?"

"You'll see soon enough. How is the pregnancy going?"

"I'm not telling you anything," Naomi snapped. "You tell me what you're talking about! Are you… are you talking about Noelle? Is *that* your wife?"

Ignoring Naomi's question, Wolfe smiled at someone off screen. "I've gotta go," he said, looking back at the camera. Ms. Parker, we'll speak again next week for your usual update on Taylor. Naomi my wife sends her best. She's looking forward to meeting her new grandchild."

After that, the line went dead. For a long moment, everyone just stood there without speaking, stunned. It took Renata a second to register that Wolfe was... *serious*. He really wasn't sending Taylor back.

"You told me he would do this," she said, tears choking her voice as she turned to Quentin, letting the phone slip from her hands and drop to the floor. "In the very beginning. You told me I was being ridiculous if I thought he was really gonna give her back, and I... I can't believe I was this stu—"

"*Stop.*" The edge in Quentin's voice made her stop speaking, as tears dripped from her eyes. She'd seen Quentin angry before — at her, at Marcus, even at Terry King — but the look on his face now... wasn't a look she *ever* wanted to see. He was *beyond* angry. His hands shook as he cupped her face, tipping her chin up to face him. "Don't you dare blame yourself for this. He's not doing this shit again. Not to you, not to Naomi, not anymore. *Not* today.

He kissed her, with a surprisingly light touch, considering the rage radiating from his skin. When he turned away, he faced the rest of them team. "Marcus, it's time."

"You're reading my mind, Q," Marcus said, his face carrying a similar — if not *more* menacing — expression as Quentin. "Kendall, Inez... y'all down?"

"Wait a minute." Renata grabbed Quentin's arm, turning him to face her. "What's going on? What are you doing?"

Quentin smiled. "We're about to go get your daughter back, *bien-aimé*. It's time we paid Wolfe a visit."

— & —

"If she's there... bring her back to me. Please."

Marcus closed his eyes, taking a breath as he pulled a clean shirt over his head. It had taken them hours to formulate a plan, and convince a few of Kendall and Inez's former unnamed-government-agency friends to accompany them, for extra man power. Now, they were simply waiting for the right time. It was best to go middle of the night, cloak of darkness. It was already night now, and time to go. Time to take the hour long flight that would get them to Wolfe's compound.

He turned to Naomi, still naked, still beautiful, with that tiny bulge in her stomach. Guilt gnawed at him. *What if I don't make it back to her?* But he couldn't really let himself think about that. He *would* eliminate Wolfe. He *would* erase that ever-present fear from her mind. And now, because she thought it was possible, he would bring her mother back to her as well.

The feeling that Wolfe was just taunting her, employing his usual emotional manipulation, came to mind. If Naomi's mother had been alive all this time... why hadn't she contacted her? Why hadn't she said anything? *Why* was she with Damien Wolfe? Of course... if she actually *was* alive, she could answer for herself. Marcus just hoped it wasn't a similar situation to Renata and Terry King — knowing your child was out there, needing you, but you simply don't care.

Approaching the bed, he sat down at the end, and pulled Naomi into his lap. She snuggled close to him, and Marcus was struck by conflicting emotions over how vulnerable she felt. He was glad that she was comfortable letting down her guard with him. Glad that she trusted him, relied on his strength. But... he also missed *her* strength. Her willingness to not back down, not let emotions rule her. He missed her *fight*.

But Marcus understood. Or at least, he was trying. Just like Renata, Naomi was dealing with blow after blow. Unexpected pregnancy, being attacked, then finding out that her father may not have been the man she thought he was… it was a *lot*.

For *anybody*.

So…instead of thinking about what he *wished* she would do, he simply stroked her back, until she'd calmed, and turned her head up to press her lips to his.

"You'd better bring your ass back," she said, moving so that she was straddling his lap. "I'm not kidding. If you don't come back to me… I will *kill* you."

Marcus chuckled, then gently swatted her on the butt. "Then I guess I'd better make sure I— wait a minute, what are you doing?"

Naomi smiled at him as she finished her swift undoing of his pants, then filled her hands with him. "Well… in case this is the last time…"

"I thought we *just* did that. You're still naked, Beautiful."

"That was a test run."

Marcus's laugh turned into a groan of pleasure as she lowered herself onto him, but it was short lived. Suddenly, the sound of muffled chaos erupted below them

Shit.

Naomi moved out his lap, scrambling for clothes as Marcus put everything away and refastened himself. By the time he turned to her, Naomi had already pulled on shorts and a tee shirt, had a gun in her

284

hand, and was tucking a second one into her waist. There was no point in telling her to stay where she was. If there were intruders in the house… she was probably safest with him.

As they exited the room and descended the stairs, he warned her to stay behind him. The commotion was coming from the garage, where they were supposed to be meeting to leave. Confusion swept him as he turned through the doorway.

A terrified-looking Taylor was in Renata's arms, sobbing on her shoulder. Another teenager, who Marcus recognized as Wolfe's daughter Kennedy stood crying nearby. Quentin, Kendall, and Inez all had their guns trained on a man in dark clothes on the floor. Startled by the sudden opening of a door, Marcus pointed his gun, finger on the trigger as Savannah — Savi — came barreling through. When she saw his gun, she stopped and raised her hands, letting her medical bag hit the floor.

"Marcus," she said, her dark eyes opened wide. "It's *me*. Inez called me!"

Inez glanced over her shoulder, noticing Marcus and Naomi's presence. "She's good Marcus. I called her to help *him*." She nodded her head at the man on the floor, and Marcus turned his gun away from Savi with a quick apology.

She quickly retrieved her bag from the floor, and rushed over to where the rest of the team stood, with Marcus and Naomi following. She dropped to her knees beside the man, and opened her bag, doing a quick examination before she used her scissors to cut open his pants leg.

Marcus moved to stand beside Kendall, and once he was there, his eyes went wide.

What the hell was *Harrison* doing here, with what appeared to be several bullet holes through his lower body?

What the hell was going on?

— & —

"You just couldn't leave it alone, could you?"

Terry King paced the floor in front of where Damien Wolfe lay immobile, thanks to the drug he'd injected in his spine, and both of his kneecaps shattered by bullets Terry had *thoroughly* enjoyed putting there. He really wanted to just get this over with, but that was too simple. That would be *way* too easy.

It would be way less pain than Damien Wolfe deserved, after what he'd done to Renata.

Terry had fucked up.

That was something he could admit.

He'd trusted Allison to do right by their child, even though she didn't understand him leaving, and she hadn't. He should have been more diligent. He should have hired someone to keep tabs on them. Maybe he shouldn't have screwed Damien out of that drug deal. Maybe... he shouldn't have screwed Damien's sister.

But, that was the distant, *distant* past. He was focused on the present, focused on the fact that King Pharma was losing investors, about to be under countless investigations, and hemorrhaging money faster than he could even keep up with. And this *bastard* had used his daughter to do it.

Terry glanced over at the love of Damien's life, tied up, bloodied and bruised. He hadn't gotten nearly as much satisfaction as he'd hoped for while making Damien watch that.

He knelt down beside his old friend, and smiled. "Nothing to say for yourself man? No response? Maybe if I get your daughter in here, give her the same... *treatment* I gave your wife... maybe then you'll have something to say."

At that, Damien laughed, although it was distorted by the drugs. "Whatever. Harrison must have gotten the girls out of here a long time ago. If not, you would've already used them against me."

"Oh, you're right," Terry said, patting Damien on the shoulder. "Your little right-hand-man escaped with your teenaged daughters."

"Exactly like I thought. You'll never get your hands on them. Harrison knows better. *I win.*"

Terry laughed, then shook his head. "No, my friend. *I* win. Because I'm not talking about them." He glanced from Damien, to Noelle, then back to Damien, and laughed again.

"I'm talking about the *thief.*"

— *the end... for now* —

I know, I know! Where's the rest, right? Be on the lookout for the continuation of the "If You Can" series, *Save Me If You Can*.

Christina C. Jones is a modern romance novelist who has penned more than 25 books. She has earned a reputation as a storyteller who seamlessly weaves the complexities of modern life into captivating tales of black romance.

Prior to her work as a full-time writer, Christina successfully ran Visual Luxe, a digital creative design studio. Coupling a burning passion for writing and the drive to hone her craft, Christina made the transition to writing full-time in 2014.

Made in the USA
Middletown, DE
02 April 2024